SHAKESPEARE'S CHANGELING:

A Fault Against the Dead

BY SYRIL LEVIN KLINE

Paperback ISBN 13: 978-1-950282-70-8

eBook ISBN 13: 978-1-950282-71-5

Library of Congress Control Number: 2013908512

Distributed by Bublish, Inc.

DEDICATION

This book is dedicated to the late David Lloyd Kreeger,
philanthropist and modern Renaissance man, who first suggested
the idea for this work and thereby sparked my quest into
the Shake-speare Oxford authorship controversy

and to

Peter Kreeger, whose steadfast friendship and generous support
enabled the fulfillment of his late father's vision by fostering the
creation of this book from the seeds of its humble beginning to
the full-flower of its completion

ACKNOWLEDGMENTS

Special thanks to Knight Kiplinger for his kindness in hailing the achievements of Oxfordian researchers over the past 15 years, and to the Shakespeare Oxford Society and Shakespeare Fellowship who continue these traditions, along with such "worthy pioneers" as Charlton Ogburn, Ruth Loyd Miller, Eva Turner Clark and other valuable contributors.

Dave Cowan provided conscientious editing and coaching. Thanks to Sally Oesterling for her insightful comments, and to Michael Wray and William Travers for suggesting some essential elements of mystery. Huzzah to Warren Gifford, Carla Malick, Michael Kline, Carrie Kline, Judy Spigle and Bob Davis who commented on earlier drafts.

Thanks to Judy Greenberg and the staff of The Kreeger Museum for helping to make our presentations so elegant, and to Richard Waugaman, who shared a delightful evening with us presenting a Freudian view of Lord Oxford's complex personality.

Eternal gratitude to my mother, Blanche Levin, who embodied the art of storytelling, and to my grandmother, Jennie Hewitt, who was never too busy to read to me. Heartfelt gratitude to Irvin Levin, my father and first spiritual teacher, and to my brother, Daniel Levin, who lent me his inner strength during some tough times. Hugs and thanks to my sons Seth Adam Lessans and Jonathan Rafael Lessans, for sharing their lives and individual artistic talents with me.

Thanks to Terry Glaser for her "weighty" contribution of *The Harvard Concordance of Shakespeare,* and to Blackfriars Theater in Staunton, Virginia, and The Stratford Festival in Canada for giving audiences the chance to see Shakespeare's famous and lesser known works, as well as those by other period playwrights.

Special thanks also to Carol Banner, Barbara Sauer and all of the Lightworkers that guided this project. To Charles Byrd of Castle Hedingham, Essex, for a memorable tour of Lord Oxford's birthplace on a pleasant summer afternoon, much thanks.

Loving gratitude to Mrs. Mildred Groner, my 7th grade English teacher, who first introduced me to Shakespeare and the idea that there were other possible candidates for the authorship.

All hail Ben Jonson for his bold skepticism about the Shakespeare authorship, and to William Shaxper for his inscrutable silence.

To Edward de Vere, 17th Earl of Oxford, Viscount Bulbec, Lord of Sandford, of Escales and of Badlesmere, Lord Great Chamberlain of England, writer of Elizabethan court masques and plays and supporter of the playhouses, whose warlike countenance on the tilt-yard shook spears, my humble gratitude for your guidance and inspiration.

Last but never least, this book would not exist without my husband, Peter Kline, who kept me working hard during this 20-year odyssey, and who allowed me to bring the Earl of Oxford into our bedroom as pillow talk.

WILLIAM SHAXPER'S PROLOGUE

New Place,
William Shaxper's Home in Stratford
June 27, 1604

"Dogs bark at me as I do halt by them . . ."
– Richard III

T he wailing of Hamnet Sadler's mongrel bitch pierced the stillness of the midsummer night, increasing the terror of the exhausted rider who had just returned home.

William Shaxper slid from his horse and looked furtively over his shoulder as he clutched a leather portfolio to his chest. He fancied the full moon glowering down at him with a prosecutor's scowl. He ran to the front door and pressed his cheek against it. He heard nothing except the incessant howling of his friend's dog. His hands trembled as he rummaged for his key, found it and turned it in the lock.

Luckily, the King's men hadn't pursued him - or perhaps they had yet to arrive.

He nervously unlocked the door and stepped inside, closing it behind him with the full weight of his anxiety. Breathing heavily, eyes darting wildly, he called out to his wife.

"Anne? Are you home?"

Silence. Relief. The house at New Place was empty.

It will be easier to hide the treasure this way, without any witnesses . . .

Like a parent protectively shielding a child from harm, he hugged the portfolio to his chest. With the glowing embers in the kitchen hearth, he lit a small lantern and carried it up three flights of stairs to the attic. He locked the door behind him, just in case, and set the bundle down among the discarded family relics that lay barely illuminated by the scant moonlight. He rummaged for a place to hide his contraband and remembered the loose floorboards under the north window where he had hidden other manuscripts he had collected from his master over the years.

He crawled on all fours to the spot and frantically pried up the boards. He gently lifted the ink-stained coverlet from beneath them and loosened the girdling knot that held its treasures. He carefully removed the papers and held them up to the light. For a moment his eyes lingered over his master's quaint penmanship. It pained him that he would see it no more, now that Death, with the help of a few assassins in royal livery, had silenced his master forever.

As if tucking his children into bed, he placed *Henry VIII* and *Twelfth Night* with the other plays. He tied the cord around them and replaced them beneath the floor. He vowed to keep them safe and crossed himself, desperate to secure God's help. He would collect the remaining provocative scripts when things calmed down – if he lived long enough – when the King no longer cared about the true identity of Shake-speare.

May his name be buried where his body is . . .

Exhausted, he sank to the floor and waited for the fearsome sound of horses. The King's Men would surely be coming for him.

LORD OXFORD'S PROLOGUE

The London Estate of
William Cecil, Lord Burghley
June 17, 1586

"Thou art a robber, a law-breaker, a villain!"
– Cymbeline

William Cecil's shrewd insight sent him streaking like a prescient comet across England's political firmament. Once a descendant of common innkeepers, his elevation to the title Lord Burghley bestowed on him the rewards of sitting at the Queen's right hand.

His meticulously well-barbed beard lent him a saintly appearance, while his Machiavellian instinct for switching allegiances allowed him, like an actor, to play many parts. As a young man inflamed by a restless passion for advancement, he abandoned his working-class roots and pushed his way into the halls of power by making himself useful to an assortment of noblemen.

From the beginning, Cecil chose his friends well. He insinuated himself among them at the right time, and by studying their ways, recognized their ambitions. As the Queen's chief advisor, he wisely made it his primary imperative to protect England's royal succession from the vast number of claims made by the spawn of their politically incestuous marriages.

Early in his career, he had supported the boy-king Edward, who had inherited the throne at the death of his father, King Henry VIII. When the youth died (some said, suspiciously, by poison), Cecil avoided any connection with the ill-fated choice of Lady Jane Grey as royal successor, despite serving as her father-in-law's secretary. When the Third Act of Succession determined that Henry's children would rule, Cecil quickly allied himself with Henry's Catholic daughter Mary, wife of Philip II of Spain. Later, even as Mary lay dying from a cancer that she had falsely hoped was a pregnancy, Cecil jockeyed into power by supporting Elizabeth Tudor, Henry's second daughter, securing her Protestant reign as England's Virgin Queen.

Cecil's chameleon-like diplomatic skills afforded him a number of opportunities. He was also proud to have been appointed Keeper of the Royal Wards, a lucrative position that granted him guardianship over England's orphaned young noblemen. One of his wards eventually became his son-in-law, and because of that, Cecil was granted the title of Lord Burghley. His fortuitous elevation had been an absolute necessity, required for his daughter's marriage to the high-ranking 17th Earl of Oxford. Clever maneuvering on Cecil's part had invalidated the 1562 match contracted between the boy's deceased father and The Earl of Huntingdon, who had promised his sister Mary to the youth in marriage.

Cecil had managed it by reminding the Queen that Oxford's ancient Plantagenet, Lancaster and York lineages threatened her Tudor regime.

Any children born from such a powerful union could easily challenge the three generation-old Tudor claim, especially when the Pope had proclaimed Elizabeth Tudor, the spawn of Anne Boleyn and King Henry VIII, as a bastard.

Horrified by Cecil's solemn warning, Her Majesty immediately nullified the match and nine years later proffered a marriage between Burghley's 15 year-old daughter and the 21 year-old Edward de Vere, Earl of Oxford. What a scoundrel Oxford had been – railing that he and his titles had been bartered away like the spoils of war! Burghley was astonished when Oxford fled to France to avoid the wedding, insisting that he would marry no one but the Queen, leaving Anne in tears at the altar. As a father, he smirked at the memory of his son-in-law being brought back to England in chains and forced to marry as Her Majesty commanded.

Despite this public embarrassment, Burghley had never imagined such an illustrious match for his daughter. He had often written about the hazards of marrying young girls off too early; but he took the current when it served, even though it meant that the Queen and Oxford could continue their impetuous love affair without Anne's knowing – a sop to Cerberus meant to assuage some of Oxford's fury. It was not without a peculiar sense of revenge that Burghley saw to it that Anne married Oxford at the same ceremony in which Huntingdon's sister was given to the Earl of Somerset. Thus the misbegotten match long ago conceived by Oxford's dead father had been cunningly aborted.

At daily prayers, Burghley assured both himself and God that he always acted with a father's best interests at heart. After all, a cowardly father never would have read his son-in-law's Last Will and Testament before Oxford's fateful trip to Italy. A powerless father never would have known that his son-in-law had bequeathed his estates – if he died without a son – leaving nothing to his wife, Anne, but only to his cousin, Horatio. A spineless father never would have intervened as he had done, especially with travel so fraught with danger and his daughter so ill and bereft at home. Back then, he had shuddered to think that Oxford, so experienced in creating theatrical illusions, might stage his own disappearance, remain in Italy, and enjoy the unabridged life of a libertine.

Burghley had recently concluded that the only way to control his obstreperous son-in-law was to control the young man's money. Days ago, he had sued in the Court of Wards to receive unpaid marriage fees and declare Oxford mentally incompetent to handle his own finances.

Sitting back to enjoy his customary glass of port, Burghley heard his son-in-law rampaging towards his library. A moment later, Oxford burst into the room.

"Infinite liar! Flesh-mongering swindler! What do you mean by humiliating me?"

"Good evening, my son," Burghley said calmly. "What's the matter?"

"Don't call me 'son'! I'd sooner have piss in my veins than an ounce of your despicable blood. You know very well what I'm talking about – you, suing in the Court of Wards to declare me incompetent. It's a diabolical lie, swearing an oath that I cannot manage my own income. Why, you're the very person who picked my pockets from the moment I entered your household. But I warn you, sir, don't cross swords with me. I'm not your cherubic little ward anymore."

"I'd hardly call you cherubic, Edward, not when you destroy an otherwise peaceable evening."

"You treacherous old serpent, how dare you spout your venom in my ears? I'm thirty six years old and you have no right to keep my inheritance from me. You're not my guardian anymore."

"You brought this action on yourself," Burghley said icily. "For fifteen years I've waited for you to pay the marriage fees for my daughter Anne and I've received nothing for the privilege."

"Do you expect me to pay for the privilege of being cuckolded?" Oxford roared.

"This isn't about my daughter or your wild accusations against her. It's about you being a spendthrift. How can I help you when you persist in selling off your estates just to present some silly plays for the Queen? It's absurd. You'll lose everything if I don't put a stop to it."

"The Queen adores my plays. She prizes them above everything."

"Do you think she prizes *you* above the other courtiers because of your scribbling? Not a whit! You've fallen out of favor with Her Majesty. I've tried to help you find your way back into her good graces, but you won't take my advice."

"Your advice is cow dung, and you can wipe your ass with your legal papers," Oxford sneered. "But fear not, old man, I have some other papers to rub your nose in."

"What papers?" Lord Burghley asked, his face twitching as he leaned forward.

"I've written another play," Oxford grinned, removing the pages from his doublet. "It's based on a book my brother-in-law brought me when he returned from Denmark. I've made some alterations to it for dramatic purposes. Listen."

"I most certainly will not," Burghley said, rising from his chair.

"Then perhaps you'd prefer to *see* it. Shall I stage it at a public play-house or present it privately before the Queen?"

Burghley reached for the papers. Oxford snatched them away.

"On second thought, don't read it. That would only spoil the surprise."

"God's blood, what surprise? Edward, what have you done?"

"What I've left *undone* is more to the point," Oxford said, as he shuffled the papers. "Let me see. We're into the second act, right before the entrance of the players at Elsinore when Hamlet says —"

"Nonsense!"

"No, that's not the line. Let me prompt you and reveal the characters with my voice. Hamlet speaks first and says, 'Oh Jephthah, Judge of

Israel, what a treasure hadst thou!' And then in the creaking voice of an old man, you say, 'What a treasure had he, my lord?' and Hamlet says, 'Why, one fair daughter and no more, the which he loved passing well. Am I not in the right, old Jephthah?' Then you say, 'If you call me Jephthah, my Lord, I have a daughter that I love passing well.' Then Hamlet says, 'Nay, that follows not,' and you say, 'What follows then, my Lord?' and Hamlet says, 'Why, as by lot God wot. And then you know, it came to pass, as most like it was.' You're familiar with the old song from church, so you know how it goes."

"Are you implying that my daughter's ravings are true?"

"Bravo, Lord Fishmonger, I can see that my words have hit their mark. You didn't think I'd ever learn about it, did you?" Oxford whispered, "but even a madwoman can speak the truth."

"Edward, you're wrong to take Anne's delusions to heart," Burghley said, as he steadied himself by placing both hands on the table. "The doctors say her ravings are caused by unhealthy humors. And as far as your income is concerned, my control over it has been an act of kindness. You simply cannot go on squandering your money on plays and players."

"But it's *my* money and I can spend it as I please!"

"Not if the Court of Wards determines otherwise."

"You preside over that court, you sanctimonious embezzler – you, who are unfit to live even on the molten outskirts of Hell! I'll teach *you* to toy with me! Consider *this* an act of kindness!"

Oxford plunged his dagger into the table between the middle and index fingers of Burghley's right hand. The old man flinched and nearly fainted. Seconds later, he opened his eyes and found that the blade had missed him by a hair's breadth.

The Earl of Oxford was gone.

ACT I
CHAPTER ONE

Thirty years later
The Scene: London to Wilton House
April 13, 1616

"A true-devoted pilgrim is not weary . . ."
– The Two Gentlemen of Verona

B en Jonson spurred his horse headlong into the wind with reckless fury. The roan gelding summoned its strength, kicking
crusts of dirt into the face of its portly rider, blurring his view
of the countryside.

The perfunctory tone and imprecise wording of his patron's summons had caused him to rush off from London on the fastest horse he
could find. Had he provoked the official censors again? He had done
so before and suffered for it. In the eyes of the government, he was a
troublemaker and a known recidivist. Although King James had named
him poet laureate, he wasn't one to be deceived by royal honors, for he

had lived long enough to see the mighty fallen and even the weapons of war perished.

As a playwright, he was considered a dangerous person, and he had plenty of reason to believe he was being watched at all times.

Riding frantically to Wilton House, Jonson shuddered to think that King James might be punishing his patrons for some inadvertent offense in one of his theater pieces; and that as its author, he would be the next in line at the gallows.

As he reined his horse to a halt in front of Wilton House, Jonson surveyed the former Benedictine convent, reborn as a magnificent estate. Decades ago, King Henry VIII had given Wilton to the Herbert dynasty as a reward for their loyalty after his split with Rome. While it glowed with elegance now, the sacking and dissolution of the convents and monasteries led the cynical Jonson to see it as nothing more than the spoils of war transferred to flatterers by an arrogant king.

Thank God the two incomparable Herbert brothers, Lords Pembroke and Montgomery, could not read his thoughts!

A servant appeared and ushered the playwright to a nearby tent while a stableman tended to his horse. A youth approached with a pitcher of water and a towel. Jonson grinned at the proffered nicety. It wouldn't do to appear slovenly before the patrons who paid his salary and held his prospects in their hands. He scrubbed his face and checked himself in the mirror for any telltale signs of the road. Even the servant seemed satisfied with the hasty renovation of his appearance.

The playwright's heavy boots echoed uncomfortably on the polished floors of Wilton. Although he'd been in the great house dozens of times, the pedestaled marble busts and oil portraits of unyielding ancestors made him nervous as they glared down from their gilded frames. He would have preferred meeting Pembroke and Montgomery in a public house like the Boar's Head, where he could relax and let his guard down; but he was sure neither nobleman had ever frequented such a place.

The library door opened onto a courtly tableau. Instantly, Jonson felt the bristly snag of his abrasive nature threatening to ruffle Lord Pembroke's smooth demeanor. He weighed Lord Montgomery's light-hearted temperament against his own choleric impatience. The nobles were ephemeral, glittery and polished where he was harsh, big-boned and hewn of peasant stock.

Lord Pembroke stood facing the window, perusing a folio of maps. He seemed startled by Jonson's presence, as if he'd forgotten his terse summons. Lord Montgomery stepped forward to greet the playwright, as if the differences in their ranks meant nothing, as if they were old friends or comrades-in-arms on an equal social footing.

Jonson wouldn't have it. He bowed low, knowing that when all was said and done, they were his superiors and expected his deference.

His gaze fell on Countess Susan. He wasn't sure why she was there to witness his imminent peril, but her radiant smile lightened his mood. She had been an attractive child, favoring her father's chestnut hair and silver eyes over her mother's pale complexion. Time had enriched her delicate features with an exquisite grace.

"My lady," he smiled, kissing her hand.

Jonson remembered his very first glimpse of her. Too young to know her father's secrets, Susan had nevertheless been old enough to eaves-drop as he helped Jonson revise the earliest version of *Sejanus*. With the Earl's hand added to his work, the novice playwright had assumed they would share credit. But when Lord Oxford insisted that Jonson publish it under his own name, the former bricklayer bristled. He hadn't understood the ban against publication by noblemen. It seemed unfair, not giving credit where it was due, since the play had been a collaborative effort. He wasn't a pirate, he said; he wanted to be known as Honest Ben Jonson.

He must have raised his voice a bit (actually, he had shouted) and frightened little Susan. She ran to her father and flung her arms around

3

him. Jonson was dumbfounded as the Earl described the Queen's literary ban while his daughter entwined herself around his neck – and Jonson's heart.

Now the years had passed, and he stood before her, waiting for his patrons to speak. Lord Pembroke cleared his throat.

"We all want to compliment you on your fine work in editing your folio of plays, Ben," he said.

"It is I who must compliment you, my lords," Jonson replied. "Not every writer has the chance to see his life's work printed in a single volume. I will always be grateful to you both for sponsoring its publication."

"*The Complete Plays of Ben Jonson* is the first collection of its kind, is it not?"

"Yes, the first of its race ever begotten in England, I'm proud to say." Jonson paused. "Why do you ask? Has there been some trouble with it?"

"Not at all. Merciful Heavens! Should we expect any?"

"No, but the tone of your letter –"

"Oh, that," Pembroke said, waving his hand dismissively. "Well, perhaps I should have been softer in my choice of words. What I meant to say is that we have a similar project in mind, and my sister-in-law here has convinced me that you're the only writer in England with the skill, education and honesty to accomplish it."

"Thank you for your confidence, my lady," Jonson said, with a bow.

"But time is of the essence," Montgomery added curtly. "We want to publish a volume similar to yours featuring the complete works of another deserving author. And, since you have done so well with the volume of your own works, we want you to act as editor."

"I am honored, my lord. But where is the author? Why can't he edit his own collection?"

"Nothing would have pleased him more -- if he were alive to do so."

"Oh, he's dead then. What grave strife, that Death prevents his undertaking," Jonson quipped. His patrons ignored the jest, all too familiar with his obtuse sense of humor.

"We're prepared to pay you a goodly sum in advance," Montgomery added.

"I'm flattered, my lords, and place myself once again at your service."

"In all fairness, Ben, you might want to think it over before you accept," the Countess said. "Publishing this particular volume could be a most dangerous assignment."

"How so, my lady?"

"We are asking you to edit a folio of my father's complete works."

Jonson looked uneasily at Pembroke and Montgomery.

"Is that permitted, Your Lordships? Has the King granted license to publish plays bearing Lord Oxford's name?"

"His Majesty knows nothing about it," the lady said.

"Not yet anyway," Montgomery added.

"How do you propose to accomplish it? And why now, after all this time?"

"The timing has never been more favorable," Pembroke said. "The King has granted me the title of Lord Chamberlain, giving me full authority over every manuscript that passes through the Stationers' Register. And with our friend George Bucke as Master of the Revels, we will control the publication and production of every play in England. For the first time, we can associate Lord Oxford's name with the famous plays."

"And what will the King say to that?" Jonson asked.

"I'm sure His Majesty will have some misgivings – he always does – but everyone knows he loves the plays."

"Maybe so, but does he love the author? The real author – not that scribe from Stratford."

"You're referring to William Shaxper, of course," the Countess said.

"Aye, my lady," Jonson nodded, breaking an awkward silence. "I haven't thought of him in years."

"You must admit, at least he was useful."

"A sponge is useful too, my lady; but oh, what filth it collects!"

Jonson read his patrons' disapproval. He discreetly changed his tone.

"It would be a great tribute to see your father's complete works published under his own name after all these years, my lady," he said. "I would be honored to oversee this great task. The Star of England deserves a stellar monument."

"Your primary task will be to find the plays, and it won't be easy," Montgomery said. "In this case, our author is dead and therefore inconveniently silent on the matter. You must collect as many manuscripts as possible, but God only knows where the originals are! After all this time, I fear they may be scattered all over England, lining baking pans or wadded up to stop bungholes. Perhaps some of the actors still have them, but whether they're foul papers or fair copies, I'm sure only you can tell."

"We've already secured the Earl's longtime friends Leonard Digges and Hugh Holland to contribute some dedicatory verses," Pembroke added. "You might want to ask Michael Drayton to pen a short tribute."

"I will, my lord."

"Well, however you manage it. And by all means, throw in some of your own verses. As editor, you can do as you wish in that regard."

Jonson grinned at the prospect.

"One other thing," Montgomery added. "We suggest that you journey to Stratford to see Mister Shaxper. Perhaps he can enlighten you on where to find the plays, and favor us with some of his own verses."

Jonson sank back into his chair. Did no one care about casting pearls before swine? Shaxper had once boasted that he could versify while butchering a calf. All Jonson could picture was the bloody cleaver.

"Pardon me, my lord, but William Shaxper is incapable of poetry," Jonson said. "It's true that he's written one or two epitaphs for tombstones since his retirement; and, well, actually, that's a good line of work for him because dead men can't ask for their money back."

Montgomery snickered. Pembroke looked baffled. Jonson tried again.

"What I mean to say is that his verses won't be in the literary style one would expect in celebrating the memory of Lord Oxford as the great Shake-speare."

Jonson knew it wasn't going to be easy, avoiding impolitic remarks that would confuse and anger his patrons. And of course, even His Majesty had no appreciation whatsoever for such clever repartee, especially on forbidden matters.

Countess Susan gently touched Jonson's hand.

"We all know how you feel about William Shaxper, Ben, but you must search everywhere for the plays. Surely the scribe knows where some of them can be found. He was entirely devoted to my father, right up to the end. We believe he might have taken some of them back to Stratford with him for safekeeping."

Jonson doubted that precise motivation, but he swallowed his opinion in deference to the rank of his benefactors. He was determined that the great plays would not suffer the same fate as Shake-speare's sonnets, purloined and published by a beguiling impostor.

He had to admit that he knew his patrons were right. The best place to look for the plays was in the home of the scribe who had made fair copies from foul papers – claiming the author's labor as his own. Perhaps he had taken some of them there after all.

Jonson bowed obediently.

"I shall leave for Stratford first thing in the morning, my lady."

CHAPTER TWO

The Scene: The road to Warwickshire

April 14, 1616

"It may be you think me an impostor . . ."

– Pericles

T he next day as Jonson rode towards his destination, second thoughts unsettled him. The jagged scar that puckered across his right hand reminded him of the branding he had received in prison. Although guilty of killing his fellow actor Gabriel Spencer, Jonson had claimed benefit of clergy as a minister's son and was granted his freedom. Nevertheless, he was branded with a hot iron and his worldly possessions were seized, pleasing both the jailers and the churchmen that justice had been done.

That mark of Cain commemorated his second brush with the law. Jonson's first offense had been for co-authoring a treasonous play with Thomas Nashe. Looking back on it, Jonson knew they had been extremely naive in not considering the consequences of their actions. They were lucky to have escaped with their lives (and their hands) for having criticized the government. When Nashe fled England, Jonson stayed behind and relied on the support of his secret patron. Lord Oxford advised him to cloak his words in cryptic language that rivaled the ancient Riddle of the Sphinx. Over the years, Jonson's prose had proven he'd gotten quite good at it.

He felt honor-bound to redeem his patron's reputation. The Earl of Oxford had taught him style and form, and Jonson remained mystified as to why publishing his works would be a crime. Other noblemen had had their books published posthumously, but this honor was forbidden to Lord Oxford. In the mind of King James, some unfathomable secret had made Oxford's case different. Twelve years after his death, Oxford had been denied his share of tributes. A rank impostor had taken credit for the entire Shake-speare canon, sonnets and all. That unfairness galled Jonson, especially since the impostor was infamous among the writers as an upstart crow.

Surely editing Oxford's folio would be considered an honorable enterprise; but then again, if King James were displeased, anyone associated with the project would suffer unspeakable punishment.

Jonson had no desire for an encore in prison, and as England's first poet laureate, there was no precedent attaching a lifetime of royal protection to that honor. He wanted to avoid death by hanging as much as Lords Pembroke and Montgomery wanted to escape beheading, the standard form of execution strictly reserved for the wealthy classes.

With Jonson's knowledge, standing by and doing nothing seemed unethical. His inaction would inevitably cause the bard's true identity to be lost forever, and no one would know that Lord Oxford had written the Shake-speare plays.

The more Jonson considered it, the more horrible it seemed not to let the author's ghost speak. If a man's name could be so easily separated from his works regardless of his literary reputation, no play or poem was safe from thievery. Every writer's labor was at risk, if a dead man's efforts could so easily be ascribed to an impostor.

Jonson swallowed his disgust for authority and turned his attention to the road.

CHAPTER THREE

The Scene: Stratford, two days later

April 16, 1616

"Writ in remembrance more than things long past . . ."

– Richard II

Stratford-on-Avon was a provincial town, much like the peasant scribe Jonson had traveled to see. The village buzzed with the incessant drone of work, offering little joy or frivolity. Farmers rose early to work the fields as tradesmen unlocked their shops for business. Carts groaned under heavy loads, mocking the muscular oxen that pulled them. Boys not yet apprenticed to the trades attended Stratford's grammar school, hoping to do more than sign their names with an anonymous mark. Mothers shared traditions of homemaking with their daughters: baking bread, sweeping hearths and tending vegetable gardens.

Only the graves at Trinity Church promised eternal peace and serenity.

Shaxper's home at New Place sat on a level plot of land. The heavily beamed façade crossed over white plaster, joining with large timbers to support its sturdy structure. Two outbuildings and a small barn stood alongside it, and a well-kept garden bordered the grounds. At the time of its purchase twenty years earlier, Shaxper had boasted that it was the second best house in Stratford, and that he'd acquired it with the proceeds from the ticket sales of *Hamlet*.

Jonson had cringed at those words, and he did so now at the sight of the imposing roof. New Place looked down on its neighbors with the same palpable contempt as its owner. According to his fellow writer Michael Drayton, Shaxper was famous in Stratford primarily for gouging the price of grain during a famine. Rumor had it that members of his own family had never seen him write anything more complicated than a receipt for barley – and an overpriced one at that.

Jonson dismounted, tied his horse to the fence and knocked on the front door. No one answered. He tried even more forcefully the second time as a crowd of children thundered down the lane chasing a big yellow dog. Still no answer. He jiggled the door but the lock held tight.

He walked around back and peeked through the window. Dark timbers lent the kitchen a dreary feeling. Dried herbs hung from the ceiling and a fire smoldered in the hearth. A skinned rabbit, seasoned and ready for roasting, lay on the table. Yet despite these modest signs of domesticity, the house seemed unwelcoming.

He pressed his nose against the glass and was startled by the sudden sensation of hot breath against his cheek. He turned and saw the yellow dog on its hind legs, panting and whining beside him. The hound dropped down and padded over to the back door, pawing it until it opened. It cocked its head at Jonson, inviting him to act as its accomplice.

Humored by the silent request, Jonson grinned and patted the dog. He followed it into the kitchen and watched as the four-legged burglar seized the rabbit from the table. Without so much as a nod in Jonson's direction, the dog ran off, escaping beyond the garden fence with its prize dangling from its jaws.

The playwright chuckled and closed the door. Immediately, he smelled a hearty stew simmering in a large kettle suspended over the hearth. He recalled that he hadn't eaten since daybreak. Seduced by the idea of satisfying his hunger, he stirred the kettle. Closing his eyes, he savored the aroma and raised the ladle to his lips.

He was suddenly distracted by a soft moan from the other room, and peered through the doorway to find its source. He saw an old man lying on a couch by the window, laid out like a corpse. Wisps of gray hair billowed from his bald head across his pillow. Was this gaunt apparition the scribe who had once been so bloated with brag and bluster? The jeweled rings on his scrawny fingers confirmed it. Jonson recognized the gaudy trophies of Shaxper's salad days when the impostor had flaunted them as symbols of his wealth and influence.

Given his condition, it was a miracle no one had stolen them.

Jonson rested the ladle against the kettle. He walked over to the couch and leaned down for a closer look. An angry voice shouted at him from behind.

"Who are you? I demand to know what you are doing here."

"I-I'm Ben Jonson, sir," he stammered, turning towards the doorway. " I'm a playwright from London, and an old associate of William Shaxper's, come to see him on a matter of the utmost importance. But if this is he, I'm afraid I may be too late."

"Too late? What, is he dead?" The gentleman rushed to the couch and knelt beside it. He rummaged through his leather bag and produced a small mirror. He held it under the old man's nose. The surface clouded with faint breath.

"Thank God, he's alive. You had me very worried, sir. I'm Dr. John Hall, William Shaxper's son-in-law. I recall his speaking of you, Jonson, and regret that my father-in-law cannot rise to greet you himself."

If he did, he'd spit in my eye, Jonson thought. Instead he said, "The kitchen door was open, so I walked in."

"We needn't lock our doors in Stratford. It's not like London. We don't have any thieves. And I'm sure *you* haven't come to steal anything, have you, Jonson?"

"Why, no. Certainly not," the playwright replied, thinking of the yellow dog who'd raced off with its plunder; and on the subject of thieves, he asked, "How is Mr. Shaxper?"

"Sad to say my father-in-law is very ill. That's why I insist that he must have absolute quiet and no visitors. I'm sorry, but I'm afraid I must ask you to leave."

"But I've come all this way to speak with him."

"Speak with him?" the doctor chuckled. "About what?"

"I want to prepare the Shake-speare plays for publication and I need his help."

"Oh, that's impossible. His days as a scribe are long past. He hasn't enough strength to scrawl his name, let alone sit up and copy out that endless content."

"Just give me a few moments to ask him if he knows where the original manuscripts are."

"Let me understand – you want to publish a complete folio of Shake-speare plays, but you don't know where the manuscripts are?"

"It does sound odd, doesn't it?" Jonson blushed. "We can't account for all of the plays – not yet, anyway. But your father-in-law's recollections could be of great help to me in finding them."

"I must say, he isn't always coherent."

"Still, I'd like to speak with him."

"He won't say much . . ."

"Perhaps. But at the very least I'd like to let him know that I came to Stratford out of respect to see him – for old times' sake."

"Don't toy with me, sir. We all know how you feel about my father-in-law. He used to regale us at the dinner table with the most shocking stories about you, and I'm sure every detail was true."

"No doubt," Jonson grinned, "a true reflection of William Shaxper as the natural child of honesty."

Hall completely missed Jonson's double meaning. "Very well, you may speak to him," the doctor concluded after a moment. "But don't upset the poor man with any talk of the public theaters. His days for that promiscuous nonsense are over. I'll have my man throw you out if he hears even one foul note of discord between you. Do you understand?"

"Yes. I understand. I promise not to upset anyone."

"My father-in-law is prone to hallucinations. You must choose your words carefully."

"Yes, I'm a writer, I can do that. He'll be fine. You'll see."

"I have other patients to look in on," Hall said. "Go and have your little talk with my father-in-law, Jonson. See if you can get anything sensible out of him."

"I will, Doctor, thank you. I'll be Wisdom and Tact personified, I swear."

"Never swear in vain, Jonson," Hall said. "I've heard that you possess neither of those qualities."

Jonson grinned awkwardly and tried to look reassuring.

Dr. Hall clutched his medical bag and went outside. Jonson saw him whisper to the brawny man pitching hay by the barn. The ruddy-faced servant wiped his sweaty brow and sat on a bench in the shade, fixing his eyes on the house as the doctor left to visit his patients.

Jonson turned and leaned over the scribe's pale body to assess his frail condition.

Suddenly, Shaxper's eyes fluttered open. The ghostly figure trembled and sat bolt upright. He stared at Jonson for a moment, recognition flickering in his cold eyes. He gasped and struggled to breathe. He gripped the playwright's shirt with his bony fists, pulling him down on top of him. The old man's rancid breath made him gag.

Jonson's voice strangled in his throat and he wrenched away, his heart pounding.

Shaxper wheezed and calmly looked into the eyes of his nemesis.

"It was worth risking a fit of apoplexy to scare the piss out of you!" he laughed.

"God damn it! You whoreson pimp!" Jonson shouted. "Was that supposed to be funny? Your man is ready to cudgel the piss out of me."

"I know, I heard. Now *that* would be entertaining," Shaxper said. "But I suppose you don't think so."

"You miserable ham! Trust you to have the bad taste to overact your own demise."

"What, have you no applause for my death scene?"

"It was mildly entertaining. Too bad it wasn't real."

"You were always jealous of my talent," Shaxper said, feigning a yawn. "Actually, it was a brilliant dress rehearsal; but alas, I'm not acting. I wrote my Last Will and Testament a month ago. I had to revise it when my daughter Judith ran off with that scoundrel Thomas Quiney, so I cut her out of it. I've left everything to my oldest girl Susanna – she's the doctor's wife – and to her mother, the untamed shrew – with one or two bequests for my theatrical friends. But don't count *your* money, Jonson. You're getting nothing. You're not even mentioned."

"That doesn't surprise me. You'd take everything with you, if you could arrange it with The Almighty. But you say you wrote your own Last Will and Testament – or did you steal the wording from someone else and clap your name on it?"

"Go to, Jonson! The legal language is common, and in my youth I prepared such documents when my father was alderman. You can spout better insults than that, you old carbuncle."

"Let's call a truce then. Tell me, what ails you, Shaxper? Why are you ill?" Jonson asked. "Has venereal disease finally caught up with you?"

"Ha! If only I had the working parts to catch it! No, it's not the Spanish disease. The doctor says I have a weak heart."

"Well, then. That confirms the long-standing opinion of England's literary men."

"God's blood, I thought we had a truce. Or shall I summon my man from the barn?" Shaxper prepared to shout.

"No, don't. We've had our differences in the past, but if you want my opinion, you're much too young to die. You're only fifty-two years old, younger than Thomas Lodge, George Chapman, Anthony Munday –"

"Ah, my contemporaries, England's great literary men," Shaxper said, sarcastically. "Are those hacks still alive?"

"Those *playwrights* are still alive, yes."

"Do they still hate me?"

"None of them would write you a glowing epitaph."

"They were always jealous of me."

"Jealous of you? They were outraged! You were trafficking in stolen manuscripts."

"I had Lord Oxford's permission to do what I did."

"Yes, during his lifetime. But we all know how you profited from his plays after his death."

"I had to earn a living. He was taken from us so suddenly."

"Aye, indeed; murdered like Marlowe," Jonson sighed.

"At home, in his own bed," Shaxper said, mournfully. He looked Jonson in the eye. "So, why did you come all the way from London to Stratford? There's always been bad blood between us, so I know you didn't come here to inquire about my health. You told my son-in-law there's a publishing venture in the works, and you need my help to accomplish it. Let's talk like businessmen. There must be some compensation in it for me."

"The Countess of Montgomery never said anything about paying you---"

"Ah, the Countess, Lord Oxford's daughter. Well, she wouldn't begrudge me a gratuity after all these years. I'll wager her husband and his brother have already contracted a publisher. The Herberts are so well connected in the literary world. There must be some money in it for me."

"Money! Is that all you ever think about? You weren't content with simply pirating Oxford's plays, but you also bought *The Second Maiden's Tragedy* from Thomas Middleton and copied it in your own hand so you could sell it as a Shakespeare play and fetch a high price. All of the writers found out what you did, so you're not in any position to make demands."

"Perhaps the Countess will allow me to make a few personal appearances as Shake-speare. I need the money. Upcoming funeral expenses, you know."

"Absolutely not. It's time for us to reveal the truth about the authorship."

"Powerful men in the government will fight you on that point," Shaxper said. "Are you ready to die with a noose around your neck?"

"The Countess has hired me to see her father's plays into print, and she believes you know where they are," Jonson said.

"She has misled you then. Too much time has passed. I know nothing."

"You stashed the papers somewhere—"

"What does it matter? The playhouses only show *Pericles* nowadays."

"I am prepared to acknowledge your unique contribution to Lord Oxford's work in our folio," Jonson bargained. "After all, you were his most faithful confidante."

"More important than his wives, his lovers, his children or his beloved Queen," Shaxper added. "I guarded his darkest secrets, any one of which could have toppled the nation when he was angry; and oh, he was angry so often! I always managed to calm him down and remind him that our secret work on behalf of England was more important."

"God's blood, he needed no reminder of that from the likes of you. Your audacity makes my head spin."

"Very well, Jonson; spin this – to hell with you *and* the Herberts *and* your Shake-speare folio. I won't summon my man, but I'll not say another word. I'll take my secrets to the grave."

Shaxper folded his arms and pursed his lips like a spoiled child.

"Forgive me," Jonson pleaded anxiously, realizing he'd gone too far. He gently grasped Shaxper by the shoulders and looked into his eyes. "I was wrong to offend you, sir. After all these years, you do deserve a proper hearing for everything you suffered as Lord Oxford's front man. I'm sure it would lighten your spirit to reveal those secrets, even to an old fire-eater like me. Let's close the rift between us. Perhaps it would mend your ailing heart to bring you to some confession of your true state, as it were."

"Yes, a deathbed confession would ease my mind," Shaxper said. "But I must warn you – the truth will be far more burdensome than you think."

Jonson ignored the warning. He sat down to listen and visualized the manuscripts drifting closer.

CHAPTER FOUR

The Scene: Southwark, London

April 8th, 1584

"O cheerful colors! See where Oxford comes!"

– Henry the Sixth, Part 3

T he cacophony of street musicians competed with church bells as Sunday morning believers transformed into afternoon revelers. Puritans prayed over the wayward multitude, hoping to turn their giddy souls away from the wicked playhouses; but their homilies fell on uncaring ears, drowned out by the rollicking merrymakers.

"Piety trampled in the gutters!" That's what John Shaxper would have said, had he known his son longed to answer that heathen call. John depended on William to take over the family grain business one day. Now that the boy was safely-married, they had come to London to learn how to increase their income by expanding their involvement in the wool trade.

John didn't know it, but William already had ambitions of his own and none of them included the wool business or the aging spinster he'd impregnated several months ago. William didn't love Anne Hathaway any more than he loved the sheep grazing in his father's field. He resented being forced to marry her simply because the bulge in his breeches required immediate relief on the day he delivered her order of grain and chose to thrust in a few seeds of his own. He loathed the idea of starting a crop of babies that would tie him down in Stratford. In London, William saw that there was hope for excitement and a life beyond the mundane.

With his father kneeling beside him in prayer, twenty-year old William heard the revelers outside and wasn't about to pass up his chance for adventure. He bowed his head, crossed himself and crept out of the church, leaving the older man to counsel with God over the success of the venture that had brought them to London.

William stepped into the street and was immediately swept along with the crowd and deposited in front of The Curtain, one of the many public theaters along the Thames. Someone thrust a crumpled handbill at him. He smoothed it out and read that Lord Oxford's Men were to perform *The Famous Victories of Henry the Fifth* at two o'clock that afternoon. People were already queuing up to see it. The leaflet boasted that the original play had been thoroughly enjoyed at Court for its audacious swordplay, satire and romance. For the cost of a penny, one could see the same spectacle that had so delighted the Queen. William was sorely tempted, having never seen anything like it in his bucolic country town.

Only yesterday, when they arrived in London, his father had railed that the playhouses were havens for whores and pickpockets.

"Actors are the minions of Satan," John Shaxper said. "A man's worst inclinations are aroused every time some beardless boy acts like a woman in a love scene."

His words aroused William's curiosity. He was sure they expressed his father's shame at the events that had transpired a year earlier on a similar trip to London.

John Shaxper had been robbed and severely beaten in an alley behind one of the playhouses. Unable to recall his name or any part of his identity, he was locked away in Bedlam as the beneficiary of charity. If his wife hadn't gone to find him, he would have been lost forever. His rescuers had been as delicate as possible in describing his condition to her.

Back home under Mary's care, John gradually recovered, although he never spoke about the mysterious London incident. William was frequently awakened by his father's nightmarish screams. Whatever had befallen him, drunkenness was now the only relief John Shaxper knew. He suffered the humiliation of being quickly removed from his post as alderman. His neighbors saw that the once-affable merchant had returned from London a battered and broken man.

Accompanied by his son this time, John had pointed out the play-houses and grumbled that each one was crowned with a colorful banner that allowed even the most illiterate simpleton to fall into Hell. Perhaps that was true, but William ignored his words. With youthful callousness, he took note of the locations and vowed to see a play as soon as pos-sible, confident that he was too smart to be lured down a dark alley, even for an exciting assignation.

He now stood amidst the revelers. They were rank and unwashed, and seemed to be a truly devilish lot. Even their Sunday garments were rancid with sweat, having no hint of the fresh lavender used for launder-ing in the country.

William gagged as the crowd pressed in tightly. Someone puffed tobacco smoke at him. A drunk jostled him and coughed in his face. As the boisterous mob clamored towards The Curtain, he wondered how the Earl of Oxford could lend his name to such a frenzied enterprise as a company of players.

And yet, like a moth seduced by candlelight, William was drawn to it, too.

A coach pulled up to the playhouse. A fashionable lord and lady stepped out and were hurriedly whisked inside. As the wealthier patrons arrived, William saw that not all theatergoers were coarse and rude. The nobles and ladies had impeccable manners and seemed none the worse for attending a playhouse. Even the Queen had survived the corrupting influence of *The Famous Victories* to give it a pleasant testimonial. William concluded that if Satan hadn't thrust Her Majesty into Hell over a theater piece, especially with the Pope so confident that she would end up there anyway, the son of a grain dealer could also escape damnation.

Now if only he had the money to see it . . .

He slid his hands into his pockets and felt what might be a penny trapped in the lining of his breeches. He fingered and pinched it until he finally captured it. He gently guided it up through the small tear and removed it carefully to avoid dropping it into the street, where it would be lost forever. He held it up to the light and saw that it was indeed a penny. He rubbed it with gratitude, unsure whether God or the Devil had just granted him his own famous victory.

A few steps away from the door, he glanced up at The Curtain's banner, unfurling in the breeze, bearing the emblem of a writer's hand thrusting through a curtain. He noted the strange design but gave no particular thought to its meaning as he dropped his penny into the admission box and stepped inside.

He was surprised to find that the interior of the playhouse looked more like a hectic marketplace than the venue for a play. Beneath the noblemen and ladies seated on the stage and in the balconies were peddlers that passed through the crowd hawking their wares. The commoners responded with greedy indulgence. Mulled wine, meat pies, herbal cures and political pamphlets swiftly changed hands. Musicians transformed the scene into a bacchanalia of commerce.

A boy ushered William to a roped-off area several feet from the stage. This was where the groundlings stood, he explained, those like William who had paid the cheapest price for admission. He suggested that he work his way through the crowd for a better view. Taking his advice, William vigorously elbowed his neighbors as they had elbowed past him on the street.

He pushed his way through, still assaulted by the dizzying stench of ale and sweat. He clutched the rope to keep his balance. The afternoon sun poured through the open roof. The putrid odors reminded him of his father's drunkenness, which had cast his mother's family into disgrace because of their neighbors' gossip. But he was in London now, not Stratford. No one here cared a whit about the personal failures that had driven John Shaxper to drink, and that those were the very same failures that had strengthened William's determination to better himself.

The adventurous young man savored the giddy atmosphere of the theater. He gazed at the galleries and wooden stage, and watched as a well-dressed gentleman placed the admission box in a small room and locked the door behind it, rattling it to make sure it was secure. William concluded that there must be a fortune worth protecting on the other side. Surely there was lots of money to be made in this new medium of the theater! Clearly, his father had been foolish to dismiss it out-of-hand.

The music stopped and the audience quieted. A refined gentleman with boundless energy burst through the curtains at the back of the stage. His white doublet and hose were elaborately trimmed with black lace and his narrow face was framed by a ruffled collar. He stood center stage and bowed with a flourish to the nobles. He directed a mischievous grin at the groundlings and blew a kiss to a lady in the gallery.

Then he flung his arms open as if embracing the audience and the crowd cheered wildly.

William maneuvered into a more comfortable spot. He overheard some random snatches of conversation among the groundlings, and suddenly, the young man next to him pointed at the stage.

"Look, it's the Earl of Oxford!"

William glanced up in awestruck admiration.

"That impudent devil!" an old crone laughed. "He'll earn some good money with this play, I'll warrant ye."

"I think not. A nobleman can't get his hands dirty earning a living like we do."

"Ha! Isn't that always their excuse for an idle life!"

"This nobleman isn't idle," another person protested. "He offers us plays just as he offers them to the Queen. That doesn't sound idle to me, not in the least."

Determined to get as close as he could to the remarkable nobleman, William brushed past the dour critics and inched towards some empty chairs at the back of the stage, hoping that no one would see him crawl under the rope and take a seat. He was delighted that instead of standing for hours, he could watch the play in comfort. He was so close to Lord Oxford now, he could see the exquisite stitching on his doublet.

Suddenly, he was yanked by the collar and hoisted into the air.

"You, groundling! You didn't pay for this seat. Get back behind the ropes or I'll throw you out." Stunned, William didn't move.

The gentleman picked him up and tossed him onto the dirt floor. The groundlings roared with laughter at his comeuppance. His head hurt, and as he slunk back under the rope, William wondered if this was a sign from God that he should have stayed in church.

Red-faced with humiliation, he dusted himself off. Just as the idea of returning to his father dawned on him, the musicians played a martial song and the show began. The audience hushed as the actors took their places to enact *The Famous Victories*.

The play opened in the aftermath of a highway robbery. Prince Hal and his accomplices were adding up the money they had stolen from the royal tax collectors while King Henry IV lay dying. That was indeed a tragedy; but the audience laughed when Prince Hal boxed the ears of the Lord Chief Justice and demanded his henchmen's freedom. They wept when the old King died, unaware of his son's deception. And when Prince Hal became king, he immediately quit his madcap ways and later emerged as the triumphant hero at Agincourt. The audience gasped at the fight scenes, hooted for the clowns and sighed at Hal's tender and strategically played romance with Lady Katherine.

When it was over, William stood in front of the empty stage. The message of the play had hit its mark: that a young man could attain great heights in spite of his youthful indiscretions. William's folly had been impregnating Anne Hathaway. He had paid for it with his life by being forced to marry her.

So if the message in *The Famous Victories* was true, William could secure a brighter future after all. His dreams of gentility suddenly seemed more attainable.

With his headache mysteriously gone, it occurred to him that he should apologize for his bad behavior. Obviously, he'd made a fool of himself; and, if he wanted to work in the theater, it wouldn't do to create a bad reputation with the nobleman who seemed to be in charge of the whole business.

He looked around for Lord Oxford but couldn't find him. Instead he saw the gentleman who had thrown him off the stage talking with the man who had delivered the admission box. Perhaps if he offered them his sincerest apologies and explained his situation, they might understand and forgive him and arrange an introduction to the flamboyant Earl of Oxford.

William listened quietly at the door, as if waiting for his cue.

"His Lordship says that the authorities will be shutting down the playhouses again," one of the men said. "For the next three months, we'll need to move our performances to the countryside."

"As he pleases, but I must say, traveling with the full company is difficult," the second man said.

"I agree, but we have no other choice. He suggests that you simplify the staging to suit more rustic tastes. We'll have to work without our usual trap doors or backstage devices, and the play is going to need a proper venue."

"Please assure His Lordship that I'll do whatever it takes to produce an excellent show, Mr. Lyly. Tell him that."

"He knows. He has great faith in you, Evans, and that's why he's paying you in advance."

William heard the sound of money changing hands.

"This is very generous, but under the present circumstances, can His Lordship really afford to pay all this?"

"Somehow there's never a shortage of money where his plays are concerned. Now, of course, we'll need wagons to convey the actors and the props, and it might prove less costly to use local tailors and carpenters to sew costumes and build platforms. That should provide some good income for the merchants in town. The village of Stratford in Warwickshire is to be our first stop, and we'll need to find a large barn or guildhall for the performances. Do you think that will be a problem?"

Surprised by the mention of Stratford, William waited for Evans' reply.

"A good-sized barn shouldn't be difficult to find, if the price is right," he heard him say.

William waited for the conversation to end. After Evans left, he framed himself in the doorway and addressed the gentleman in the chair.

"I beg your pardon, sir. May I have a word with you about this afternoon's performance?"

"Indeed you may," John Lyly said. He introduced himself as manager of The Curtain and secretary to the Earl of Oxford. "I am at your service, sir. Come in, come in. Do you have a good review of this performance?"

"Oh, yes. It was marvelous, Mr. Lyly, watching history triumph on the stage. You must tell His Lordship so, and send him my greatest compliments."

A look of recognition shone in the gentleman's eyes.

"Aren't you the ruffian I chucked off the stage?"

"Well, yes and no . . ."

"What do you mean, yes and no? What kind of an answer is that?"

"To be precise, sir, yes, I was on the stage. But no, I'm not a ruffian."

"Is that supposed to be clever? What do you want?"

"I want to apologize to you, to the entire company and especially to His Lordship for my rude behavior this afternoon. Can you pass that message on for me?"

"I shall, sir. But whom shall I say is sending such winning approval? What is your name, sir?"

"Forgive me," William said, stammering an introduction. He prattled on about his passion for the theater and how it had enticed him away from church.

"Well, I do have to admit that you greatly amused Lord Oxford," Lyly laughed. "He thinks we should pay you to be thrown off the stage at every performance! Good clowns are hard to find, and we always sell more tickets when the groundlings think such antics are part of the show. If you were trying to impress the Earl of Oxford, I'd say you succeeded rather well."

Eager to be taken seriously, William said, "I'd rather impress him with the fact that I see theater as a profitable business enterprise."

"Is that so? His Lordship sees it as an art."

"Rightly so, theater *is* an art; and thank Heaven it has a patron like Lord Oxford to support it. But while he and other noblemen aren't permitted to earn an income in business, the rest of us must work for our daily bread, isn't that true? Even the actors must receive some salary."

"And the tailors and the carpenters and the musicians and the copyists," Lyly sighed. "Everyone must be compensated. We consider ourselves fortunate when we can convert even a small profit, however meager, into a new play. Production is costly, even for country tastes."

"That's why I want to offer you my services," William said. "While I was waiting to speak with you, I overheard you say that you were bringing this play to Stratford. Pardon my boldness, but my father owns a thriving grain business there and we have a barn that's virtually empty at this time of year. I can rent it to his Lordship's company – for the right price."

"A *fair* price," Lyly insisted.

"It will be fair for all of us," William said, wondering how his father would react to the prospect of renting his barn to a congregation of heathens.

Lyly studied the young man, observing that his confidence had grown during their brief talk. Behind his rustic manners lurked a shrewd tradesman who could strike a clever bargain.

"I can ride out with Evans and look at your barn," Lyly said, "and if it suits our purposes, we will rent it. The final decision rests with Lord Oxford, of course."

"Of course," William said firmly, trying not to betray the vital importance of his next request. "There is one more thing, sir. I wonder if the Earl of Oxford would be generous enough to grant me a small favor."

"And what is that?"

"To permit me to learn how a play is built."

"Oh, I'm sure His Lordship wouldn't mind letting you work among the carpenters."

"Not with hammers and nails, sir, but with pen and ink," William said. Fearing a refusal, he quickly explained. "I'd like to learn how a play is built from the time it is written until the time it is acted upon the stage, so I can inform myself about every aspect of this business."

Lyly stared at him in disbelief.

"I'm afraid that's impossible, sir. Our company has been cursed with an abundance of spies who try to discredit His Lordship's loyalty because of his interest in the theater. With all due respect, as far as I know, you could be one of them. The Earl of Oxford would never agree to meet you or let you see his work unless you could convince him that you are trustworthy. But first, you'll have to convince me."

"I will do that in Stratford, sir. My friends and neighbors will vouch for me. And I can sell them tickets to the play in advance, if you would allow it."

"Sell tickets in advance? An interesting prospect," Lyly said, thoughtfully. "No one has ever done such a thing. I suppose we could pay you a percentage of your sales. Let me think about it and convey your ideas on commerce to the Earl of Oxford."

"Thank you, sir. I am honored that you would consider doing so," William fawned. "I hope you have forgiven me for my reckless behavior earlier this afternoon."

"I have, sir. I'll consider it nothing more than a round of youthful exuberance. I'm sure that your enterprising spirit will allow you to earn enough money to afford better seating at The Curtain next time," Lyly said, as he ushered the young man from the playhouse.

On the way out, William nodded politely to Henry Evans and fancied that he saw Fortune smiling back at him.

CHAPTER FIVE

The Scene: Stratford-on-Avon
two weeks later, April 23, 1584

"Now I play a merchant's part . . ."
– The Taming of the Shrew

S tratford had seen its share of traveling farces, religious pageants
and puppet shows, but it had never seen anything like *The
Famous Victories,* with its clever mix of comedy, tragedy and
history.

When John Lyly agreed to pay him an extra incentive for tickets
sold in advance, William Shaxper became a relentless promoter. He
impressed his neighbors with the importance of seeing the same play
that had delighted the Queen, and warned them that companies like Lord
Oxford's Men would bypass the village in the future if it didn't support
the players. Fortunately, the hardworking people of Stratford appreciated a good diversion. Tickets were quickly sold and Lyly was pleased.
William could hardly wait for his introduction to the Earl of Oxford.

As the money poured in, he began to envision himself a theatrical impresario, garnering hefty profits by importing the latest cultural sensations into Stratford. Even his skeptical wife Anne admitted that his trip to London had emboldened him. The growing popularity of the playhouses proved that theater was indeed a lucrative business, despite John Shaxper's insistence that it was a godless waste of time.

Beyond that, William never lost sight of his ultimate goal: a proper introduction to the Earl of Oxford, with whom, he had come to feel, his fortunes rested.

His hopes for an impending meeting were quickly dashed when he learned that Lord Oxford would not be traveling with the company. In spite of this sudden disappointment, William's strong determination allowed him to carry on with his plans.

Excitement spread when the play wagons rolled into Stratford. The villagers applauded the motley juggler and the small black dog that jumped through a row of hoops. A crier waved The Curtain's enigmatic flag and shouted that *The Famous Victories of Henry the Fifth* would be performed the very next day at Shaxper's barn on Henley Street.

No one was more startled to hear that than John Shaxper. Barely recovered from a drinking binge, he cornered his son behind the pub.

"What do you mean by renting my barn to those heathens?"

William ignored the bitter words and wiped the old man's face. "You've been drunk for a month now, Father. The ale is leaching out of your pores. Don't you think it's time to stop?"

"Bloody hell! I'll drink when I please, and I'll not have my boy telling me to stop. Show me the respect I deserve as your father."

"I'm sorry, sir, but you whipped it out of me years ago. And what you did to Mother was a disgrace."

"I never hurt your mother, not once –"

"No, not once, but many times," William said. "You foolishly lost her inheritance and forced us all into debt. You were seen drunk in public and dismissed from your post as alderman. You tormented our neighbors by piling a dung heap next to their door. You were disgraced and jailed so often, it broke Mother's heart. Well, I'm not going to follow in your footsteps. See this, Father?" he asked, dangling a purse in front of him. "I earned all this money in one week - *in one week*, for selling our neighbors tickets to a play! And I'll earn even greater riches, now that I'm working my way into Lord Oxford's good graces. You should be proud of me, Father. I've made a neat little profit for myself and this is only the beginning."

John Shaxper grabbed for the purse. William tucked it safely into his own pocket.

"When I was a boy, I knew you loved me, Father," he said. "But everything changed when you came back from London bruised and battered, and the decent life you had worked so hard to build crumbled all around you. You found your courage in kegs of ale, but I don't believe that's how a man should live in this world. I found my courage with the players, Father, and I'm determined to work hard for the rest of my life to make a name for myself. I am terribly sorry for whatever happened to you behind that playhouse, but as long as I live, I swear I'll never drown my sorrows in hogsheads of ale the way you do."

"You think you know what the world is, boy," the old man grumbled, "but you're a blind, stumbling puppy in a pack of hungry wolves. You'll learn what evil is, if you persist in associating with that deviant band of miscreant players --"

John Shaxper lunged at his son, lost his balance and fell.

He lay on the ground in a heap, waiting for William to pick him up and dust him off, and perhaps pay him to go on his way as he had so many other times. He was such a good boy, William, a regular milksop, driven by the same gentle compassion his mother showed even to the smallest of God's creatures.

William stared at the pathetic figure in the dirt. Despite his anger, he pulled his father up, dusted him off and slipped him some coins.

"Get along, Father. Go home, and give this money to Mother."

"No, not yet . . . best swallow more courage before The Bull closes tonight."

John Shaxper grinned and turned away. He spat on the ground and lurched off towards the pub.

For two straight days *The Famous Victories* drew appreciative audiences. When the final performance ended, William watched as the theatrical illusions vanished before his eyes. Gone was the envisioned battlefield. Actors were no longer princes or warriors, but ordinary men spending their pay at The Bull. The local tailors and carpenters drank and supped beside them, as if the play itself had forged them into a company of brothers. Props and costumes were packed onto wagons for travel the next day.

With the closing of the play and the barn emptied, William felt abandoned and useless. Things hadn't gone the way he'd planned, and he longed for a happy ending to his own story. Now he was even more confused about how he (or any man) could undertake a career in the theater. If there were books to read, he would find them. If there was a school to attend, he would apply to it. If he had to serve an apprenticeship, he would slavishly endure it. But if his path to success was barred, he would be trapped in the pitiful existence his termagant wife and drunken father had carved out for him in Stratford.

Worst of all, it seemed as if John Lyly had forgotten to commend him to the Earl of Oxford.

The town grew quiet. Lanterns flickered in the descending night. Suddenly, a stentorian voice boomed from a nearby tent.

"Good my Lord of Oxford, go see who hath done this deed!"

Perhaps His Lordship had come to Stratford after all!

William struggled to control his excitement as he ran towards the tent, aware that he couldn't miss this miraculous opportunity. It had already been proven that he couldn't count on John Lyly to put him forward. He must take matters into his own hands, as the proverb said, and manage his own destiny.

Words whirled in his head like chaff in the wind. He imagined explaining his numerous ticket sales to Lord Oxford, followed by an ardent declaration of his love for the theater and why it would make him an excellent player. And then Lord Oxford would graciously accept him into the company, and his fortune would be made for the rest of his life. William was sure it would work; and then he hoped it would work. And finally, he *had* to make it work before his certainty faded altogether.

William straightened his shirt, ran his fingers through his hair and hesitated at the entrance. He said a prayer to bolster his confidence, eased the tent flap slightly and peaked inside.

In the shadows, he recognized William Browne, the distinguished actor who had portrayed Prince Hal, removing his makeup in front of a mirror. Browne gently slid off Prince Hal's false nose, revealing his own underneath. He pulled off his bowl-cut wig and shook out his reddish-brown hair. He peeled off round cheekbones to expose his angular face. He mimicked lines from the play to John Lyly, who stood nearby.

"If it please your Grace, the crown is taken away."

"Good my Lord of Oxford, go see who hath done this deed. No doubt 'tis some vile traitor that hath done it, to deprive my son. They that would do it now would seek to scrape and scrawl for it after my death!"

William quickly realized that Browne had dissolved, and in his place was the Earl of Oxford, the elegant courtier who had opened his arms to embrace the audience at The Curtain. John Lyly stood by, holding a pair of gloves and a walking stick.

The great nobleman had disguised himself to come to Stratford with the actors; but why? William chose to eavesdrop on the strange scene unfolding before him.

"The Roman god Janus had two faces; but for me as a player-within-a-player, it's a difficult task," Oxford said.

"Quite so, my lord," Lyly replied, "and once again, you've skirted the Queen's ban. I can only imagine how she'll feel about it, if she finds out."

"I've skirted her before and she never complained," Oxford laughed, offering a double meaning. "At least she can't dispute the historical accuracy of the play. The Earl of Oxford fought beside King Henry V at Agincourt."

"But he was the 11th earl, my lord, and you are the 17th. And if you persist in ignoring the Queen's ban against noblemen acting and play-writing, you could be the last."

"I'm not afraid of that," Oxford sighed. "God knows, it might be a relief to be a little less noble and a little more common so that I can move about my life with greater ease. This time I wrote my noble name Oxford *into* the play instead of *on* it, which covers my identity as play-wright and suggests it, all at the same time."

"Even so, my lord, if the public discovers that you indulge in base pursuits--"

"*Base pursuits?* By my word, Lyly, whether I perform at Her Majesty's Court or in the public playhouses, what royal tastes find sweet won't sour in the public appetite."

"But acting in barns? You must admit that's quite beneath your dig-nified rank. You shouldn't have done it, my lord. It's demeaning. You shouldn't have come to Stratford."

"Nonsense. I played the role of a great king."

"Against the odor of animal dung. Did you see the size of that dung-hill outside? I heard it's the talk of the town and the subject of a lawsuit against the family that owns this barn."

William blushed.

"Rank is rank," Oxford said, "and it smells rank when I'm forbidden to live as I please."

"If you anger the Queen, she'll spike your head on London Bridge."

"Oh, I think not. Heaven knows I've given her cause many times, but Eliza has always protected me, ever since she cloaked my transla-tion of Ovid under my Uncle Golding's name so it could be published without scandal. She has loved me since I was a boy -- in more ways than one."

William was astounded by the bawdy tone of the innuendo. He strained to hear Lyly's reply.

"The risk is great, my lord. Your words have a unique stamp. You reveal yourself with each one and spare neither friend nor foe in your comic satires. The Queen barely tolerates it."

"Perhaps Her Majesty is offended because I taunt everyone equally."

"Prince Hal is the perfect example. You boast that your play is his-torically accurate, and then you write in it that Prince Hal and his men robbed the King's receivers at Gad's Hill. Well, that never happened, my lord. From the time he was Prince Hal until the time he became King Henry V, he did no such thing."

"That's true. Prince Hal and his men never committed robbery at Gad's Hill."

"No, but you and your men did," Lyly whispered.

"It was a theatrical event, a staged outdoor performance."

"It didn't amuse Lord Burghley. It was his money stolen. He com-plained to the Queen."

"And do you know what she did? She laughed herself silly during our pillow talk! She mocked Burghley's complaint and then laughed when I went to the foot of our bed and portrayed how his men groveled, dropped the money and fled. It was probably my money that we stole back, for he winnowed a large part of my inheritance away from me over the years. Gad's Hill will always be a sacred place for me, Lyly," Oxford sighed dramatically. "It was there that I witnessed the miraculous conversion of Lord Burghley's men from receivers into givers."

"That's all well enough, my lord, but I do wish you'd take my concerns seriously."

"There is nothing to fear. The Queen has sworn to protect me."

"For as long as she lives, my lord, and who knows how long that will be with her health so precarious?"

"Come now, you know it's against the law to contemplate the death of a monarch . . ."

Realizing he'd heard too much, William turned and tripped over a tent spike. He winced as he hit the ground.

"What was that?" Oxford asked. "Did you hear a noise?"

"Indeed, my lord. It was close by. I'll have a look."

William pressed himself into the grass, wishing the night would render him invisible. From the corner of his eye, he saw Lyly a few feet away, moving a lantern from side to side. Its rays sought William, but by some miracle, the light didn't betray him.

"Nothing there, my lord," Lyly reported. "It must have been the wind."

"I suppose it's safe for me to leave under the cloak of night," Oxford said. "Please pack Prince Hal carefully. Verily, he is a man of parts, with his nose here and his cheeks there and his bowl-cut tresses resting on the table."

"I'll take good care of him, my lord, and meet you back at the inn."

William stood up and dusted himself off. As he did, his elbow lightly brushed the tent.

Lyly caught the gentle rustle of the cloth. He opened the tent flap and shoved a lantern towards William's face. Lord Oxford grabbed the intruder and leveled a dagger at his throat.

"Who are you, sirrah? Speak before I strike you!"

"Forgive me, my lord. I didn't mean to trespass on your privacy."

"I should gut you like a salmon and toss your fishified flesh into the river. Who are you? Who sent you to spy on me?"

"N-no one," William stammered. "I'm not a spy. I'm the man who rented you the barn."

"And so he is," Lyly confirmed. "He's been pestering me for weeks for an introduction to you."

"So, sirrah, you have met me," Oxford said. "Tell me, is this the cordial encounter you desired? It occurs to me that you eavesdrop behind curtains in the same tedious fashion as my father-in-law. You must be one of his spies."

"No, my lord, I am not. I came to talk with you about joining your acting company. I am very sad to learn that you're forced to disguise yourself --"

"This man is mad, Lyly. He's imagining things. We must send him to a madhouse or cut his throat so he won't distress anyone with his wild ravings."

"On my honor," William said, his voice creaking with fear, "I'll swear an oath never to reveal anything I saw or heard here."

"I don't believe you. You look like a man who'd sell his mother to the devil for a ducat, and then join him for supper on her parboiled remains."

"Please!" William sobbed, as Oxford pressed the knife deeper. "I'm just a grain merchant with a wife and children. I'm nothing, I'm nobody! Please let me go."

"Swear on your mother's virtue that you'll keep silent."

"On my mother's virtue, I swear I'll never utter a word!"

William closed his eyes. He felt Oxford's breath against his face just above the knife.

An eternity seemed to pass before Oxford released his grip and pushed William from the tent.

"Get out of here, villain, before I learn that you're a liar and your mother is the town whore!"

William fled amidst the sounds of mocking laughter. Lanterns flickered as the night distorted familiar landmarks into ghostly silhouettes. He cursed himself for looking like an imbecile in front of the Earl of Oxford, for losing his chance to join the players, and for failing at everything he tried. What, he wondered, had ever deluded him into thinking he could better himself?

The answer came to him, and he stopped in his tracks.

The road to his success was paved with a courtier's secret.

CHAPTER SIX

The Scene: London
Several months later, October 19, 1584

"By indirections find directions out."
– Hamlet

When his mother casually revealed that her family was distantly related to the Earls of Oxford, William stared at her in disbelief.

She'd never spoken of it before, and never had cause to mention it, but his incessant chattering about the players must have raised the association in her mind. William was thrilled to discover that his Arden family tree bore a fruitful connection to Elizabeth Trussel, wife of the 15th Earl of Oxford, and thus Lord Oxford's grandmother. Certainly, that would improve his chances of having his apology accepted in light of the frightening turn of events inside the tent. All he had to do now was declare his kinship, impress His Lordship with his unrivaled talent and his fortune would be insured, thanks to the unbounded blessing his mother had bestowed on him with a few casual words.

William wrote a letter to his old schoolmate, Richard Field. Originally apprenticed to the London printer George Bishop, Richard now worked for Thomas Vautrollier, one of the city's finest publishers. His life had vastly improved since leaving Stratford, and William hoped some of that success would rub off on him. The next day he said a hasty farewell to his wife Anne and promised to return home as soon as possible. He rode to London in the hope of finding a job in Vautrollier's shop at the sign of the white greyhound near St. Paul's.

Clad in a former employer's doublet, Shaxper walked down cobblestone streets until he found the proprietor's shingle. He smiled, pushed open the weathered door and stepped inside. The bell above jingled a courteous welcome.

The shop was filled with morning sunlight. In one corner, pens, paper and parchment were wrapped and ready for sale and the smell of ink permeated the room. Books published by Vautrollier lined some tall shelves along one wall and a few scattered benches encouraged customers to sit and browse. Only the wealthy had the time and money to afford such luxuries. While he envisioned a glowing future for himself, at present William only had enough money to pay for his lodgings, unless Richard felt inclined to be generous.

He wandered to the back of the shop and peeked through the doorway. At the printing press he saw Richard receiving some instructions from a man, apparently his employer.

"There are too many errors on the last few pages, Richard," he said. "You must always insist on perfection from the compositors. Each man must be accountable for his work. If we fail to be accurate, we must do the job again and that becomes far too costly. *Comprenez-vous?*"

"Yes, Monsieur Vautrollier, I understand."

William heard the floorboards creak behind him. He turned to see a petite, businesslike woman offering him a welcoming smile.

"Good day, sir. May I help you find a particular book today?"

"N-no, I-I'm not here to buy a book," he stammered. "My name is William Shaxper and I've come to see my friend, Richard Field."

"Ah yes, Richard told us all about you," she said. "Your friend is a very hard worker."

"He always worked hard, especially in school. But as for myself, I cannot say the same."

"I'm sure you're being modest, sir. Allow me to introduce myself. I am Jacqueline Vautrollier, proprietor of this shop."

"You own this shop?"

"My husband and I are partners in marriage and in business. Why do you look so surprised?" she laughed. "I'm sure there are marriages in Stratford."

"Yes, but no publishing partnerships. Most of Stratford's women are housewives."

"Most of London's female publishers are widows, which is a fate we all hope to avoid since we are married to our work. Oh, but it's time for Monsieur's medicine. Richard!" she called. "Your friend from Stratford is here. Come and visit while Monsieur and I take our herbs."

When the couple had gone, the two sworn brothers from the country school in Stratford greeted each other with friendly fisticuffs.

"Why, Willy Nilly!" Richard shouted. "I can't believe you're finally here!"

"I haven't heard that nickname in years, Dickie."

"But look at you. Where in God's name did you get that doublet?"

"I stole it from a corpse."

"God's blood, you didn't!"

"Well, that's partly true. Mister Houghton left it to me in his will."

"Alexander Houghton of Lea Hall, the man who hired us to sing?"

"The same. He stipulated that I make good use of it. Well, what do you think? Have I followed his wishes?"

"He certainly left you well suited," Richard quipped. "Remember that secret maze of tunnels under his house and how we celebrated Mass underground? We were so young and foolhardy, toying with the authorities who would have arrested us in the middle of our prayers."

"How true," William sighed. "It seems like another lifetime. But since then, I've made some exciting new plans."

"I know. I've been fascinated by your letters. Why the sudden change in your career? Will you be moving Anne and the family to London?"

"Not exactly. I'll explain everything in a moment. But I can see you've been secretive, too. Your letters rambled on about your success, but you never mentioned anything about the beautiful Jacqueline Vautrollier."

"She's a good wife. She takes excellent care of my master. He hasn't been well lately, but his condition is improving."

"It sounded serious in your letters. Maybe you'll get lucky and he'll die and you can take over the shop."

"Quiet, Willy, she'll hear you. Show some respect. She's my master's wife, for God's sake."

"She told me herself that she's married to the printing business. You may not have noticed, but I saw the way she smiled at you."

"She's grateful, that's all," Richard replied. "She has depended on me to run the shop during Monsieur's illness. They have been very good to me over the years."

"But you never know. It may only be a matter of time before you're left to comfort the grieving widow – and this is a very profitable business."

"You haven't changed a bit, still the same vulgar mind," Richard said, shaking his head.

"What you call 'vulgar' I call practical. Money is everything, especially when you don't have it. Or have you forgotten our impecunious childhoods?"

"I haven't forgotten anything."

"Good. Then you've spoken to Vautrollier about a job for me."

"Not in those exact words, but I have spoken about you . . ."

"Well, does he have a position for me or not?"

Richard rubbed the back of his neck and looked down at the floor. "The proper time to ask him hasn't presented itself yet."

"The proper time? I told you, Dickie, I'm moving to London and I need to find work."

"I'm well aware of that. Your letters suggest that you think this shop will give you access to the Earl of Oxford. Even if you do manage to get his attention, you're too unpolished to be employed by such a man, unless you want a job holding horses outside his playhouse."

"All I asked was that you help me."

"I don't think Monsieur Vautrollier's shop is the right place for you."

"*You* don't think –"

"You give the appearance of an upstart crow: plenty of squawk and no song."

William felt the deadly sting of Richard's words.

"I thought we were friends, Dickie. Thanks for nothing."

He turned to go. Richard grabbed his arm.

"Listen, Willy, even if you go now, you won't get far with that attitude. Take a look at yourself in the mirror over there and tell me what you see."

"I see a prosperous gentleman in a silk doublet," he replied.

"Nonsense. You're a straw man in a stuffed shirt. If you want to succeed among London's nobility, you must walk, talk and act with a measure of dignity. You must educate yourself in all aspects of their society or no one will ever respect you."

"What's wrong with the way I talk?"

"You talk like a country bumpkin. And you're about as tactful as that dunghill your father shoveled too close to the neighbors."

"Oh, that," William said. "That's why I came here, Dickie, for you to tell me these things and give me your best advice. You've always known the right thing to do, even when we were children. It was like magic."

"I'm not a magician, and I haven't got the power to turn a horse's ass into a golden fleece."

"Listen, I need your help, that's all. I can't afford to starve to death while I'm unfolding my plans with Lord Oxford. At least introduce me to Vautrollier. I promise I won't make any lewd remarks about his wife."

"I don't know if I can trust you . . . "

"Richard, where are your manners? Aren't you going to present your boyhood friend to me?"

Leaning on a walking stick, Monsieur Vautrollier made his way into the room. Caught off guard, Richard quickly fetched him a chair and made the introductions.

"What a delightful shop you have, Monsieur," William Shaxper said, in a suddenly cultivated tone that startled Richard. "I see you have books by Lord Burghley and Arthur Golding on your shelves. And that volume of Ovid is a masterpiece."

"*Merci*," Vautrollier said. "I'm proud to say we published them all. I've always tried to impress on Richard that printing is an art, and I believe he has come to espouse the idea – oh, I almost forgot, speaking of spouses, Jacqueline needs your help at the press. Go and attend to things, Richard, while I take your friend on a tour of our shop."

"I will, Monsieur, but are you certain? Perhaps you should rest."

"How can I rest when there is so much to be done?" Vautrollier coughed. "I will show your friend around the shop and prove that I still have ink pulsing through my veins. Go, go, *allez, allez*. Jacqueline needs you. Run along and be useful."

William winked at Richard as he left the room.

"With these delightful books to your credit, Monsieur," he said, in his most charming voice, "I wonder if you've ever met the Earl of Oxford. He's kin to the very authors you display here."

"*Mais oui.* In fact, the Earl of Oxford is my best customer. He comes into the shop often. There are so many stories I could tell you about our friendship over the years."

"Oh, please, Monsieur, tell me one. I would so like to hear it."

William saw that flattery would sway the Frenchman to his desires.

"*Vraiment?* Truly?" Vautrollier's eyes glowed as he summoned the memory. "It was the most astonishing day I've ever had in this shop. The Earl of Oxford rushed in, having heard that I'd acquired a rare Italian manuscript. He had just completed his official duties as Lord Great Chamberlain at some royal ceremony – but I don't recall which one – and he sat in his finery at this very table, browsing through the manuscript as if he had no greater demands on his time. The Queen's men came to collect the Sword of State, which he had set down here as if it were a mere trifle. They couldn't pry him away from the folio, not even to attend to the Queen. He said he preferred the company of books and paid me to keep the shop open after hours. He was more than generous in doing so, I must say."

William ran his hands along the table as if it had magical powers to bestow.

"Lord Oxford is famous for his literary work. He is the glass of fashion, a champion of the tilt-yard, a true celebrity . . . and a celebrity customer is good for business," Vautrollier concluded.

"But he openly supports the playhouses," William whispered.

"Yes. I myself have warned him that there is no dignity in it, and I pray that his passion for the theater will not be the cause of his undoing. At the same time, he is an illustrious man, a scholar and a poet who has translated books into various languages. He supports a number of other literary men in the publication of their work. For example, if you read Latin, you might enjoy Bartholomew Clerke's translation of *The Courtier* with its superb preface by the Earl of Oxford. No nobleman has ever written a tribute like it. The book instructs young men on the proper etiquette at the royal court."

"Then I'm sure it will instruct me, too," Will said, vowing to study it. "Most of all, I enjoy reading about England's history."

"Then you'll want to read Hall's *Chronicles*. It's on the second shelf to the right."

"I'm very familiar with Hall's *Chronicles*, having read it at the home of a former employer."

"It's wonderful to see a young man interested in improving his mind. When do you find the time to read, having to work every day?"

"I haven't worked in a while. I've just arrived in London and haven't had time to seek employment yet."

"What kind of work do you do?"

"My father taught me the business of tanning leather," he said, resorting to his practiced speech. "I was a glove maker and grain dealer in Stratford, and used to copy out legal documents for my father when he was alderman. I sang tenor for a former employer in Lancashire. I have a fine secretarial hand, or so I am told. I hope these skills will help me find work in London rather quickly."

"I wonder why Richard said nothing about this," Vautrollier mused. "He knows I need to hire men who can read, and they're scarce in London."

"Are you hiring, Monsieur?" Will asked, trying to conceal his excitement. "I would work my hands raw for you if I could be surrounded by these masterpieces."

"I need a man with a sense of accuracy. The tasks of a compositor require strict attention to detail."

"I've had experience copying out legal documents," Will said, "and as a tanner I can dress your books in the most excellent covers."

"Perhaps Richard has underestimated the skills of his boyhood friend."

William decided to let the remark pass.

"Let me assure you that if you hire me, Monsieur, you'll never be disappointed. I am an ardent bibliophile and would undertake my tasks here with great care and precision."

"You speak well and make an excellent impression," the printer concluded. "I believe you would be a credit to my shop, helping customers and serving as needed. You can start tomorrow, if you wish."

"Thank you, Monsieur. That will give me the rest of the day to find a place to live."

"Of course, you have no home in London yet. I can offer you an attic room, if you'd like. It's small, but it will serve a single unmarried man. You have no family, *n'est-ce pas*?"

"None," Will replied, picturing his awkward wife and unwanted children back in Stratford. "How kind of you," he continued, "to offer me a home under your own roof. I am humbled by your kindness, Monsieur, and am honored to be working for London's most respected publisher."

Richard returned to find his employer and boyhood friend agreeing to terms.

William went to work as a compositor, setting type before it went to press. He spent his leisure time studying the inventory of books that belonged to his masters. Soon, thanks to his skillful diplomacy with the customers, business was brisk. Vautrollier was delighted that his new hire shared his goals for the shop.

But William Shaxper also had goals of his own. He studied *The Courtier* and took copious notes on the etiquette Richard had found lacking in him. He read about the virtues of the Italian Renaissance. He practiced bowing in the mirror, hoping that eventually he would develop the grace he needed to win his way into Lord Oxford's employ. Richard laughed and said he looked pretentious.

During his off-hours, he pored over *Euphues and His England*, written by John Lyly and dedicated to Lord Oxford. In it he found a guiding principle: *Be humble to thy superiors, gentle to thy equals, favorable to thy inferiors, envy not thy betters, jostle not thy fellows, and oppress not the poor.* Thinking about those words, he could understand for the first time some of Richard's criticism of him.

William continued to harvest information from the books in Vautrollier's shop. After a great deal of research, he could diagram the de Vere ancestral history from memory. He began with the marriage of William the Conqueror to the sister of Alberic de Vere, whose grandson became the first Earl of Oxford. The Second Earl built Hedingham Castle in Essex, and the Third Earl was one of the rebellious barons who forced King John to sign the Magna Carta. Family fortunes ebbed and flowed throughout British history, as various Earls of Oxford fought in the battles of Crecy, Poitiers, Agincourt and Bosworth. At the height of their power, de Vere family landholdings sprawled across ten counties.

King Richard II had named the Ninth Earl of Oxford Duke of Ireland. It was sadly ironic that this same earl had survived a daring dive on horseback into the Thames to escape an enemy, only to be gored to death by a wild boar on the grounds of his own estate.

The Thirteenth Earl had helped Henry Tudor become King Henry VII. The ungrateful king later fined his benefactor for having too many followers, and the family fortunes sharply declined once again. Orphaned at an early age, the Fourteenth Earl served King Henry VIII; but when he died young and childless, the title passed to his uncle's family. His cousin John de Vere became the Fifteenth Earl of Oxford and was given the honor of carrying the crown at Anne Boleyn's coronation. He married Elizabeth Trussel, Shaxper's shadowy kinswoman from the Arden family. Their son, also named John, became the Sixteenth Earl. His only son was Edward de Vere, Seventeenth Earl of Oxford: courtier, poet, scholar and theatrical impresario, as well as William Shaxper's newly discovered kinsman.

Of all the books Vautrollier recommended, William found Cardanus' *Comforte* the most compelling. Its translator, Thomas Bedingfield, had written a self-effacing letter to the Earl in the book, thanking him for his support. William nearly fell off his chair when he read Lord Oxford's response, declaring that he had sponsored publication as an "eternal monument" to Bedingfield. This was unheard of, endowing a literary monument to a man of modest means simply because he had translated an antique book into English.

By now, William concluded that Lord Oxford liked rewarding his friends. Literary immortality was only one of the generous gifts he could bestow upon his followers. William's heart pounded as he read the concluding lines of Lord Oxford's dedication:

For when all things else forsake us, Virtue will ever abide with us; and when our bodies fall into the bowels of the earth, it shall mount with our minds into the highest Heavens. – E. Oxenforde

William shivered at the prospect of his own immortality. Surely Lord Oxford, so eager to give everlasting fame to Bedingfield, might also give some to him. When he became Lord Oxford's most obedient and trusted servant, William knew that there would be no limit to the rewards of fame and fortune that would come his way.

Turning to other books, he skimmed over the dedications to Lord Oxford in *Calvin's Version of the Psalms of David* by Arthur Golding, and John Brooke's *The Staff of Christian Faith*. Both praised the Earl of Oxford's scholarly achievements, but Golding's words reflected the concern of an uncle hoping to discourage his nephew's mischievous leanings. William wondered if Golding had been privy to his nephew's theatrical inclinations. These would have seemed blasphemous to a rigid Puritan like Golding, if he'd ever suspected that his nephew had not only written *The Famous Victories,* but also had the unmitigated gall to disguise himself and act in it.

After a few months, London's fickle weather took its toll on Vautrollier's health. When his physician suggested that certain flower remedies might prove helpful, Jacqueline bundled up her husband and asked Richard to accompany them to France. In their absence, William managed the shop.

When they returned home, it became clear that "business as usual" was a thing of the past. Jacqueline and Richard discussed the accounts and concluded that the shop would temporarily close to save money needed to pay the doctor's fee. No new work was taken in and William and three others were dismissed.

Far from upset, William viewed his dismissal as fortuitous. After sending money home to his wife, he had set aside enough for himself to live for a while. The time had come for him to speak with members of Lord Oxford's inner circle, those who knew best the private side of the public man.

CHAPTER SEVEN

The Scene: London
March 15, 1585

"But like a drunkard I must vomit them . . ."
— Titus Andronicus

After some false starts, William's inquiries led him to The Golden Lion in Shoreditch. The barkeep pointed to a rotund, brick-faced fellow sitting by the fire, showing off his war wounds. That was Robert Greene, the ruffian with the beefy arms raising his shirt to display his scars, the least discreet member of Lord Oxford's band of playwrights, a man likely to disclose anything to anyone who bought him a drink. William thanked the barkeep and paid for two pints of ale, an easy investment in his future.

Ambition overruled William's disgust for having to talk to such a man. He slowly approached the braggart and offered him a drink. Greene interrupted his story, squinted at this unforeseen act of kindness and boisterously thanked his benefactor. He struggled to recall where he and William Shaxper had met before, but William assured him they had not.

Greene's small captive audience trickled away during the interruption, and soon William was the sole listener. He smiled and nodded as Greene continued his epic war stories. The drunken playwright grunted and rambled on, occasionally wiping his mouth with his sleeve. When he rolled up his shirt to give William a closer look at his scars, the young man controlled his urge to vomit.

"Scotland was ablaze like the bowels of Hell!" Greene exclaimed. "Have you ever fought in a war, Shaxper?"

"No. I've never had the opportunity."

"What, are you a coward?"

"No. I've always fancied I'd do more harm to myself than to the enemy."

Greene clapped him on the back. "Ha! I like a man who can tell a good joke."

William stiffened. He hadn't meant to be funny.

"I've heard that the Earl of Oxford writes comedies at Her Majesty's Court," he ventured, "and that he is your patron. Is it true?"

"Aye. His Lordship and I are sworn brothers . . . we're close, like this." He crossed his fingers to illustrate the bond.

"Perhaps you can tell me how to join his troupe of actors," William continued.

"I suppose you think being an actor is thrilling."

"Oh, yes. With all my heart, I do."

"Well, it isn't," Greene snapped. "No one has any respect for the common players."

"Why not? Being a player is more respectable than selling grain or tanning leather."

"Not by much. No hardworking commoner is ever respected, unless a generous nobleman desires to purchase his services."

William was delighted to have his instincts confirmed.

"Lord Oxford respects his actors or he would never sponsor them," he countered.

"He respects us playwrights more," Greene said, between burps. "The actors would have no thoughts in their heads without us playwrights putting 'em there."

"I don't believe it," William chuckled. "Only wise and clever men can learn someone else's words and bring them to life. Actors must step beyond themselves to portray their characters."

"Tush, man," Greene laughed. "Actors are fools. They travel around the countryside all summer long, jostled about in rickety wagons, shouting bombasts and clashing swords, dripping sweat into their heavy helmets and woolen cloaks. Would you call that clever? We playwrights are the clever ones, sitting comfortably around Lord Oxford's table at the Savoy, eating and drinking his food, writing and revising our work. Without us, the playhouses would have no plays and the actors would have nothing to say. Take my word for it."

William didn't recall hearing any of the traveling players complain about the hardships of the road. They were simply glad to be paid for their hard work.

And as he well knew, playwrights, players and playhouses were England's newest commercial enterprise. Lord Oxford's role as their sponsor was precarious, in light of his political and family connections – and worse yet, if he indulged his whims with the lowly pursuits of writing and acting.

"Who are the playwrights around Lord Oxford's table?" William asked.

"You've probably never heard of 'em, as most people don't know the names of our playwrights nowadays, nor do they bloody well care. But there's me and Lord Oxford, John Lyly, Thomas Watson the poet, Thomas Kyd, Christopher Marlowe . . . have you ever written a play?"

"No," William said, taken aback. "I've never given it any thought."

"Well, at least you're a literate man, which is more than I can say for most of our countrymen. You say you want to become a player? Well, the truth is, Lord Oxford doesn't need any more players now. What he truly needs are playwrights with an interest in history. He's going to need a lot of history plays very quickly. He told me so himself."

"Why? Is there a holiday or some patriotic event coming up?"

"Nothing that I know of," Greene belched.

"Are audiences demanding to see more history plays?"

"Not that I can tell."

"Is it a matter of money then? Will history plays draw in larger audiences?"

"I don't know. I'm not a businessman."

"Then apparently, the Earl of Oxford *doesn't* tell you everything," William said, immediately regretting his words.

An awkward silence fell. William handed Greene the second pint of ale. The liquid apology brought the necessary forgiveness to loosen the playwright's tongue in response to more crafty questioning.

"I saw Lord Oxford at a history play once," William said. "Is it true, what they say about him?"

"Is *what* true?"

"You know . . . the buzz of those vile and persistent rumors."

Greene looked confused, and then suddenly, his drunken words fell like withered leaves.

"The rumor-mongers feed on his defiance like parasites. They know Lord Oxford leads a scandalous life, thanks to his father-in-law's public bruiting of it. Lord Burghley is furious at his son-in-law's antics, and never knows what secrets he's going to reveal. Did you know that the Queen supported a ban against publication by noblemen? It was meant to stop Lord Oxford, but it hasn't worked. He simply conjures his poison and hides it under a different label."

"What poison? What label? I don't understand."

"He pays us to act as his go-betweens," Greene whispered. "We sign our names to his work so it can be approved for public performance. Several recent books have noted that the Earl of Oxford writes excellent comedies, if he could be allowed to take credit for them. But a nobleman cannot be seen as a clown, making people laugh at the expense of his rank. So he dons a disguise. He plays the chameleon."

"You mean he writes under someone else's name."

"Aye, or as the more widely-known Anonymous. Bear in mind that Lord Oxford is also a serious writer. He transforms ordinary words into iambs, turning leaden prose into golden poetry, like this: daDA daDA daDA daDa daDA," Greene said, banging out five beats on the table. "His Lordship tries to teach us how to write full plays in iambic verse, but so far none of us have come up to his standards."

"I saw his players perform *The Famous Victories* in London and in Stratford."

"Ah, then perhaps you know who wrote it."

"It was an anonymous play, I believe," William said, trying to recall the precise wording of the handbill.

"Aye, all according to Her Majesty's orders," Greene chuckled. "She knows Lord Oxford wrote every word of it. She's afraid of exposing his authorship, even though audiences don't care who a playwright is, as long as he offers a motley swarm of bawdy fools and vile assassins. Never mind that Lord Oxford draws his characters from real life. They're all people he knows, some of them quite well, like Lord Burghley."

"I can't imagine any man being so brazen as to make an enemy out of Lord Burghley."

"Imagine it, sir, and that man would be Lord Oxford," Greene said, pleased at having snagged William's curiosity. "The two men had a terrible falling-out that started years ago, when Lord Oxford was orphaned and sent to Lord Burghley's home as a royal ward. The old man objected whenever the spendthrift youth wrote and presented court masques for the Queen. He didn't care that a courtier's duty is to give Her Majesty expensive gifts and tributes, and that she desires a rousing entertainment more than anything else. The Queen owns all the gold and jewels she could want, and even as a youth, Lord Oxford was the only one among her noble bucks able to devise a provocative diversion."

"But you said she banned his plays."

"Not at the royal court," Greene explained. "Those masques are very private affairs. The after-dinner audiences are small and selective, entirely different from the *hoi polloi* at the public playhouses. I watched a court masque once, from behind the curtain on the gallery stairs. It won't do for our nation's commoners to learn the truth about their superiors in a comedy, tragedy or history play -- even though, as they say, the truth will out."

"I'm beginning to understand," William sighed.

"Well done," Greene laughed, "for by God's Blood, I swear I never shall!!"

Greene's expression suddenly changed from besotted amusement to complete seriousness. He leaned forward and whispered.

"A few years ago, His Lordship drove the Queen into a violent fury, and he had the gall to put it on stage for all the world to see."

"What happened? What did he do?"

"He was sent to the Tower for fathering a bastard with one of the Queen's ladies."

"By Heavens! Is that a crime?"

"No, but the Queen is ruled by a jealous heart. Lord Oxford was the first of her courtiers to suffer such a consequence."

"And what became of the lady and her child?"

"She and her newborn were also immediately imprisoned in the Tower. It was a terrible time for all of them, but if you ask Lord Oxford about it, he'll tell you the Queen was quite merciful."

"Merciful? How merciful can such dark imprisonment be?"

"It seems that the royal mercy rains differently on some than on others. The Queen allowed Lord Oxford to have pen, ink and paper in his cell, that he should not go mad, as he feared, with the tedious passage of time. He wrote about the ordeal and it became an anonymous piece for the playhouses. I've always said that he was lucky the Queen didn't discover his authorship, or else she would have chopped off his head measure by measure and spiked it on London Bridge, to the delight of the crows that feast on traitors' meat."

William knew this penalty was far more gruesome than being forced to marry Anne Hathaway, who'd been pregnant with his child.

"Noblemen father bastards every day and never go to prison for it," Greene snickered. "And despite her peculiar mercy, the Queen made Lord Oxford suffer for his errant romance. When she learned that he and his mistress had exchanged secret vows to marry after he was granted the divorce from his adulterous wife, the Queen denied it to him. She had no desire to see Catholicism persist in any of England's noble families, and since Lord Oxford's mistress was Catholic, he was forced to abandon her and return to his Protestant wife. Within days after he did so, all were freed from the Tower, but the lady and her kinsmen were enraged by Lord Oxford's breach of promise. A blood feud erupted between the two households. Knife fights spilled out onto the streets, and even the Queen was powerless to stop them. And then came the dreadful night Lord Oxford was stabbed in an alley behind Blackfriars."

"Behind a theater . . . like my father," William muttered.

"What's that?"

"Nothing. I pray you, continue, sir. What happened next?"

"Lord Oxford went back to his wife and to this day, he suffers from the wound in his leg. He is a spectacular champion in the tilt-yard, but despite that enormous skill, he's forced to rely occasionally on a walking stick. Still, some days are better than others, and through it all, he counts himself lucky to be alive. He blames Lord Burghley for that particular tragic declension of events, and has sworn to avenge himself with his pen. He's doing it now, in a play called *Hamlet*. He's continuously revising it and adding further delicious fulsomeness to it."

"It's dangerous, being Catholic in England. Best hide one's religion, if you ask me," William said.

"Aye, that's best," Greene nodded.

"I wonder, sir," William said, summoning his courage, "if you could introduce me to the Earl of Oxford."

Greene stood up, sweating profusely. He tugged at his collar.

"Is it hot in here?" he asked.

"Not particularly, no."

"Then by God's teeth, I'm going to be sick. Fetch me the slop bucket."

"I-I don't see a slop bucket anywhere," William said, looking around nervously. "I'm sure it's outside. They wouldn't keep such a disgusting thing in here --"

"Point me towards the door then, damn ye! I can't wait--"

William steered him towards the back of the pub. The patrons scattered as the barkeep threw the door open and slammed it behind them. Greene broke away in the encroaching darkness and stumbled towards a tree. He bent over and retched. William gagged at the repulsive odor.

"I need to see Monsieur Riche," Greene sputtered, after a few moments.

"Who?"

"Monsieur Riche, His Lordship's apothecary. Let's pound on his door. Riche, Riche, Monsieur Riche!"

"Calm yourself, sir. I'll take you there, but first, tell me where Lord Oxford may be found."

"Where the books are . . . at the Savoy, away from Burghley's spies . . . when he was a boy at Hedingham Castle . . ."

Greene slumped onto William's shoulder. Together, they hobbled down the lane towards the apothecary.

CHAPTER EIGHT

The Scene: The Vine & Fig,
Village of Castle Hedingham
April 1585

"O, how full of briers is this working-day world!"
— As You Like It

onfident now that he could succeed by forging a powerful
connection with his illustrious (and somewhat infamous)
cousin, William Shaxper set out for Lord Oxford's ancestral
home.

He marveled at Hedingham Castle's ancient keep and its expansive
view of the countryside, its narrow windows peering like watchman's
eyes at the village below. That same tower had protected the castle
against King John's siege of 1216 after he had been forced by the 3rd
Earl of Oxford and twenty-four other powerful barons to sign a document granting them new rights and protections from royal abuses. The
Magna Carta inspired a radical sense of freedom in the land, causing
men of all social rank to consider rising above their stations. Success

could be achieved if a man worked hard, planned well and, as William Shaxper knew, attached himself to the right patron.

He asked around the village for a man named Pinch, the former jester in the household of Lord Oxford's father. Several townspeople pointed to The Vine & Fig, a venerable old inn staunchly planted below the castle; and ready to mark the end of their workday with a few drinks, they escorted him there. They told William all about the inn, and how it had come down to Meg Bucklesbury as an inheritance from her father. Pinch, they said, had also claimed the inheritance by marrying Meg and settling into his new career as a tavern keeper.

Shaxper thanked them for the information and found himself a table by the hearth. He ordered something to eat and watched Meg from a distance. Her eyes sparkled with mischief as she poured drinks for her customers and leveled soft jests at them. In the ebb and flow of the neighborly banter that criss-crossed the bar, Shaxper heard the country pleasantries he knew so well. He realized they were as abundant in Hedingham as they were in Stratford, but they *were* absent, he thought, from the hustle-bustle of city life.

As the afternoon wore on and business became less hectic, Shaxper invited Meg to join him at his table.

"Ah, at last a chance to rest these old bones," she said, as she wiped her hands on her apron and arranged for one of the serving girls to take her place behind the bar. With a heavy sigh, Meg plunked herself onto the bench and brushed the hair from her eyes. "It's been quite a day, as you can see," she said, fanning herself with her hand.

"Is it always this busy in here?" Shaxper asked.

"Oh, aye. There's seldom a moment's peace. Mind you, we've been in business since Noah's Flood, and I've always been given to believe that it was my father who stepped up to the Old Navigator as he left the Ark and offered him the first drink he'd had in 40 days and 40 nights. Well, sir, is our food to your liking? Is there anything else we can get for you?"

"Small beer, I pray you, but bring a pitcher of water so I can mix it myself," Shaxper said. When the serving girl brought his order, Shaxper watered down his drink, sipped it and grinned.

"Not much for strong drink, are you?" Meg laughed. "The Vine & Fig won't be making much money on you, I'll warrant; not with a child's drink."

"I-I know small beer is for children," Shaxper stammered, "but I can quench my thirst as often as I like and never get drunk, and that should keep my money flowing into your till, shouldn't it?"

"Upon my honor, sir, forgive me. My tongue is ofttimes quicker than my brain and I deserve your gentle rebuke. I meant you no offense," Meg said.

"I am not offended, madam, but I have every reason to be sober and keep my wits about me."

"As you wish, sir. But madam-me-not, for it makes me feel old. Call me Meg, as everyone else does. Is this your first time in Hedingham?"

"Yes. In fact, I've come all the way from London to see your husband, hoping he would teach me about the art of comedy. Is it true that he was the jester to Lord John de Vere, the 16th Earl of Oxford?"

"Aye, Pinch was his household fool. People said he was the funniest man in England once . . . well, more than once, I'd say. He also led Lord John's company of players. But that was long ago, back when Pinch claimed he had the best hire-and-salary in the world."

"I would agree with him. I myself am looking for work in the London theaters."

"Mark you, Pinch *used* to say it – you won't hear such talk from him anymore."

"Why not?"

"It was the talk of the village that he was mightily abused by Lady Margery, Lord John's widow. She dismissed the players after His Lordship's death and Pinch was so despondent over her cruelty, he threw himself off the tower. A hay wagon broke his fall, and I stepped in to nurse his wounds. We'd known each other as children, you see, and that sort of love never dies. Pinch would not recommend serving as a player in a noble household to anyone. He would quickly disabuse you of the notion that it's a marvelous life."

"I'm not sure even a man of his talents could do that," Shaxper said.

"Ah, but you do seem like a such a level-headed youth," Meg said, reaching for his hand.

"What are you doing?"

"I'm reading your fortune," she said, studying his palm. "I can see in an instant whether your true heart's desire lies within your grasp, or whether you're deceiving yourself . . . you see, the palm is called the table because your destiny has been set and all things rest upon it and – oh, yes. I see. It's partly what you've said, but not exactly what I expected to see."

"What do you see? Is it my death?"

"Yes," she smiled, "but not yours alone, for we'll all die someday, sooner or later. I do see that you have a heroic purpose ahead of you, receiving great fame and fortune for creating illusions. And from the looks of it, you're not alone in that either."

"Then the playhouses truly are in my future."

"Indeed they are, but there's a darker side – pretense, I'd say. Fame and Fortune are written on your palm, but I also see an old man burdened by a terrible secret."

"What old man? Is it me?"

"That's a mystery, too," she said, as Shaxper gently slid his hand away from hers. "There's only so much we poor mortals can see, but it would be a shame for you to condemn yourself to a player's life when there's no glory in it. That's what Pinch would say."

"But by reputation, he was funnier than Will Somers, King Henry VIII's fool. Pinch must have found some glory in that fame."

"Aye, he did – and Lady Margery destroyed it."

Shaxper raised a curious eyebrow.

"You see," Meg continued, "no other jester in England at that time ever commanded a cry of players. Most noblemen were entertained by dolts or dwarfs that were mocked for their imbecilities and deformities, a practice that I find most cruel."

"But noblemen also maintained musicians as their servants."

"Aye, but they didn't maintain resident companies of actors - men who were literate, able to understand and learn their lines. Lord John was different from other noblemen. His castle had a chapel *and* a theater in it. It was that very thing that captured his son's attention."

"By his son, you must mean Edward, Earl of Oxford, patron of the London theaters," Shaxper said, delighted at this turn in the conversation.

"Aye, that's him," Meg nodded. "I remember when he was born, a little lordling-viscount with a whole string of titles to his name. He was a precocious child, and once terrified Pinch by dancing barefoot on the bulwark of the old tower with no regard for his safety. Pinch gave him scenes to translate from the comedies of Terence and Plautus, and soon the lad took parts in them. Edward was so well disguised, his parents never knew they were applauding their own son among the players. They wouldn't have approved if they'd known, especially Lady Margery. Pinch took a big risk by indulging the boy."

"Why would his mother care if her son took to the stage in private?"

"Because Edward was wild and impetuous, like a stallion that defies his paddock and bolts haphazardly to distant pastures. He refused to be tethered and constrained to give up writing and acting because of his noble rank."

"I always thought a nobleman could do whatever he desired."

"Not so," Meg said, with confidence. "You and me, we can muck about in life all we want, and no one cares if we get dirty. But if we were titled nobility, our actions would be grist for the gossip mills. Edward always said that the plainest commoner enjoyed more freedom than he did, and he was twelve when he said it, and he was probably correct. But look, here comes Pinch now, and he can tell you the rest."

Meg stood up and waved at the dissipated old curmudgeon in the doorway. Several rowdy customers greeted him, and Pinch scowled back with feigned annoyance. He shuffled towards the table and lightly kissed Meg on the cheek.

Shaxper could hardly believe that the wretched man had once been a popular jester.

"It's about time you arrived, my love," Meg chided. "I was beginning to think you'd left me."

"Nonsense, sweeting, whither would I go? And who have we here? One of your many admirers, I suppose."

"Pinch, this is Mister William Shaxper, come all the way from London to see you. He wants to be an actor."

"Accept my condolences, sirrah," Pinch sneered. "I'd rather express them to you now, instead of to the audience, later."

"Say what you will, sir," Shaxper chuckled, politely, "but my feet are set upon the stage."

"Well, don't set your heart upon it," Pinch grumbled. "I did that once, and look at me."

"Mister Shaxper sought you out so he can learn comedy from a master," Meg said. "It'll do both of you good to let him apprentice his ears to you for a while. I'll go tend to our customers and have one of the girls fetch you some ale." Before Pinch could object, Meg kissed him on the cheek and toddled towards the bar.

Now that he was alone with Shaxper, the fool's suspicion was palpable.

"You can drop all that rubbish about learning comedy from a master," Pinch growled, as he drank his ale. "That's not the real reason you came to Hedingham, is it?"

"No, not really," Shaxper replied.

"You've been asking a lot of questions in the village. I've got big ears, and it's easy to catch my neighbors in the act of gossip. I'm sure they've told you that the Earl of Oxford and I haven't spoken in years, not since his wedding to Lord Burghley's daughter."

"You knew him as boy –"

"Has Meg been gossiping, too? She should leave the past where it is, dead and buried."

"I'm willing to pay you for what you know," Shaxper said, sliding a few coins across the table.

"Oh, I see - planning a bit of mayhem against Lord Oxford, are you? Well, your money's no good here. Edward and I may be estranged, but I wish him no harm. Surely Meg told you that."

"She did . . . and she also said you encouraged his acting."

"Until his debauched mother drove us apart and sent him to live under Lord Burghley's strict governance. My heart has never mended over Edward's tragic departure. It was nearly the death of me."

Shaxper wondered if that had caused the jester's suicide attempt. Instead, he said, "The young earl was lucky to have lived with such a brilliant and powerful man as Lord Burghley."

"Is that what you think?" Pinch glared. "Well, you're right - Lord Burghley has unlimited power. That self-aggrandizing opportunist shifted political alliances every time the wind changed. He supported each one of King Henry VIII's children, whichever one looked to be the next monarch. First, he supported the boy King Edward VI, and then his Catholic sister Mary and finally, our Protestant Elizabeth. It didn't matter, as long as the situation yielded him advancement."

"I intend to rise from the common ranks as Burghley did," Shaxper said.

"What, by becoming an actor? Ha! If you believe that, you're more fool than I am."

"Meg assured me of it. She read my fortune in my palm."

"Did she? Well, never mind what she says. The poor woman's illiterate. She seems wise, but her seams unravel quickly."

Pinch signaled for another ale. When it arrived, he took a long drink, set his tankard down and stared into it, his face a portrait of self-pity. Shaxper felt he could almost see his tongue loosening.

"Some people don't recognize treachery when they see it," the old jester said. "Lord John was a fool in that respect, and perhaps a greater fool than I ever was."

"What do you mean by that?"

"Lord John should have worn the cuckold's horns from the moment he let Charles Tyrell into his household," Pinch said, his memories unraveling. "He arrived one day like a Greek bearing gifts. The Queen required her gentleman pensioners to be handsome, and Tyrell was no exception. Lady Margery soon fell under his spell and the two became lovers while Lord John was at Court. But there was more to it than adultery, more to it than simply alienating the affections of a husband and his wife."

Shaxper's heart beat wildly.

"History is full of kings and noblemen who murder to usurp a fortune," Pinch said. "And poison is that monstrously convenient plague that breaks out among the nobility from time to time. Surely you recognize the name Tyrell from our country's history as belonging to two different cold-blooded assassins. I know for a fact that Lord John was in good health when he left to attend the Queen, but when he came home, he was dead within a week. As I see it, there was only one cause for such a rapid decline. Lord John had been poisoned."

"Poisoned!" Shaxper gasped. "And you still believe it, after all these years?" He searched the jester's face. "Yes, indeed. I can tell by your eyes that you do."

"Edward believed it, too. Imagine the dark thoughts that crossed his mind when one month after his father's funeral, his mother married the suspected assassin. The entire village was stunned when food from the funeral was served at the wedding feast. Edward was packed off to London, and Lady Margery dismissed the players, saying we had destroyed the dignity of her household – as if she ever had any dignity, making the beast with two backs with her husband's murderer! My heart broke when she refused to let me accompany Edward to London. Perhaps our lives would have been different if I had gone, for Edward was a vulnerable orphan at 12 who suddenly became Earl of Oxford."

"But as his guardian, it's well known that Lord Burghley gave him a fine education."

"Ah, Lord Burghley made that known. But when Lord John was alive, he also provided his son with the finest tutors in England. Edward was raised in the noble traditions of chivalry and honor. He was not yet five years-old when he rode to the home of Sir Thomas Smith to begin his studies. Did you know that three of his uncles were poets and literary men?"

"I know that one was Arthur Golding, who translated Ovid's *Metamorphoses* from Latin into English," Shaxper said.

"You've read it then?"

"Yes, enough to know there are no Christian virtues in it."

"It's not exactly the Calvinist text one would expect from a Puritan like Golding, is it?"

"Hardly."

"That's because Golding didn't translate it – Edward did," Pinch said, his inebriated voice dripping with pride. "It took Edward several years to translate fifteen volumes of Latin ribaldry into rhyming couplets of English hexameter, but he did it. Golding admired the quality and Edward wanted to publish it, but Lady Margery insisted that her half-brother, as uncle-tutor, put his name on it to protect the dignity of her household, or some such nonsense. I always thought it was a shame that Edward hadn't been born a commoner. He would have been a brilliant jester, if men of rank weren't required to be so serious. Some of 'em would rather kill you than endure a well-deserved mocking."

"You said his other uncles were also literary men. Who were they?"

"The Earl of Surrey refined the sonnet form and wrote poetry that was published ten years after his death. And Sheffield was a poet, although none of his work has survived, most likely because it was never published. Both of these men died before Edward was born, but their private papers had a great influence on him. He took his degrees at Cambridge and Gray's Inn, did you know that? Edward is fluent in six languages."

"Oh, that's as many tongues as the Queen has."

"What do you mean by that, sirrah?"

"In terms of language, of course," Shaxper said. "What else could it mean?"

"I thought you had a double meaning," Pinch said, in an intoxicated whisper. "Everything has a double meaning. Edward told me so himself the night before his wedding, when he was drunk and railed whirling words about his affair with the Queen, who had arranged his match with Burghley's daughter so they could continue their torrid affair in the royal bedchamber. But as far as I know, their passions faded quickly. I lost touch with Edward after the wedding, but by all accounts his marriage to Burghley's daughter was a disaster. Still, the old man profited by it. He arranged it that way."

"I don't believe it," Shaxper said. "You've had too much to drink."

"That's your opinion, sirrah. Take what you think is the truth, or leave your doubt where it lies, I don't care," the jester said, his face darkening. "Revenge, aye - now there's the root of an engaging drama. It wasn't just Lord Burghley stealing the orphaned earl's money and titles. Edward's own half-sister sued to have him declared a bastard, saying that Lord John and Lady Margery were never married. Edward stood to lose everything: his titles, his income, his good name. I remember, he wrote about his grief. It seemed like the end of the world, but the Queen protected him and the suit was dismissed. And when Edward accidentally killed a man during a fencing match, the coroner ruled it self-defense. Someone always protects the Earl of Oxford. He's fortunate that way, unlike the rest of us."

"I see," Shaxper said, making a mental note about the special treatment accorded men of rank and privilege. "I hope to join his acting company in London."

"Well, let me give you fair warning, sirrah. The Earl of Oxford has no patience for frauds and flatterers. He has great contempt for dissemblers. Remember that, if you hope to stay on his good side."

"I'll do my best. Thank you for the warning."

"I think you've gotten what you came for," Pinch said, squinting at Shaxper. "But I'll wager none of it was funny. Edward and I may be estranged, but that's how it is and it doesn't bother me, as long as you don't do him any harm."

"No harm intended," Shaxper said, holding up both hands as if to block danger itself.

Pinch rose unsteadily, nodded a gruff goodnight and meandered towards the bar.

Shaxper briskly rubbed his palms together, wondering why the room had suddenly gone cold.

CHAPTER NINE

The Scene: Stratford-on-Avon, Warwickshire

June 1586

"The toe of the peasant comes so near the heel of the courtier . . ."

– Hamlet

S haxper returned home to his wife bearing a wealth of determination and a purse full of savings. With an obstinate mixture of guilt and respect, he had come to deliver his hard-earned wages to Anne in person, rather than send them home in a tightly wrapped and coldly worded farewell letter.

It was the least he could do to spare her feelings, he thought, for he had no intention of staying in his accidental marriage any longer. He was impatient to get back to London but he didn't want to seem cruel, so he lingered to say a proper goodbye to his children. Three year-old Susanna might miss him, he thought, for she was old enough now to sit on his lap and bury her face in his chest. He was sure that his colicky twins Hamnet and Judith didn't care who he was or where he was. Still, he swore to return to them as soon as he was financially secure, and they were old enough to care who he was, and to understand how he had improved their lives by allying himself with his theatrical kinsman, Lord Oxford.

He promised to send Anne money regularly. He had expected her to be grateful for this boon, and for the reassurance by his presence that he wasn't simply staying on in London and abandoning her and the children completely.

But Anne refused to make his departure an easy one. She wept in the doorway with the twins in her arms and pleaded with him not to go.

"I'll be back before you know it, I swear," he called over his shoulder "And I'll return to you with a small fortune, I promise."

"How can you leave me like this, William?" Anne cried. "What will the neighbors say?"

"It's not my business what they say," he replied, recalling their wicked gossip about his father.

"They'll say you abandoned me because of the twins."

"But I've assured you that's not true. In London, I can earn a fortune. I can't possibly do that in Stratford, and now we have two more hungry mouths to feed."

"Dear God, what's to become of me and the children?"

"God will take care of you. And Hamnet Sadler – I've asked him to look in on you."

"At least leave me some more money."

"I can't. I need to pay my travel expenses. I'll send you more money when Lord Oxford pays me my advance."

"What advance? He doesn't even know you. What makes you think he'll ever know you?"

"He'll know me . . . and he'll need me, I'm sure of it. But I have to act now, I can't wait any longer. I stayed until the twins were baptized and I must say, it's been the longest month of my life."

"What about little Susanna? She loves you, she's devastated, just look at her, William."

Anne stepped aside, revealing Susanna sobbing behind her skirts.

Shaxper sighed and knelt down. Susanna ran into his arms.

"I'll make it up to her," he said, as he kissed the little girl and handed her back to her mother.

"And how will you do that?" Anne asked. "Why in God's name would the Earl of Oxford pay any attention to you? Because of some distant family kinship? That's absurd!"

"I told you," Shaxper said, as he tightened his satchel and mounted his horse. "I'll send you my earnings as soon as I'm employed as a player in Lord Oxford's Men. What more do you want?"

"I want you, William. I love you. Don't you love me?"

Anne Whatley's face flashed through Shaxper's mind. She was the maiden he really loved, and if he hadn't gotten Anne Hathaway pregnant and been hauled before the parish priest to marry her, his life would have been different. Anne Whatley of Temple Grafton would have understood his feelings about London. She might have joined him there, if he knew where she was after all this time.

"Be quiet, Anne" he scolded, "the neighbors will hear you."

"You've got some whore stashed away in London, haven't you?" Anne shouted angrily. "Go to her then! Go and make a fool out of yourself, but you'd better send the money you promised me or I'll sue you for it!" Anne clutched the twins and kneed Susanna into the house. She slammed the door behind them.

Relieved to be quitting Stratford, he turned his horse towards London. He noted how sad it was that his harridan of a wife had no sense of Fortune or Destiny.

Anne Whatley would have understood.

Beyond the outskirts of Stratford, two men crouched in a roadside ditch concealed by low bushes. Engaged in the lucrative business of robbing travelers on the way to London, the highwaymen used a tall tree at the fork in the road to spot their victims, whose bulging satchels offered a tempting invitation to collect whatever booty they desired.

To dispel the afternoon's eerie silence, Shaxper whistled *Greensleeves* as he rounded the bend. Just as he came under the tree, the screech of a crow pierced the tender melody of his tune. The villain hidden in the leaves let out a blood-curdling scream and dropped down onto Shaxper's horse. His partners leapt up from the ditch and tried to wrestle the reins away from Shaxper. They grappled over the satchel. The terrified horse reared and galloped down the road.

Shaxper felt a searing pain rip through his shoulder. From the corner of his eye, he caught the flicker of a knife's blade at his back. He felt dizzy, but the thought of losing his satchel and the money he'd earned emboldened him to fight. Roaring with anger, he kicked off his assailant and scrambled into the underbrush like an animal on all fours, frantically searching for a place to hide. With each step, thorny vines scratched and tore at his flesh.

As he stumbled into the brier patch, a shot rang out and a bullet grazed his leg. He could almost feel the thieves breathing down his neck. His shoulder throbbed and he was sure his life was over. He fell to the ground and lay on his back, eyes closed and teeth clenched. He thought of his mother Mary and little Susanna. He gripped his bag as if his life depended on it.

Hearing a rustling nearby, he opened his eyes to see the thieves towering over him.

"What do you want?" he quavered.

"Your money, sir, and quickly."

"But this is all I have in the world," he begged, as he clutched the satchel. "Please don't take it."

"Kill him, Poley. Let's take it and be done."

You might as well be dead, Shaxper told himself. You'll never get to London now. You'll never be famous. You'll never make a name for yourself. No one will ever hear of William Shaxper except as the victim of an infamous murder on the highway . . . if your body is ever to be found in such a place.

"Here," Shaxper said, thrusting the satchel forward. "Take my money, but please don't kill me. Leave me in peace, I beg you."

Someone laughed and yanked the satchel away. Shaxper felt a pistol at his head. He whispered a prayer as he heard the trigger being cocked. He wondered how long it would take for the maggots to devour his flesh once he was dead, and how far across the field the animals would scatter his bones. Would his soul be allowed to enter Heaven without a priest or a proper burial? He was a simple man, and didn't know the answer to such questions. He prayed for Jesus' sake that his death would be a quick and painless one.

He closed his eyes and heard his empty satchel landing in the bushes behind him. He heard the mocking laughter of his assailants as their feet crunched through the thicket and into the distance.

He felt a stunning blow to his head. A death-like sleep crept upon him in the warm sunshine.

He rolled over and let it come.

ACT II
CHAPTER TEN

The Scene: Cecil House
May 4, 1586

"Who makes the fairest show means most deceit . . ."
– Pericles

S eated in his library enjoying his wine, William Cecil, Lord Burghley, thanked God for having made him a clever man.

By befriending young Elizabeth during her dark days as a political prisoner under her sister Mary's rule, he had earned the Princess' everlasting gratitude. But his real rise to power had come shortly after young King Edward's untimely death. Sadly, the boy-king had indulged in the misguided whim of naming his cousin, Lady Jane Grey, to be his royal successor. It took only nine days for the Privy Council to reject her claim in favor of Edward's sister Mary. Poor Lady Jane was beheaded on Tower Green, a victim of the boy-king's naivete and her own family's lust for power. Then years later, after Mary's agonizing death, Fortune finally put the crown on Elizabeth's head.

No one had expected this turn of events. Despite the fact that the Pope had declared her a bastard, Fortune had raised the lowly Princess Elizabeth from the dust and set her on a glittering throne. As payment for his loyalty, the new Queen elevated Burghley to the rank of chief advisor. He congratulated himself for that fact every day, confident that not even the astrologer John Dee could have acted with better foresight.

He was sure this had happened because in his youth he had read Machiavelli's *The Prince* to guide him in rising from the middle classes to commanding power of his own. He was awed to think that Fortune governed only half of a man's fate, while the other half was ruled by Will.

To move the idea from his thoughts into his actions, he personified it, as he did with most of his studies. Fortune became a charming but fickle woman, with Will as her forceful, masculine consort. Together they conspired to control a man's destiny; but to avoid being crushed by Fortune's Wheel, a man must use his force of Will to steer events in his direction. Machiavelli had said that if a man neglects what *must* be done in favor of what *ought* to be done, he will bring about his own ruin rather than his security. Lord Burghley had not only embraced the precept, but he lived and breathed it.

Just like Elizabeth, Fortune favored decisive men over meek ones. She had brazenly offered herself to him during her imprisonment, seeking to express her gratitude for his tenderness with lust. But he sublimated his natural urges, and instead of stiffening with desire, he stiffened his resolve and gently refused her, decisively calming her bewildering cravings with sweet and sympathetic words.

He didn't tell her that he knew that Thomas Seymour, married to King Henry VIII's widow Catherine Parr, had taken Elizabeth's virginity when she was only 15 and living under her stepmother's roof. Seymour's incestuous visits to her bed had left her shocked and confused, churning with mixed emotions. A major scandal was avoided at the time only because no one thought Elizabeth was of any importance. Her virginity didn't matter, since a suitable husband from a noble family could always be found for such a girl.

But Fortune intervened, and in an ironic twist, Elizabeth rewarded Burghley for his decisive refusal of her sexual favors because, in her words, he had "safeguarded her dignity at the crossroads of her fate." Elizabeth valued him as an incorruptible and cautious advisor. While she never again tried to seduce him, she cast her erotic desires on younger men, many of whom sought political advancement in her bed. He had to protect her from these dangerous entanglements and undesirable unions, particularly because his son-in-law, the Earl of Oxford, was her favorite.

The two of them were always behind closed doors, loving and singing and dancing and laughing and speaking foreign languages, sharing a colorful world of court masques and theatrical illusions, which Burghley detested as sinful and unholy rubbish. Sometimes it was more than he could bear, listening to them from behind a tapestry while they sang duets or read scenes from Oxford's plays as a prelude to their long nights of unabridged passion. Why couldn't Oxford just go home to his wife?

Damn those plays! The historical ones weren't bad, and Burghley had survived the humiliation of having his habits caricatured at Court, but he never knew when he or other members of his family would be mocked on the public stage. He had survived the obvious reference to the robbery at Gad's Hill in *The Famous Victories* because the play had been presented anonymously. He had even survived the embarrassment at his daughter's wedding when Edward revealed the private financial proposals of her rejected suitors in his play, _The Merry Courtship of Mistress Anne_.

Burghley's most recent fear was the prospect of being exposed for conniving a consensual, albeit incestuous, union with Anne in a play called *Hamlet*. He confessed as much to the Queen in a mysterious letter, begging for her royal mercy but leaving his precise crime unnamed. He hoped she wouldn't recognize his sin entwined in the clever lines of *Hamlet,* for he was sure Edward had put it there. If so, Burghley knew his career would be over and Edward would have won his revenge.

But the Queen only wanted history plays from Edward now, strictly for political purposes, so perhaps Burghley had nothing more to fear. Historical figures were cut in marble and didn't inspire the intense scrutiny of the living. Julius Caesar, Pericles and Coriolanus, being mortal men, had outlived their sins as Burghley knew he himself would, when he lay in his grave.

It was unfortunate that the bad blood between himself and Edward, Earl of Oxford, had simmered gradually during his ward's adolescence and boiled over into his unhappy marriage to Anne. As a royal guardian, Burghley always believed that he had done his best to balance Edward's needs with England's wellbeing. If it turned out that the young man's interests were secondary to maintaining England's welfare, sacrifices on Edward's part were mere trifles to be expected.

As if to prove himself correct in his thinking, he turned to his well-worn journal and opened it to the terse entries written at the start of his stormy relationship with the Earl of Oxford.

> *August 1561 – Hedingham Castle, Day four of H.M.'s*
> *royal progress. Hot. Trouble ahead with young de Vere.*
> *E. stood too close to him, rested her hands on his shoulders*
> *for too long. Flirted with him most shamefully in front*
> *of the courtiers and ladies. Boy remarkably poised for 11*
> *years- part prodigy, part prodigal.*

Thinking back to the day, Burghley knew his assessment had been accurate, even prescient. At the time, the boy's anger had not yet surfaced. His father was alive and his family still intact. The very next entry a year later referred obliquely to the tragedy that had ensued.

August 1562 - Funeral of Lord John de Vere - his son to become the first royal ward placed in my care. He seems distressed and possibly outraged, claims his father was murdered and his mother married the assassin. He will not easily be made pliable.

Burghley shook his head. "Pliable" was hardly the word to describe his son-in-law. He turned the page and read on.

Sept.1562 - Edward loses everything if his half-sister prevails in her suit to declare him a bastard.

The Queen had understood Edward's agony over the charges of bastardy; for as a child, she had endured the same tragedy. She personally intervened to save Edward's good name. She made sure the court legally upheld his legitimacy as the rightful heir of Lord John de Vere and his wife, Lady Margery. The charges of bastardy were dismissed and Burghley breathed a sigh of relief.

Notwithstanding the Queen's intercession and de Vere's uncanny luck, the 17th Earl of Oxford had seemed determined to flirt with scandal. Perhaps the astrologers were right and such matters were written in the stars. Maybe Edward de Vere was destined to live with a wounded name.

But Time did not stand still and the stars moved in their spheres. Lord Burghley turned the pages.

July 7, 1565 - Against my advice, young Oxford appointed Keeper of Royal Ewer. Proximity to E's evening bath worrisome. He is precocious and impressionable.

Burghley shook his head and recalled the night his fears had been realized. He'd spent it with his ear against the Queen's bedchamber door, listening to her ruthless seduction of the boy.

July 12, 1565 – De Vere initiated into royal bed. I predict he will surrender whenever she summons him and will quickly learn to profit by it. In time, she will grow weary of him and their passion will die a natural death; for now, must assess possibilities.

The old man sat back and tapped his fingers against the table. He recalled that he'd been able to make good use of the Queen's passion for Oxford while it had thrived. He crossed the room and opened his own personal journal, the one he'd written shortly before the execution of Oxford's uncle, the Duke of Norfolk.

1571 – Oxford's foolhardy attempt to rescue Norfolk thwarted. The Queen has announced that I will be titled Baron Burghley when Edward marries my daughter. I will reap high honors for my work, all or most of it done in secret . . .

There had been so many secrets, and Burghley had kept track of them all. He noted how many times the Queen had jailed Norfolk for treason and then suddenly released him, thanks to Oxford's gentle persuasion. Apparently, a few flattering sonnets went a long way in softening her heart. Almost immediately after Leicester, her former favorite, fell from grace, Oxford, the Queen's new favorite, found that entertaining in the royal bedchamber had its rewards. Burghley had grown nervous as his daughter's wedding day approached. It seemed clear that the Queen intended to keep the Earl of Oxford tightly gripped in her talons.

July 1571 – H.M. has proclaimed it, according to plan; Anne is to have a husband, a star beyond her reach. Let the jealous vixens at Court weep with envy! She will wed my former ward within a month. We will be showered

*with riches and glory for her sake, and she will become
Countess of Oxford.*

Remembering what happened next, he found a corresponding entry
in his journal about Lord Oxford.

*August 1571 – There will be no wedding. The rascal has
abandoned my sweet girl at the altar! He will be arrested
and forced under pressure to reconsider his priorities.*

The Queen had feared that her lover Oxford had met with some
danger; what else, she thought, could have prevented him from taking his marriage vows to Anne? It was a ridiculous notion, but such
were her delusions. When the errant bridegroom was found escaping to France, the Queen ordered his return and placed him under
house arrest, where he could be watched at all times. She plied him
with some delicious promises and vowed to love him forever. He
trusted her word, and the wedding was rescheduled to take place
after Christmas. Anne was a radiant bride. Burghley cast his eyes
over his bittersweet recollections.

*December 1571 – Westminster Abbey was lavishly deco-
rated at the bridegroom's expense. He offered one of his
comedies called <u>The Merry Courtship of Mistress Anne</u>,
by way of an entertainment. Dr. Caius of Cambridge was
insulted at being portrayed as one of Anne's rejected suitors. A character named Slender was done up like Philip
Sidney, and the secret details of his proposal to my daughter were revealed to the whole world! My wife and I were
shocked, Sidney was angry . . . and the Queen was much
amused.*

My youngest son Robert acted the part of a pageboy quite well. He made the Queen laugh and since then, she has called him her Dwarf. I wonder, was she laughing at his words or at his deformity? Damn the wretched nurse who dropped him down the stairs and caused his crooked back! But my Robert loves his new brother-in-law Edward and would do anything in the world to please him.

Oxford's marriage will be consummated in three years, when Anne turns 18.

Burghley had known that hot-blooded Oxford couldn't wait for Anne, and that the Queen's unbridled passion wouldn't wait either. Her Majesty hid their affair behind the reticent and lovesick girl, offering the glittering marriage as a reward. Burghley wondered, had he really sacrificed his daughter at age 15 while publicly stating that marriages arranged in childhood always ended badly? Absolutely not! He was a caring and thoughtful father who had arranged the best possible match for his plain, unassertive daughter, and he was thankful the Queen supported it.

And over the years, his son Robert, who had once loved Edward so well, had grown furious at his brother-in-law's callous treatment of his sister.

December 1572 – Despite the difference in their ages, the amour between E. and O. has intensified. Love has erased all reason from her mind. I tell her that romantic insensibility is a risky course, and that for a queen, it can prove fatal. Meanwhile, it has been a year since Anne's marriage. She laments Oxford's absence and resents his platonic visits. I believe she knows what's going on behind her back . . .

He did his best to mollify her. He kept his ear to the Queen's door and lost a great deal of sleep when he overheard her promise to marry her young paramour and release him from his ill-contrived, unconsummated wedlock with Anne. The entry from his own journal reflected his agitation:

> *January 1573 – Love has stolen her senses! Does she truly imagine ruling beside the Earl of Oxford, whose nature is so volatile, he can scarcely govern his own impulses? The nobles will certainly rebel if he is named King Consort, and his preference for Catholicism will pose a serious threat to national security.*

Upon reflection, he had to admit he hadn't thought about his daughter at all. He'd merely kept silent; and in concert with the Queen's other advisors, he had urged Elizabeth to marry so that she could produce an heir. He had suggested several matches with foreign kings or princes, all of them capable of strengthening England's political alliances. And how did she respond to his judicious counsel? By toying with these suitors, mocking them in pillow talk with Oxford and sending them home empty-handed.

He referred again to his journal.

> *September 7, 1573 – The Queen turns 40. She complains that she is barren while her Scottish cousin has a son. With no heir apparent, revolution is a dangerous possibility. More than a dozen nobles have legitimate claims and all are prepared to fight for the throne. My Treasons Act will protect her; legitimate or not, E.'s child will become her successor whenever she decrees it.*

Burghley recalled how his scheme had been too dangerous to set down on paper.

It began with the fact that Oxford's lineage united the highest royal bloodlines of the land: Plantagenet, Lancaster and York. If he sired a child with the Queen, who was a descendant of the more recent Tudor line, their offspring would have an indisputable claim to the throne. Without naming names, Burghley had insured that the Treasons Act he had championed through Parliament would sanction this remarkable possibility by making the Queen sole arbiter of her successor. It mandated execution for anyone who, during her lifetime, even questioned who her successor might be.

Burghley had realized that such an action must be taken, along with all of its consequences. The Queen continued to reject all of her suitors, and if she died without an heir, the country would be torn apart with civil strife. The only victors in the ensuing struggle would be France and Spain.

If the Virgin Queen gave birth out of wedlock, she would jeopardize her honor and her throne; and in that case, too, the country would be torn apart. If she had a child at all, the infant itself would have to be concealed for its own safety until Her Majesty's death. This meant that she could name an heir, bastard or not, either on her death bed or by royal decree after her death. Anyone who challenged such a decree would be executed under the Treasons Act, and only by this means would the royal lineage be assured.

There was no alternative but to provide the country with a future king. Since the need for a royal successor was of greater importance than Anne's marriage to Lord Oxford, she would be shunted aside. Burghley saw no other way out of the dilemma. He read his cryptic words:

October 1573 - The Queen and Oxford stop at Lambeth with the Archbishop.

Burghley looked out the window and noticed that darkness had fallen. He rubbed his eyes, remembering how easy it had been to set aside his daughter's marriage and allow her husband to serve as breeding stock.

He hadn't been sure the Queen would conceive, but Oxford was strong and lusty. The Archbishop was well rewarded for sanctifying the secret union, and if a child was born from it, the Queen would give Oxford the title of King Consort and his marriage to Anne would be annulled. Power had a way of making all things possible.

April 15, 1574 - The Queen is in seclusion.

Burghley had listened from behind a curtain when the pregnant Queen dismissed Lord Oxford and thanked him for his "official service." Oxford flew into a rage as she waved the marriage contract to Anne in his face and ordered him to go home and honor it. The Queen carried his child in her womb and it was just beginning to show. The infant belonged to England and no rascal would ever live to claim it. She was sure he understood exactly what that meant.

Oxford was forcibly escorted home, where he had raged into the night, overturning furniture, ripping tapestries and threatening revenge at being ill used.

In due time, without regal fanfare or cannon fire, the Queen gave birth to a boy. The infant was given to the grieving Countess of Southampton in place of her own baby, which had recently died. The good lady swore to carry the secret of the changeling to her grave; and so far, she had kept her oath.

Ultimately, Oxford consummated his marriage to Anne, for there was little else he could do. He settled down as much as his volatile and tempestuous spirit would allow, and immersed himself in literary pursuits. The Queen continued to call on him to present plays and masques, but her favor had fallen on Sir Christopher Hatton, a newcomer at court who enjoyed the pleasures of her bed.

Burghley turned the page and confronted the tragedy that had changed their fortunes.

January 1, 1575 - Anne is several months pregnant with Oxford's child.

But almost immediately, Fate dealt her a miserable blow. Burghley trembled as the memories returned.

The Queen had finally granted Lord Oxford permission for his long-desired journey to France, Germany and Italy, but Anne, being pregnant, could not go with him. Almost immediately after his departure, she suffered a miscarriage and, despondent with fear, worried that her hedonistic husband would abandon her. Burghley believed it too, since it was no secret to anyone that the Earl of Oxford was not in love with her.

As soon as the doctors assured Burghley that Anne would be able to have more children, he wrote several letters to Lord Oxford, warning him about the dwindling state of his finances. He implored him to come home, but said nothing about the death of his baby or Anne's declining health. Burghley and Anne were certain the presumptuous courtier would stay beyond their reach in Italy and demand his freedom from the unhappy marriage, if he knew there was no child to bind him to it.

Oxford wrote back, refusing to come home merely because of money matters, which Lord Burghley was quite capable of managing on his behalf. The unwary Earl of Oxford surprised everyone by extending his stay, ignorant of what was happening at home.

And then Burghley remembered Lord Oxford's will, written before his marriage, stipulating that if he died childless, his fortune and titles would pass to his cousin Horatio. Thus, Anne would be left with nothing.

Burghley had sought guidance in the Bible, opening it at random to the story of Lot's widowed daughters. He had slammed it shut when he came to the part where they had gotten their father drunk to steal his seed so they could bear children. He took a deep breath and opened the Bible again. This time the pages fell open to the story of Jephthah, who sacrificed his daughter by taking her virginity to satisfy a bargain with the Lord. Reasoning that this was a form of Divine Guidance, Burghley made a terrible decision.

> *September 1575 –I wrote Oxford of the birth of his daughter.*

Burghley recalled how the afflictions of Anne's second pregnancy, the result of one consensual act between them, had disastrously clouded her mind. She had almost destroyed them both when she told the Queen that her husband would know the child was not his. She said it before witnesses and would have said more, if Burghley hadn't stopped her. He didn't like locking her away as the gossip rampaged through the Court. Everyone mocked powerful Lord Oxford for being a cuckold, deceived by Lord Burghley's meek and unassuming daughter. When he heard the news in France, Lord Oxford sped home, ranting and raving about the unfaithful wife who had betrayed him. He cast her off as damaged goods and sent her home to her father.

Burghley turned again to the records he kept on his former ward.

> *1576 – Oxford claims I've turned his private life into a public scandal. If he appeals to the Queen for a divorce from Anne, all is lost.*

Lord Burghley had covered his tracks. He shook the journal gently and a yellowed paper fell out. On it was his copy of the rambling confession he'd written to the Queen.

> *1576 – Whereas I, by God's visitation with some infirmity, cannot do my duty at this time, and my daughter, the Countess of Oxford, is also absent from Court, the reason for her non-appearance may be reported differently to Your Majesty. I finish with the humble request that if I have offered myself with dishonesty, I may have your*

> *Majesty's princely favor to seek my just defense for me
> and mine.*

It had been ten long years since he'd written those words, and his sin had remained concealed. Anne had gone mad, and no one paid attention to her wild accusations of incest against him. But this play called *Hamlet* thundered revenge. Burghley cringed at the humiliation he'd felt at the point of Oxford's knife, and wondered whether it would be less painful to feel the end of his distinguished career, just one more malicious strike against his well-ordered world.

Burghley reviewed his achievements, confident that no other man had equaled them. Certainly none of the Queen's lovers could have placed her on the pedestal he had carefully carved out for her. All those years ago, lust had ruled her senses while Burghley had remained clearheaded, guiding her with no thought of carnal reward. His love for Elizabeth Tudor was an abiding affection that no one else could match, not even Lord Oxford with volumes full of passionate sonnets.

Burghley clenched his fists. He had no intention of being undone by a vengeful playwright and a vicious theater piece.

There were more pressing problems to consider. If Spain carried out its threats of war, England could fall to its fierce Armada with no fleet of ships to protect its own shores. Burghley wondered what would happen if the nation perished under his watch because none of its men would rally to defend it. What would history say about his strategies, if his beloved Queen were killed or taken prisoner and ransomed?

But perhaps it wouldn't come to that, if the plays could be persuasive. After all, Lord Oxford was a patriot. He had fought in the wars in Scotland and had undertaken several secret missions inside Catholic strongholds within foreign countries. In Italy, with his innate charisma, he had negotiated a truce between two warring factions. Perhaps that, coupled with the lessons in statesmanship Burghley had taught him, would make the history plays a propaganda success.

Torn between admiration and dismay for his son-in-law, Burghley recalled a play he'd seen as a child, an uncomplicated religious allegory about the eternal struggle between Good and Evil, a battle portrayed in terms of absolute values. If only such theatrical clarity were possible in the real world, so that England's citizens would see the immediate need to defend it.

Burghley had seen Lord Oxford raise dead kings in the playhouses along the Thames, sending shivers of awe from the nobles to the groundlings. But until that very moment, he had never imagined that Oxford's theatrical bent could prove politically advantageous. The Queen needed her subjects' support and Parliament had to act quickly to levy higher taxes and call men to arms. Perhaps the nation's historical struggles against her enemies, set on stage in the context of Good versus Evil, would stir his countrymen.

Not since Virgil had written the *Aeneid* to promote ancient Rome's military agenda had anyone used propaganda on such a scale. Only Lord Oxford was capable of forging his words into a battle cry that would arouse the masses to defend their nation at all costs.

But beyond the erratic side of Oxford's nature was the problem of his authorship. If the commoners discovered (or even suspected) that they were being manipulated by a member of the aristocracy, Burghley feared they would turn against the Queen and destroy England from within.

The public playhouses were becoming increasingly popular. This meant that Lord Oxford would need a pen name to perform his service to the state. He would also need a front man to stand in for him. The commoners would be pleased that the compelling new playwright had spontaneously sprung up from among their numbers. The impostor himself would have to be modest and responsible, a relative stranger to London's social sphere, and perhaps a graduate of one of the new country schools, someone who could deliver the plays to the censor and to the playhouses without raising suspicion.

Burghley pondered how to pay for this undertaking, having seen Lord Oxford spend large sums of his own income producing plays for the Queen. He decided that a stipend of one thousand pounds a year would underwrite expenses, and that it must be kept completely off the record as far as the Exchequer was concerned. More writers, scribes and actors could be employed to expedite the propaganda plays and all would be managed by the impostor under the masterful literary guidance of Lord Oxford.

Grinning with satisfaction, Lord Burghley gathered up his papers, meticulously checking to see that none lay about for curious eyes. He placed the journals in the vault behind the tapestry. He blew out the candles and went to his bedchamber.

He would present his plan to the Queen in the morning.

CHAPTER ELEVEN

The Scene:London
June 15, 1586

"In Nature's infinite book of secrecy
A little I can read."

— Antony and Cleopatra

"How dare you turn your back on me!" the Queen shouted at Lord Oxford as he barged out of the room, limping slightly because of the old wound in his leg. He used his walking stick to push past the courtiers and ladies in the anteroom, leaving a trail of whispers in his wake. John Lyly had to run to catch up with him.

"My lord, wait! Where are you going?"

"I'm going to The Boar's Head. I need a drink."

"My lord, if you will only consider some way to obey her majesty's command. . ."

"I will *not* let her treat me like a menial."

"Her Majesty never called you that."

"She refused to lift the ban on publication."

"But she made you a much better offer, my lord."

Oxford grabbed Lyly by the collar and shoved him up against a wall.

"Perhaps you didn't understand," he said, exaggerating every syllable, as if talking to a child. "Her subtle proposal was an insult. It's outrageous, ordering me to write history plays for hire and salary, as if I were a tailor custom-making doublets!"

"But you can spend the money any way you wish. That's the best part. The Queen has offered to sponsor your playwriting. She's going to pay your production costs. All right, maybe she is asking you to write propaganda plays, and maybe you won't be identified as the author, but everything else will be kept confidential, strictly off the record, without even so much as an accounting to the Exchequer. What more do you want?"

"It still reduces me to the level of a common tradesman. It's an insult! Don't you see what's at the heart of her bargain? She intends to control everything I write for political purposes. She's trying to silence me by offering me my heart's desire . . . on *her* terms."

"But she wants to sponsor your plays. What possible harm can that do?"

Oxford stared, appalled at his secretary's naiveté.

"I'll be at The Boar's Head. You can either join me or go hang yourself."

A week later, tired and hungry, Shaxper trudged into London with only a crumpled letter of introduction in his pocket. He was more determined than ever to succeed, having had plenty of time to convince himself that surviving the robbery was a confirmation of Divine Intervention.

Taking a deep breath, he joined the hurly-burly in the crowded streets, the familiar stench of the city once again filling his nostrils. He avoided looking at the severed heads on London Bridge, their jaws agape with death, a stern warning to all treasonous Catholics. He made a mental note to keep his mouth shut and emulate those who survived.

He bumped against the merchants who hauled their wares into the streets as he picked his way through the crowd. He overheard tidings of the New World wafting from the open windows of the taverns. Adventurers boasted about the exotic animals and spices they had seen on their travels. Musicians sang the latest songs, and the strange new smell of tobacco drifted onto the lane. Surrounded by the bustle of enterprise, Shaxper took heart. London still represented the brave new world of his dreams. By the grace of God, he would find ready employment with the Earl of Oxford and refill his purse as quickly as possible.

Feet aching, he sat down to rest in front of The Boar's Head and watched as its intoxicated patrons stumbled out onto the street. Whores and pickpockets busily plied their trades, grateful for the easy commerce. A commotion broke out on the next block, and he craned his neck to see what was going on.

Curiosity overruled his pain. He rose to investigate. Moving towards the noise, he recognized John Lyly pushing aside the sea of flatterers that encircled the Earl of Oxford. The mob was loud and raucous, everyone making brazen attempts to get as close to the glittering celebrity as possible. Shaxper edged in, too, unwilling to miss his chance. He trailed the swarm of revelers into the pub and watched as every creature in the place – drunk or sober – hovered around the charismatic Earl.

At first Lord Oxford greeted everyone graciously, but as the riffraff pressed closer, he gripped his walking stick and deftly used it to distance himself. Smiling and nodding, he worked his way towards the stairs.

"Will it be the usual, my lord?" the barkeep called.

"Yes, yes. Send up a tray, and quickly, too."

Then dashing up the stairs, he disappeared with Lyly right behind him.

Shaxper elbowed his way to the foot of the staircase.

"I used to enjoy these crowds at my tournaments," he heard the Earl say, "but since the stabbing at Blackfriars, I feel like Julius Caesar on the steps of the Senate . . ."

The door closed behind them.

Shaxper looked over his shoulder and saw that the barkeep was busy tending to his customers. Veiled by smoke, he seized his chance and took the stairs three at a time. He halted on the landing, realizing he had no idea which room was Oxford's. Whispering a prayer, he chose a door and put his ear to it. His heart soared when he recognized Oxford's sonorous voice inside.

"God's body, I wish Audrey would hurry up with that ale. My hands are shaking. I need to write, but my hands are shaking."

"Perhaps you should lie down."

"No. Go tell her to hurry."

"But you only just gave the order —"

"If we're having *the usual*, it should be ready by now!"

"It will come."

"As much as I trust Audrey, you must remember to taste everything before I do."

"I will. I always do. I haven't died of poisoning yet, and neither have you."

Hearing the serving wench on the stairs, Shaxper quickly moved away from the door. Affecting nonchalance, he pretended to gaze out the window and then turned as if heading downstairs.

"Aaaaauuudrey!" the Earl bellowed from inside the room. "Where the hell is my ale?"

"Here, my lord. Open the door."

When the door flew open, Audrey quickly stepped inside as the eavesdropper ducked into an alcove. Within seconds, the door opened again. Lyly stuck his head into the hallway and looked around.

"There's no one out here now, Audrey, but keep your eyes open just the same."

"Yes, sir, I will."

The door closed. Shaxper watched as Audrey stuffed some coins into her apron and went downstairs. He once again took up his position outside the door. He could feel Oxford's panic through it.

"Are you sure no one's out there?"

"No one, my lord."

"None of the Queen's stooges or Burghley's agents?"

"Not a soul, I swear."

"God's blood! This time the Queen has me by the balls! Do you know that?"

"Calm down, my lord. Have a drink."

"And then what?"

"And then you'll stop trembling. You'll be able to work."

"I can't work today. And I can't drink this stuff. It smells like horse piss."

"Nonsense. It's your usual."

"Are you saying I usually drink horse piss?"

"No, I—"

"Perhaps it's royal piss. She'll do anything to humiliate me now."

"I don't believe it. Her Majesty needs you to write history plays."

"You don't know that woman the way I do. She always says one thing and does another. What am I supposed to make of it?"

"For the moment, nothing, my lord. Have a drink."

"Taste it first. What the hell do you think I'm paying you for?"

There was a long pause. A few unintelligible words were exchanged before Shaxper could hear again clearly.

"It's not piss *or* poison," Lyly said. "It's ale, and quite good actually."

"Well, are you going to drink the whole pitcher yourself? Pour me some."

"Yes, my lord."

There was another silence, broken again by Lyly.

"You haven't told me everything, have you, my lord? What did the Queen say when you two were alone?"

"She swears she loves me!" Oxford laughed. "Isn't that rich? She's been swearing that since I was twelve, but it really doesn't matter. She swore the same oath to Seymour and Leicester and Hatton and a battalion of her other minions. I know that now; I'm not a dazed orphan anymore. Twice she's made love to me before imprisoning me in the Tower. She practically swoons with passion every time she gives the decree. 'Oh, my poor dear Oxford, once again your devilish nature has left me no choice,'" he mimicked.

"No choice? What does she mean?"

"Each time it means something different. This time it means that if I don't comply with her order to write those damned history plays, she'll brand me a traitor and stake my head on London Bridge. History will set me down as a villain. Does that sound like love to you?"

There was a brief silence. Shaxper flattened his ear against the door. He heard the sound of agitated pacing; then, Oxford's voice: "I'm to be expelled from Court under a cloud of disgrace. That's the cover story. I'm supposed to limp back to the countryside like a beaten dog, live under clouds of presumptuous gossip and scratch out reams of propaganda for the playhouses, and no one must know my mission. We're at war, and England needs a fleet of ships."

"So there really is no choice."

"None at all. I'll be little better than an anonymous pamphleteer hiding behind a pseudonym like our Martin Marprelate, and the Queen demands a huge volume of work – a whole series of plays to be performed one after another, in a short space of time, at each of the playhouses. It's a Herculean task: writing plays in repertory, copying out rolls for the actors, training and rehearsing swordsmen, hiring musicians, sewing costumes, building sets . . ."

"It's not at all like pamphleteering."

"And it carries a sentence of death, if I fail. There's no escape. Unless . . ."

"Unless what?"

"Unless every playhouse in England suddenly and mysteriously burns to the ground. I'll torch them myself —"

"That's absurd. You worked so hard to create them."

"But I must do something. I can't write these plays alone; and under penalty of death, how could I ask anyone to help me?"

Shaxper knew it was time to make his entrance. His fate depended on it, danger be damned. He cleared his throat, squared his shoulders and knocked on the door.

Lyly answered.

"Yes? What is it?"

"My name is William Shaxper, sir. I've come to see Lord Oxford."

"Not now. We're busy."

"But it's a matter of urgency."

"You didn't really expect to see His Lordship, just by walking in off the street, did you?"

"Wait! I have a letter of introduction," Shaxper said. He reached into his doublet and gave the letter to Lyly. The secretary skimmed it and handed it back.

"This is a letter from a dead man. Thomas Vautrollier passed away a year ago."

"I-I'm sorry, I didn't know.

"Then you weren't as close to him as this letter suggests, were you? That's not a very convincing recommendation."

"I can get you a letter from Richard Field, if you want. He runs the shop now."

"That won't be necessary." Lyly peered at Shaxper. "I must say, you look familiar. Have we met before?"

"Ohhh, I don't think so," Shaxper lied. "I'd certainly remember a gentleman like you, sir."

"Save your flattery. I'm a busy man, and so is the Earl of Oxford. Good day now."

He started to close the door, but Shaxper's foot was quicker. "It won't be a good day for anybody unless you let me see the Earl right now."

"Why, you impudent knave! Who do you think you are?"

Shaxper summoned his courage. "His Lordship and I are kinsmen. He won't take kindly to your showing me the door this way."

A voice came from within. "Who is it, Lyly? He sounds like he's from Warwickshire. His accent's as thick as porridge."

The door swung open and the Earl of Oxford stood before him. Shaxper promptly forgot every rule of etiquette he'd learned, except for his well-practiced bow.

"My lord, it's truly an honor –"

"Stop groveling, my good man. Don't bob up and down like a game-cock. Lyly, give him alms. Don't let the beggar go away empty handed."

"I'm not a beggar, my lord," Shaxper bristled. "I'm looking for work – gainful employment."

"God's blood, not another actor!" Lyly snorted.

Shaxper had to think fast.

"With all my heart, my lord, I am *not* an actor."

"What are you then?"

"A copyist with fine penmanship, looking for work as a scribe, my lord."

"What makes you think I need another scribe?"

"Perhaps not for your personal correspondence, but the theater business is booming. Surely you must need schooled and literate men to copy out scripts for the players."

"Must I?" Oxford growled.

"Yes. It's a lot of work. Anyone with half a brain could see that."

At Oxford's nod, Lyly pulled Shaxper into the room and closed the door. Wary and uncertain, the Stratfordian upstart nonetheless congratulated himself for having come this far. He began to sweat.

His eyes darted around the room. It was spacious and richly furnished, lit by three large windows that overlooked the street. Two immense tapestries, one displaying a scene of falconry, the other showing jesters entertaining at a banquet, hung on opposite sides, stark contrasts seconded by dark beams and whitewashed walls. Several chairs with red cushions and clawed feet looked inviting. The tray of food sent by the barkeep rested on the table, overflowing with fruit, honey, bread and cheese. Beyond the hearth was a second room lined with bookshelves. In the center was a table cluttered with pens, papers, inkwells and opened books. Lyly closed the door as if guarding a secret.

"Sit down," Oxford said. "Have Audrey bring up another flagon of ale for our guest, and let's hear what this fellow has to say."

"Thank you, my lord," Shaxper said, "but I don't drink ale. I prefer small beer."

"Drinking a child's drink? Now that's a tragedy."

"Actually, most of the tragedies in my childhood have been the result of drunkenness - but not *my* drunkenness."

"That sounds like a riddle," Oxford chuckled.

"I'll have the ale, but only if it's watered down."

Lyly poured another drink for Oxford and himself. He grimaced while adding water to the ale and handed it to Shaxper.

"So you seek work as a scribe?" the Earl asked.

"Yes, my lord. That's why I came to London."

"I don't believe it. Who sent you?"

"No one sent me. I came here on my own."

"All the way from Warwickshire?"

"Yes, from Stratford-on-Avon."

"Why? Aren't there any jobs in Stratford? Don't you have a profession?"

"Oh, there's plenty of work in town, if you're a farmer or a merchant or a grain dealer. But I'm better educated than most of the people there, so I've come to London to improve my prospects."

"An admirable decision. You must be ambitious."

"I am," Shaxper said proudly, "but not dangerously so."

"Have you ever *seen* a play?" Lyly asked.

"Yes. I've stood among the groundlings . . ."

"Oh, well, what further theatrical experience could a man need?" he snipped.

"I know what plays I like and what plays I don't like," Shaxper said, defensively.

"Really? And how many plays have you seen?" Oxford asked.

"Seven."

"How were they? Did you like them?"

"No. They were church plays – most of them about burning in Hell for one's sins."

Oxford burst out laughing. Shaxper blanched.

"My lord, this talk is rubbish!" Lyly sneered.

"Actually, I find his candor quaint. Since he's a regular theatergoer, he knows what he likes. I seldom have a chance to hear unmitigated honesty. Well then, what kind of play holds your interest, sir?"

"The best play I ever saw was *The Famous Victories*. I saw it four times, twice in London and twice more when your company came to Stratford—"

Shaxper bit his tongue. Surely they'd recognize him now, as the village idiot, the one they'd held at knifepoint!

Oxford's eyes widened.

"You saw *The Famous Victories* four times? Did you hear that, Lyly?"

The secretary nodded. Oxford leaned forward, flattered and intrigued.

"I'm actually reworking that play right now, polishing its historical accuracy at the Queen's request, though I'm sure you can see it stands on its own, just as it is now. Tell me, what did you think of it? Better still, what did you think of William Browne?"

"Well, I –"

"Wait a minute!" Lyly exclaimed. "I know you! You're the broker from Stratford who rented us the barn."

"Yes, I did, but —"

"Why didn't you say so?" Oxford asked. "Did we neglect to pay you? Is that why you're here?"

"No, you paid me very handsomely, my lord. Thank you."

The conversation came to a dead halt. Shaxper waited for Oxford or Lyly to throw him out. *Could both men have forgotten how they'd tormented him?* He summoned his courage and came in on cue, changing the subject.

"As I told Mr. Lyly, I worked for Monsieur Vautrollier a few years ago, on my last stay in London. His apprentice was my boyhood friend, Richard Field. Perhaps you've heard of him."

"Yes, he's making quite a name for himself. Of course, it didn't hurt that he married Vautrollier's widow and took over the publishing business."

"That's one way for a peasant to improve his prospects," Lyly snorted. "Why don't you ask Field for a job?"

"I'm not interested in printing, I want to work in the theater."

"Can you imagine what would happen if publishers began printing plays?" Oxford speculated. "Every rude mechanical in London would try to put them on. Nothing would be sacred, not even the playwright's good name."

"Or the profits," Lyly said.

"One worry at a time, please."

"Money certainly worries me," Shaxper sighed. "I have a wife and three children back home. I've learned that a man must seek his fortune, and not wait for his fortune to seek him. Theater is a golden cow waiting to be milked."

Oxford winked at Lyly. "That sounds so mercenary. I always fancied theater to be an Art."

"Oh, it is," Shaxper replied, "but look at all those commoners building playhouses along the Thames."

"Isn't that strange?" Oxford laughed. "How do you suppose an ordinary man suddenly acquires that much money? You said yourself it isn't easy."

"I suppose if he's desperate, he commits a crime," Shaxper said.

"No. There are legal means."

"He could find a patron . . ."

"Or the patron could find him," Oxford said. "Money changes hands all the time."

"Does it?" Shaxper said, his heart skipping a beat.

"Yes, take my word for it. A courtier can own a company of players, but if he owns a playhouse that charges a penny-a-head to see a play, even if it's a classic virtuous epic, he's considered lewd and amoral. I know because it happened to me."

"Besides, virtue doesn't sell," Lyly smirked. "Audiences love corruption."

"Just recently I signed my ownership of Blackfriars over to Lyly," Oxford said. "He and several others own those playhouses on the Thames. I've had to become invisible by order of the Queen to avoid damaging my reputation. That's why the actors call me their ghost. On payday, it's become a tradition to say the ghost walks."

"But you've been a theatrical sponsor for years; everyone knows it," Shaxper said.

"My plays and playhouses are like bastard children," Oxford replied. "I can father them and provide for them, but can never officially tell the world they're mine. The Queen has forbidden it."

"God's blood!" Lyly leapt to his feet. "I've completely lost track of the time! The writers will be arriving any minute and I'd best get them settled before Marlowe and young Ben Jonson start arguing again."

"Is Ben the bricklayer coming to repair the hearth?" Oxford asked.

"Yes, but I think he really wants to listen to the first reading of *Tamburlaine*."

"Let him listen then," Oxford said, as he turned to Shaxper. "We could use another scribe around the table, couldn't we, Lyly?"

The secretary ignored the question and hurried away, leaving the noble playwright and the hopeful scribe in awkward silence.

"Did you have a good journey to London, Mr. Shaxper?"

"Not good at all, my lord. I was robbed by a band of highwaymen just outside Stratford."

"You were lucky. At least the thieves let you keep your greatest treasure."

"What's that, my lord?"

"Why, your life, man. Your life."

"Oh yes, I'm alive," Shaxper moaned. "But I have no money, and without money, one might as well be dead."

"How much did they steal?"

"They took my horse and my entire life savings, five pounds, everything I had on me."

"Then replace it with this." He tossed Shaxper a heavy purse.

"My lord, I – I can't accept this money."

"Yes, you can. I came by it honestly, and now so have you."

"But I can't accept charity."

"It's not charity. It's a salary. I will need your help, but for more important work than scribing."

Shaxper bowed modestly. It was the moment he'd been waiting for.

"How can I help you, my lord?"

"The Queen has asked me to perform a service . . . ."

"What kind of service, my lord?"

He waited for Oxford to disclose the dangerous life-or-death proposition he'd overheard on the other side of the door, but the Earl revealed none of it.

"As I said, Her Majesty has asked me to rewrite *The Famous Victories*. She demands that I make the play more historically accurate. But I won't have time to read for details. Perhaps you could read a history book for me and make some annotations in the margins of my book to help me with the play's unfolding. Then I can decide whether or not to hire you, based on the quality of your research. Would you be willing to try?"

"Gladly, my lord. What book shall I read?"

Oxford walked over to the window and slid a huge volume from the shelf.

"I'd like you to take a look at Hall's *Chronicles*."

"I've read it!" Shaxper cried excitedly. "That book and I are old friends."

"Excellent! If you do a good job, you can keep it."

"Thank you, my lord. I'm truly honored. I'll be very thorough," he promised. "You can depend on me—you'll see."

"I'm sure of it," Oxford said, as he walked the newcomer to the door. "I'm sure of it. I'll see you on Friday then with your notations. Good day, sir, I look forward to our sharing a long and profitable relationship."

As if in a dream, Shaxper found himself back in the hallway, clutching the book and a purse full of money, more than enough to keep him in a boarding house for a good long time. The fact that he hadn't pressed the issue of his kinship didn't matter. It had suddenly become clear to him that being in the right place at the right time had deposited his future directly into his hands.

CHAPTER TWELVE

The Scene: Westminster Tilt-Yard

March 1587

"There is a tide in the affairs of men
Which, taken at the flood, leads on to Fortune."

– Julius Caesar

Outside the Westminster tilt-yard, the hellish claws of a roaring fire tore at heaven. Shaxper and several others coughed at the smoke and stepped around the angry mob, which had been preached into a frenzy by a group of Puritan clergy. Men and women, their faces contorted with hate and prejudice, shrieked like demons as they furiously tore apart Catholic books and tossed them into the fire. Shaxper was certain that none of them could read the books they were intent on destroying. It then occurred to him that in all of his time in London, he had never seen a book burning before, and the mass hysteria of the violent rabble terrified him. Forgive them, he reasoned, for they know not what they do.

He was running late, too late perhaps to help Lord Oxford prepare for the joust or to quietly rehearse the lines he had been asked to present to the Queen. As he entered the tilt-yard, Shaxper was stunned by the fairytale pageantry before him. Trumpets blared as spectators climbed the nearest hillside to watch the tournament. Powerful horses richly caparisoned with heraldic symbols pawed at the ground, anxious for the contest. Banners rippled in the breeze as lords and ladies dined on the fresh delicacies for which he had only recently acquired a taste.

For several years, Shaxper's recent employer had been England's most celebrated tournament champion. At this, his final joust, he would face a number of challengers, including Sir Henry Lee, who had taken Lady Vavasor, Oxford's former mistress, as his newest lover. With all of the animosity between the two men, Shaxper was concerned for his master's safety – if he were to die on the field as jousters sometimes did, their partnership would come to an abrupt end and Shaxper would be thrust back into his bucolic obscurity. He would lose his income as the Earl's scribe and front man, and never find his place as a player in the company.

During the past year, he had become Oxford's most dependable servant. He had eased himself into the Earl's good graces, replacing Lyly as his trusted secretary. The best boon was that Oxford had begun teaching him the art of oratory, a subject never taught in the simple country school in Stratford. Shaxper learned how to stand and emote with proper diction, how to pitch his voice and avoid distracting movements and facial expressions. He practiced often, thrilled at the new sensations he felt when reciting ancient speeches or epic poetry. It was a feeling beyond religious ecstasy, taking on the essence of other men's thoughts and feelings and making them his own.

In the meantime, Shaxper earned his living by supervising other writers in what he called the play factory, copying out Oxford's roles and manuscripts. Normally, he handed them over to the official censor before passing them on to the playhouses, but sometimes he was advised to skip that step. He was delighted when the theater managers also paid him for his deliveries, and he kept these gratuities without a word to anyone. Oxford had no interest in such fees; his concerns over the content of the history propaganda plays were more complex. He often defied the Queen's explicit laws concerning publication, but time and again Her Majesty looked the other way, which saved him from arrest.

Shaxper sometimes quailed at his master's lack of discretion and the risks he was asked to take as the middleman. The Earl's latest piece of roguery, a play called *Edmund Ironside*, had Shaxper's secretarial hand all over it. Unwilling to disobey his master, he had delivered it to the censor with Oxford's name affixed as author and he hadn't had a peaceful night since. The Queen's command for anonymity was clear, but Oxford had simply ignored it.

To appease her, His Lordship had prepared a dazzling entertainment for the interval in today's tournament. He had granted Shaxper the privilege of delivering the accompanying oration. With the bearing of a showman, Shaxper assured himself that he was impeccably well dressed and barbered. He hoped to make a good impression on the Queen and the other denizens seated on the royal dais. He had practiced classical rhetoric for weeks, but had been forced to rest his voice before he strained it.

Shaxper fancied that reciting Oxford's verses was indeed an honor that no one else in the play factory could rise to. The rest of Oxford's Men were rank scoundrels, men of grosser clay who tried to pass themselves off as poets. Not even Anthony Munday, Oxford's earliest hire, had the requisite finesse to accomplish such a recitation. While Munday had taken down parts of *Sir Thomas More* strictly from Oxford's dictation, he was no orator or actor. Shaxper, on the other hand, was a jack-of-all-trades, willing to perform any service for a price. He took it as a compliment when Oxford relied on him and called him his *Johannes Factotum,* even though the others mocked him for it.

Shaxper was sure his rapid advancement was the result of his ready compliance. He aped every aspect of the Earl's finery, to the extent that his salary afforded, while Oxford's Men, drinking and gambling a short distance away, didn't care how they looked to the world. Shaxper watched as Kit Marlowe spat on the ground and tried to wrestle his ill-gotten winnings away from Robert Greene. A brawl broke out and the constables were called. Young Ben Jonson, the bricklayer's son, quickly pocketed Marlowe's crooked dice as Thomas Kyd dragged him away to avoid their arrests as well.

Shaxper wondered what Jonson was doing there anyway, when the youth should have been helping his stepfather earn a living. Ben had no talent beyond slapping loam and rough-cast with a trowel to build a wall, and yet Lord Oxford's Men treated him like a mascot. He couldn't understand why they encouraged the awkward youth's feeble attempts at playwriting, which seemed as hopeless as breathing life into a corpse.

But there was no time to dwell on men of poor character. Shaxper turned his attention to the tournament commemorating Oxford's transition into private life. Tomorrow he would quit his courtly duties and draw the cloak over his work, retiring to the countryside to conceal it. He hadn't shared the truth of his secret service with anyone except Shaxper, the loyal scribe who had packed up his library and maintained a vested interest in his affairs.

Nonetheless, gossip about Oxford's retirement buzzed on the breeze. Some suspected he had outraged the Queen once too often, while others wagered on the date of his execution. Still others said he'd squandered his inheritance and could no longer afford to pay the tributes demanded by the Queen. Sir Henry Lee and Lady Vavasor were confident that Oxford's wounded leg made it difficult for him to stand for hours attending Her Majesty's pleasure, making his service as a courtier impossible.

Lee intended to take full advantage of his injury. Lady Vavasor herself knew the full extent of it: with a cry of revenge, her own cousin had stabbed Oxford in the alley outside Blackfriars and left him for dead. The Earl was lucky to have survived.

Perhaps Oxford's participation in the joust was one last bit of courtly vanity, marking the end of a swashbuckling career as champion with the lance. At nearly 37, he claimed to be as fit as ever, but Shaxper had seen him limp like a crab when he thought no one was looking, and then consume rivers of ale to dull the pain.

A blast of trumpets heralded the Queen's arrival, jarring Shaxper from his thoughts. Everyone bowed as Her Majesty took her place on the shaded dais followed by her entourage. Lord Burghley's disfigured son, 25-year old Robert Cecil, sat on her left, generating a flurry of whispers as she ordered his father to sit further off. Henry Wriothesley, the Queen's adolescent ward, haughtily took his chair on her right.

Shaxper imagined himself sitting beside Her Majesty some day, soaking up honors like a sponge, but first he had to get through this presentation. He anxiously patted his doublet to be sure the poetic recitation he'd been given hadn't fallen through the hole he'd neglected to mend. Oxford's impassioned words threatened to burn right through it! Shaxper blushed and began to sweat. He wondered whether the Queen would be furious when she heard her lover's words coming out of his mouth. He saw the smoke from the book burning rising above the fence and suddenly feared being punished for words he hadn't written and didn't understand. But then he nervously cleared his throat and regained his composure. He wasn't about to let fear ruin his chance for advancement. He skirted the tilt-yard and waited in front of the Earl's tent for his cue.

A crier stepped forward to announce the rules but was immediately interrupted by the din of trumpets. Hautboys from Blackfriars stepped forward dressed in Oxford's livery, blaring a fanfare in front of his tent. The crimson flaps were drawn aside, and Oxford stepped onto the field wearing a suit of golden armor. The spectators cheered as he was hoisted atop Agincourt, his well-trained charger. Suddenly, the tent was collapsed to reveal a tall bay tree completely layered in gold. Oxford and Agincourt posed before it, giving the appearance of a scene from a medieval tapestry.

The crowd gasped and broke into cheers that resounded across the field. This was the cue Shaxper had been waiting for. He reached into his pocket and pulled out his script. He walked up the steps towards the Queen as musicians from the theater played an interlude.

He stopped respectfully just inches away, and found himself staring at her shoes. He trembled but summoned his courage, determined not to look foolish. Robert Cecil and Henry Wriothesley exchanged mocking glances and stifled their laughter. Shaxper looked up at Her Majesty, who smiled at him with anticipation. Instantly, he choked up again and in his protracted silence, the royal smile disappeared.

"Is this one of your son-in-law's jokes?" the Queen asked, turning to Lord Burghley. "What does Oxford mean, sending a mute to deliver a speech?"

Burghley leaned forward. "Your Majesty, this is his secretary, William Shaxper. I'm sure he's as articulate as you or I. Aren't you, my good man?"

"Y-yes, my lord," Shaxper stammered. "I sp-speak as well as you do."

Henry Wriothesley laughed. The Queen slapped his wrist with her fan.

"Don't be afraid, Master Shaxper," Her Majesty said crisply. "Come closer, I won't bite you, although Henry here might. Is Shaxper your true surname?"

"Yes, Your Majesty, it is."

"Did your master ever tell you the nickname I once gave him?"

Shaxper shook his head, although Lord Oxford had mentioned the Queen's affinity for nicknames. He was sure she was toying with him now, and felt like the quarry at a bear baiting.

"I christened him 'Shake-Spear,'" she grinned cunningly, "because he's our reigning tournament champion and it's been said that his countenance shakes spears. I understand you're to deliver an oration concerning the glittering *tableau* he presents before us today. Kindly proceed. You mustn't keep us waiting."

A short distance away, the golden knight, his brilliant charger and the gilded bay tree shone, resplendent in the bright sunlight.

Shaxper squared his shoulders and began his recitation:

> *When Phoebus scarce the dewy morn enhanced,*
> *And halcyon hues on leafy cowslips danced,*
> *A dauntless knight through hoary forest chanced.*
> *His new-bold quest to verdant woodlands dim,*
> *In sylvan glade, espied a hermit grim*
> *Near lost in leaves beside the brook's green brim.*
> *The ancient pilgrim clad in monkish hood,*
> *Half-hidden in the still cathedral wood,*
> *Rose from his prayers, thrice crossed, and humbly stood.*
> *Then quoth the puissant knight with brazen sway,*
> *"O, gentle reverend friar, I prithee say*
> *Where does the tree of Truth and Beauty stay?*
> *What seeds of Truth are grafted in that place*
> *To Beauty's stalk; what fallen buds of grace*
> *Can Providence to Eden's path retrace?"*
> *"O, ornament of knighthood, heaven blessed!"*
> *The friar quoth, "Sir Knight, be not distressed*
> *For neither are by mankind yet possessed."*
> *"Have Truth and Beauty left thee so undone?*

Perchance your quest for Truth you must now shun,
For Beauty's blossom fades in torrid sun.
For this much I have heard, and do allow:
Like golden leaves composted by the plow,
Love maketh man forsworn of every vow."
The mournful knight fell on the shore and wept,
His tears of sorrow by the harsh winds swept
His quondam quest, he feared, could not be kept.
"Though yet forsworn," quoth he, "I'll constant prove;
Temptations never more my heart can move.
Endangered pleasures find no other groove.
If Knowledge be the mark, it must suffice;
Well learnéd is the tongue that forswears Vice;
But ignorant the soul that gains the price
Of vanity and evil-hearted plunder.
Her eye Jove's lightning strikes, her voice, his thunder,
Thus Truth and Beauty are both torn asunder."
The saintly hermit pitied this sad shift.
"Redeem thyself; accept this precious gift."
A spear of light the molten rock gan rift,
The rumbling rocks burst forth the secret lair.
Behold, a tree of sun with golden flare,
Its roots effulgent, radiant with glare.
"In lofty nest good Vesta's bird doth perch,
In vain do Cupid's arrows leap and lurch,
But Phoenix will not e'er abide the search.
Dwell here, beneath the brilliance of its shade
For here no trial or troubles shall invade
The love of Truth, where Beauty's gently made."
The Knight received the pilgrim's blessed boon
Then suddenly, he fell into a swoon

And did not wake until the morrow's noon.
By then the friar was gone from hence, forsooth
But now he knew that Beauty without Truth
Is nothing but a parody uncouth.
The knight did vow that glorious golden tree
Was destin'd as the force to set him free.
Its thoughts, his thoughts, would make all sorrows flee.
One only sun can shine upon this sight,
One only root take nurture from this light,
One only trunk to give majestic might.
This tree is our Most Virtuous Queen so fair;
There is but one to serve this monarch rare,
And live and die in her protective care.
Behold, the Earl of Oxford, it is he
Whose life may end, but ne'er his loyalty,
His head, his hand, his heart he pledges thee.

The Queen was deeply moved.

"One son," she whispered, glancing at Henry Wriothesley. She blew a kiss to the Earl.

Before Shaxper knew what was happening, Lord Burghley came forward to address him.

"You have a talent for recitation," he intoned, holding out a handful of gold coins. "Kindly accept this gift on behalf of Her Majesty."

Shaxper bowed humbly, trying not to appear too eager as he accepted the coins. He bowed to the Queen and nodded at her followers. He left the dais, hurrying across the field to his employer.

"I trust you delivered the poem exactly as I wrote it," Oxford said, looking down from his impatient charger.

"Word for word, master; although I didn't understand it," Shaxper said.

"That matters not, as long as she embraced my meaning."

"She did have the look of love about her, my lord."

"Then I have been victorious on the battlefield of Venus," Oxford said. "And now, to do battle against Mars." He put on his helmet, lowered the visor and waited for the Queen to signal the start of the joust.

Shaxper hadn't noticed Thomas Kyd sidling up to him.

"Shouldn't you be standing at the other end of the horse?" Kyd sneered.

"What are you doing here?" Shaxper asked.

"I came to wish His Lordship luck."

"He can't hear you, now that he's put on his helmet," Shaxper said. "Besides, he'll win this challenge with or without your good wishes. Now piss off!"

"Mind yourself, copy boy," Kyd sneered. "You may be the one Lord Oxford sends before the Queen today, but it's only a matter of time before he kicks you into the gutter. I'm the one who's going to take your place."

"That's highly unlikely. You're just jealous of me."

"Mark my words; he'll toss you away like he did John Lyly."

"Lyly left of his own accord."

"That's not what I heard. Lyly wanted a measure of security and Lord Burghley made him a better offer. Now he's being paid to keep watch over our beloved master at Blackfriars. Lord Oxford always treads on dangerous ground. You'd better look sharp; a man in his service could end up dead."

"I don't see you running for your life."

"Copying out his plays suits me for now, but I have other aspirations."

"I'm going to remain loyal to the Earl of Oxford," Shaxper said.

"You'll be the only one then. Sir Francis Walsingham is paying the others to report back to him, and Oxford will be summoned to explain some of his writings before the Star Chamber."

"That can't be! The Queen has fully sanctioned his work. You're lying!"

"I've given you fair warning. If you value your life, you'd better pay attention. The rest is up to you."

The smoke from the book burning beyond the fence curled up towards the sky.

Oxford's heart pounded as every muscle in his body tensed for combat. He scrutinized his opponent for signs of vulnerability, a skill he had learned as a child while training for this sport. Lee was a formidable adversary, a man of unflagging strength who had recently taken Oxford's bastard son and perjured mistress to live under his roof, leaving Oxford with wildly conflicted feelings of gratitude and resentment.

Not only did Lady Vavasor prevent Oxford from seeing his son, but the Queen had also forbidden it. Oxford complied, if only to keep his head from rolling on the block. It was a cruel penalty, but he endured it, just as he had endured the other injuries the Queen had inflicted upon him. His paternity of the royal heir was the most dangerous secret of all, and the most cruel penalty was that Wriothesley did not know of it. On pain of death, Oxford was forbidden to speak to the youth or go near him. The agony of unspoken truth clenched Oxford's throat and often seemed as if it would strangle him.

He glanced towards the royal dais, and saw Henry Wriothesley resting his head on the Queen's lap. She curled his hair in her fingers and fed him morsels of food as if he were a lapdog. Wriothesley daintily licked the palms of her hands and the Queen giggled like a young girl. As she kissed Wriothesley full on the mouth, Robert Cecil snickered like a voyeur. Lord Burghley turned and looked the other way.

Oxford couldn't believe how spoiled his secret son, now styled 3rd Earl of Southampton, had become. Wriothesley certainly didn't seem educated in how to govern himself, much less govern a nation. As an infant, he had been placed with the Countess of Southampton, whose husband, imprisoned in the Tower, had never known about the deception. The boy had become a wastrel, which was Burghley's fault as Keeper of the Royal Wards, for having looked the other way once too often. Wriothesley was now slightly younger than Oxford had been, when the Queen had corrupted him in her bed. Burghley had turned a blind eye to that, too.

But what was done could never be undone. Wriothesley seemed ready to advance at Court via the same libidinous route Oxford and many other young men had taken. Unfortunately, he was coming dangerously close to committing incest, and there was no one to warn him. His mother seemed completely unconcerned.

The crier announced the start of the tournament, signaled by a gentle drop of the Queen's handkerchief. Oxford spurred Agincourt down the list and leveled his lance at his opponent. The powerful chargers galloped at breakneck speed. Lee aimed his lance at Oxford's chest, but the Earl deflected the thrust, striking Lee in the shoulder. His opponent reeled backwards but quickly steadied himself. The crowd cheered as the competitors returned to opposite sides of the tilt-yard.

When the signal was given, the foaming steeds snorted and swiftly obeyed their masters' commands. Oxford controlled Agincourt with eloquent grace. He turned and leveled his lance as the sun blazed off his golden armor, threatening to blind his opponent. Despite the glare, Lee charged ahead, aiming a powerful blow to the Earl's chest. Instead of resisting the oncoming force, Oxford allowed his body to roll with it. The crowd held its breath as he reeled, recovered and turned his horse. They applauded, knowing the mighty blow could have killed a less agile warrior.

Like wild bulls testing each other's strength, Lee and Oxford charged again. Oxford struck his adversary's lance and broke it, hitting Lee squarely in the chest. The force of the blow, coupled with the weight of his armor, sent Lee crashing to the ground. Sensing victory, Agincourt circled the fallen warrior, allowing the Earl to pin the defeated nobleman to the earth with his lance. The contest was over.

Lee was carried from the field. The spectators cheered as a brief intermission was called. Broken lances were hauled away as the lists were prepared for the next set of contenders. Refreshments were served to the royals while purveyors of food and drink hawked their wares among the swelling throng of commoners. No one seemed to notice the shifty-eyed opportunists who left the crowd to have a closer look at the gold-leaf bay tree.

Oxford savored the crowd's adoration. He removed his helmet and walked up the steps to the Queen. Drenched with sweat, he knelt before her and smiled into her loving eyes. The courtiers and ladies applauded.

Wriothesley shot to his feet and eagerly congratulated him. Oxford tried not to let his glance linger on his son's features or betray any signs of fatherly affection; he would save his sentiments for his sonnets.

He couldn't help noticing for the first time that the boy's angular face, keen eyes and auburn hair bore an uncanny resemblance to Eliza, right down to the slender fingers that removed his gauntlets. Oxford was astonished that no one else had noticed this; or perhaps they had, but wisely kept their thoughts to themselves.

He quickly looked away. He smiled at his brother-in-law Robert, who returned only a sour expression, and nodded towards Lord Burghley. A herald approached with his prize on a velvet cushion. The Queen took it onto her lap and smiled.

"Arise, my Lord of Oxenforde. I trust you will not give away this diamond writing tablet as callously as you discarded the last one I gave you."

"I have learned my lesson since then, Your Majesty."

"Remember that you learned it in the Tower. Shame on you, for giving my gift to your mistress. It was rude and inconsiderate – beneath the manners of a commoner."

"Indeed, it was. I humbly beg your pardon."

"Ah, but you are accustomed to begging my pardon after doing precisely as you please, isn't that so?"

"I'm a rascal, Eliza. You've often said you like it when I'm on my knees."

The Queen dismissed her entourage with a wave of her hand. Lord Burghley was the last to go. He bristled as he stepped down among the commoners and the curtains were drawn.

"We're alone now," Eliza smiled. "Come sit beside me. Burghley can't see us now."

"Ah, but he'll find a post where he can listen. He always does."

"How are you, Edward? Are you hurt?"

"No, but I dare not say the same for Sir Henry Lee."

"I'm sure he'll heal under Lady Vavasor's tender care."

Oxford paled at the mention of her name. The Queen coyly took his hand.

"You must have spent a fortune on that *tableau.* Is that tree layered in real gold, or is it one of your theatrical effects?"

"Pure gold . . . to match my words."

"Your modesty hasn't been wounded," she laughed. "Whatever am I going to do with a golden tree?"

"Tell the Spanish ambassador our pirates stole it from one of their ships. That would surely enrage King Philip, the little cockerel!"

"Indeed. But I must say, your secretary delivered the poem most eloquently. Burghley informs me he's your most trusted servant."

"My father-in-law must be a mind reader. We've never discussed any of my servants, but it's true, the fellow is an excellent scribe and serves me devotedly. I'd trust him with my life."

"You haven't always chosen your servants wisely," the Queen scolded. "Too many of them have stolen from you in the past. What makes you think this man is different?"

"Shaxper claims to be my kinsman," Oxford said. "It wouldn't serve his purposes to cheat me. We share a connection between my paternal grandmother Elizabeth Trussel and his mother's family, the Robert Ardens of Wilmcote."

"Where did you find him?"

"In faith, he found me, and just when I needed help with our plays. You know how it is. You've promoted many cousins in your time."

"Yes, but I don't always trust them."

On the tilt-yard below, thundering horses tore up the earth. The royal draperies rippled in the breeze.

"Upon my honor," Oxford said, "Shaxper is honest and enterprising. His chief desire is to become an actor."

"And will he command the stage like you do?"

"Honestly, Eliza. I don't know what you're talking about."

"Yes, you do. You can costume yourself as Hamlet's ghost in the public playhouses from now until doomsday, and you can pass yourself off as William Browne from Kent as often as you like, but when you're on the public stage, you're not invisible to me."

"My motives are transparent . . ."

He kissed her as the combatants clashed in the lists.

"Heed my advice," she cautioned lovingly. "Have Shaxper pay your theatrical debts from the stipend so that you don't appear to have any hand in it. He must be the master of the plays in the eyes of the public, not you – for obvious reasons. And you mustn't squander your personal income on the production of plays any further."

"That sounds like one of Burghley's requests."

"It is."

"Well, he should stay the hell out of it! My masques are meant to please you, not him."

"You mustn't offer any plays or masques to me in your own name, ever again. Consider your position and cut your losses. Lord Burghley is worried about the three thousand pounds you recently lost on Captain Frobisher's failed sea expedition."

"It was a disaster. Frobisher lied to me about the investment, the Venetian moneylenders bled me like leeches, and the entire crew perished in the shipwreck."

"It was a tragic turn of events--"

"Well, you can tell Burghley not to worry," Oxford sneered. "His inconstant daughter will be well taken care of, whether you allow me to divorce her or not."

"Listen to me, Edward. I don't want you to be troubled by your losses."

"How can you say that, Eliza, when you deny me the right to acknowledge my sons?"

"I've denied you nothing," the Queen said, angrily. "I've merely secured England's interests."

"If I can't speak to Wriothesley, at least allow me to see young Edward."

"Lady Vavasor's bastard? I think not."

"You cannot deny me that right!"

"I can deny you anything I please!"

"Can you?" he said, pulling her to him. "You've forgotten how to play this game, Eliza. You're the one who taught me the rules of seduction when I was a terrified orphan."

"Don't be a fool. All I have to do is summon my guards —"

"But you won't, because you enjoy being taken . . . or at least the illusion of it."

"What do you want?"

"An order allowing me to see my son."

"Is that all?"

"Yes, and your blessing sealed with a kiss."

"I shan't give it to you."

"Then I'll play the role of Tarquin, and take it."

He pressed his lips against hers and she did not resist him. A riotous roar erupted from the tilt-yard. Lord Oxford parted the curtain, expecting to see an injured jouster. The Queen clung to his arm, astonished by the rampage below.

Hundreds of people surged towards the golden tree, tearing at its gilded leaves, toppling its naked frame to the ground. The innocent were crushed underfoot. Mothers screamed and shielded their children. At the sound of firing pistols, the mob quickly scattered, leaving the injured moaning and writhing on the ground.

Beyond the fence, the book burning had died down.

CHAPTER THIRTEEN

The Scene: Oxford's Rooms at the Savoy

May 3, 1588

"You blocks, you stones, you worse than senseless things."

– Julius Caesar

The Earl of Oxford tossed the battered manuscript of *Edmund Ironside* across the table. Before Shaxper could get his hands on it, Kyd lurched forward and grabbed it. He thumbed through the dog-eared, scrawled-over pages and shook his head.

"What has he done to your play, my lord?"

"It's quite simple," Oxford shrugged. "The censor won't allow us to show it."

"After all our hard work? That can't be true, my lord."

"Let me have a look," Shaxper said. He nervously perused the revisions.

"It's true, Will," the Earl sighed. "We might as well chuck it into the flames."

"But surely it deserves a reprieve, my lord. It's worthy of one."

"Not this time. The Queen says it's too controversial. She won't allow us to portray holy men as frauds and dissemblers, and she's furious about the part where the Saxons and the Vikings divide England and rule it together – as if suggesting that she should share the monarchy! And she strongly objected to Canute's men hiding down the privy hole to assassinate King Edmund when he sat down to take a crap."

"A bloody end," Kyd smirked.

"And a bloody end to this wretched script!" Oxford said. He tore several pages from the binding and Shaxper had to restrain him from throwing them into the fire.

"But it's historically accurate, my lord," Shaxper pleaded, pointing to the pages of annotations he had made. "I took careful notes, just as you instructed. I gave you all the facts exactly as they happened."

"What difference does that make?" Oxford said, angrily. "The play has been deemed too incendiary; and to see whether it's true, we must find out how well it burns . . ."

"Please, stop! We can revise it."

"Why go to all that trouble? Even with the assassination scene taken out, the censor still won't pass it and that's his final word. I can't do anything more."

"But what about history? What about the truth?"

"To hell with the truth," Kyd laughed. "Let's have a drink and the truth be damned."

Shaxper abstained when the bottle was passed.

"Will there be no new plays this season, my lord?" he asked.

"Damn it! I forgot to give you the good news. *Sir Thomas More* has been approved for the public playhouses – with a few alterations, of course."

"The censor certainly took his time about it," Kyd growled. "Well, when would you like me to start on the fair copy, my lord?"

"Actually, this time I'm going to use Will's tactful diplomacy and have him take dictation on the new scenes. You can write out the rolls for the actors."

"Thanks for bestowing such confidence in me, my lord," Shaxper said crisply, as Kyd looked crestfallen. "I'll start first thing in the morning and consult with you promptly if I find anything questionable."

"Good. I know I can depend on your excellent judgment."

"Is *this* play going to be historically accurate?" Kyd snickered. "How can there be history plays without any history in them?"

"Her Majesty was very direct on that point," Oxford said. "She desires entertainment, not academe. She says we can take the history of England and serve it up with bread and circuses for all she cares, as long as the plays inspire her subjects with enough pride to defend their homeland at whatever cost. Historical accuracy is irrelevant, since the base-minded commoners won't know the difference. So that's our job, gentlemen, serving bread and circuses in the cockpit."

"But what about *Edmund Ironside?*"

"Bury it with the rest of the dung."

"But my lord —"

"A pox on that play! There's no cure for it! Do what you will! I wash my hands of it!"

Kyd and Shaxper rose as Oxford left the room.

"It's his own fault we can't put on this bloody play," Kyd grumbled, as he rolled up the disgraced manuscript and thumped it against the table. "He should have known what he was doing when he wrote it, and bent over backwards to please the censor. We worked for over a month to copy it out, and what did we get? Stabbed in the arse like old King Edmund!"

"At least we got paid," Shaxper said.

"Ah, yes; and some of us got paid twice."

"What do you mean?"

"I'm talking about those extra little gratuities you've picked up along the way. I've got a good mind to tell His Lordship that you're using his acting lessons to impress the theater owners and skim off some of the profits for yourself."

"You're crazy!"

"Oh, am I? I've watched you fawn over Burbage and Alleyn. Exactly how many masters do you intend to serve?"

"That's none of your business. Why don't you go ahead and tell Lord Oxford. He won't begrudge me a penny, and he'd be glad to know I was personally attending to his clients. He's not in this for the money like the rest of us, so don't waste your time trying to knock me off my pedestal. You won't be able to do it."

"Don't be so sure," Kyd laughed, as he rose from the table. "I'll bide my time. But be careful, or you might find yourself crushed under the Wheel of Fortune when it starts to turn my way."

He quickly finished his drink and wiped his mouth with his sleeve. Catching Shaxper's eye on his way out, he grinned malevolently and tossed the manuscript into the fire.

As soon as Kyd was gone, Shaxper frantically rushed to the hearth and gingerly snatched *Edmund Ironside* from the flames. He had a feeling it might be worth something someday, especially if he took the trouble to make a fair copy of it and pass it off as his own. That seemed only right, since Lord Oxford had disowned the play, and he wasn't in it for the money anyway.

As it turned out, the pages were barely singed.

CHAPTER FOURTEEN

The Scene: Oxford's Home at Fisher's Folly

May 12, 1588

You had a father, let your son say so."

— Sonnet 13

L ord Oxford poured himself another drink and perused the latest letter from his father-in-law. He read it over several times, making sure he understood its perplexing message – the bizarre terms of a proposed match between his wife's firstborn daughter Elizabeth de Vere and Henry Wriothesley, Earl of Southampton.

With sheer incredulity, he shook the letter as if he fancied that the words might somehow rearrange themselves in a more logical order, or perhaps let the secrets locked within them fall out and scatter across the floor, like links in a broken chain.

He wondered why Burghley would proffer the match now, and what events were happening behind the scenes to encompass it. Just last week, the Queen had summoned Oxford to her side. They were like old friends again, and she complained about her increasing worries and ill health. Although it was against the law to discuss a monarch's death, she confessed her vulnerability to it. He was taken aback when she quickly agreed to name their secret son as her successor to protect the Tudor regime, and yet she made no mention of the match that Burghley was proposing between Henry and Elizabeth, the daughter Oxford had been compelled to accept as his own. In supporting the match, Burghley would put an end to fifteen years of silence about Oxford's secret marriage to the Queen, which had been performed to legitimize the child they hoped would one day rule England.

He wondered whether Burghley would also be ready to admit his role in covering up his daughter Anne's betrayal. After 13 years, Oxford still did not know the name of the scoundrel who had impregnated her while he was in Italy. It had taken him five years to accept Anne and her daughter into his life. If the proposed match were to take place, the true parents of both Elizabeth and Henry must be made known, since revealing only Henry's story would render it a seemingly incestuous union.

The thought of "incest" made him cringe. Poor Anne, locked away for her madness, with no chance of a cure. No one believed her wild accusations against her father. Lord Burghley was, after all, to most people, an honorable man. Everyone at court, including the Queen, considered it an act of kindness that Burghley had assumed all of the expenses and complete charge of Anne's care, and they were saddened that her madness made her oblivious to his efforts. The louder Anne raved against her father about incest, the heavier were the chains he forged for her door.

Oxford still hoped to push past the clouds of melancholia that enshrouded her mind and learn the truth from her someday. In the meantime, he had to protect his other living daughters, Bridget and Susan, and the son Edward he had conceived with Lady Vavasor. All of his children shared his distinguished lineage, the very prize Burghley had coveted when he grafted his stalk to Oxford's family tree. Not only would the blend of the Plantagenet, Lancaster and York lineages strengthen Henry's Tudor claim to the throne, but Burghley's own granddaughter would replace her tormented mother as his best hope for a regal future for his descendants.

Then, with that thought, Oxford suddenly understood Burghley's motive: with his granddaughter marrying the future King of England, he would be elevated to the highest rank a commoner could reach. Oxford imagined the old man in a state of euphoria, paying Shaxper handsomely for a Shake-speare play to commemorate the event!

Distracted by a noise outside, he turned towards the window and saw Shaxper coming up the walk. It wasn't wise to leave Burghley's letter where his scribe could see it, so he placed it in a book of poetry and waited for his secretary's knock on the door.

"You sent for me, my lord?" Shaxper asked.

"Yes, Will. I'd like you to take a look at the newly revised third act for *Sir Thomas More.* Tell me what you think of it."

"As you wish, my lord. I'll take it with me and bring it back tomorrow."

"No, no, that won't do. Stay here and read it. I want to know what you think of it as soon as possible."

"Very well," Shaxper replied. He sat by the opposite window and began reading. After a few minutes he shifted uneasily, realizing that Oxford's eyes had never left him.

"Well?" the Earl asked. "What's the verdict?

"The censor has slashed this one to pieces, too," Shaxper sighed. "I shall have to work harder to copy it out."

"That's unfortunate. Like you, the censor also happens to be my kinsman. I can't even acknowledge that I'm the playwright. Not that it matters, really . . ."

"Begging your pardon, my lord, but are you saying that you are related to Sir Edmund Tilney, the hardboiled censor we've been trying so hard to please? Why didn't you say so? Perhaps he could have helped us."

"He might have made things worse."

"I beg to differ, my lord; not with me acting as your front man."

"Perhaps, but I can't say so for certain," Oxford sighed. "Surely you've observed that England's nobility is one big consortium of cousins who often despise each other in their lust for power. Everyone is related to everyone else by marriage, or some less holy assignation. Tilney happens to be my cousin on the Howard side, and they have despicable tendencies like back-stabbing and poisoning their friends and neighbors. English history is full of such cousins."

"I'm not that sort of cousin, my lord."

"You're proven your good intentions, Will. But I must say, I have more cousins than there are stars in the sky, and sometimes they fall to earth, just to cozen me. I suppose it can't be helped. There isn't a man alive who doesn't feel the intoxicating pulse of advancement coursing through his veins. You've said so yourself."

"B-but I would never do anything to harm you, my lord," Shaxper protested.

"Most cousins would jump at the chance to sponge off their vacuous, blue-blooded relatives, if the opportunity fell into their hands," Oxford laughed. "Well, enough of that. What did you think of the third act?"

Shaxper took a deep breath to clear his head.

"I see that you've rewritten More's characterization," he said. "It's a complete departure from the rest of the play. You've made him bold and conspicuous, but he's not like that in the earlier scenes."

"That's true. He lacked a certain amount of fire, so I lent him mine."

"But don't you think it's dangerous to conjure up the ghost of Sir Thomas More on the public stage, when he openly defied King Henry VIII for marrying Anne Boleyn? For God's sake, she was the Queen's own mother! And More was beheaded for his insolence."

"Of course it's dangerous," Oxford snapped. "But ghosts sell tickets and audiences love them."

"The Queen won't like it," Shaxper said. "She'll make a ghost out of you - out of both of us - if you infuriate her with this play, especially now that you've cast Sir Thomas More so prominently in your image. You might as well sign your name to it, because everyone will know you wrote this play."

"It's your job to protect me. If you don't think I'm paying you enough --"

"I didn't say that, my lord. I did my best with the notations you gave me."

"And you did your job well. You're not to blame for my words. I'm the playwright and my characters speak through me."

"Not if the Queen demands your head," Shaxper muttered.

"God's blood, man!" Oxford roared. "The Queen loves me more than she's willing to admit, so don't lose your nerve. She's protected us thus far, and there's no reason to believe she'll stop now. I'll see to that."

"If you say so, my lord."

"Now tell me, what do you think about the play-within-the play?"

"Inserting those lines from *The Marriage of Wit and Wisdom* is a good choice. But I wonder, is it right for Sir Thomas More to choose a play for his banquet?"

"Why not? I've done so. Even in my father's day, we commanded after-dinner entertainment from the resident players when we dined at the castle. I have Hamlet choosing *The Murder of Gonzago* and Theseus requesting those rude mechanicals to perform *The Most Lamentable Comedy and Most Cruel Death of Pyramus and Thisby.* Noblemen and kings always have entertainers at hand."

"Ordinary people have no such luxury. You were very fortunate."

"Indeed I was, for twelve years, with the help of an old Fool named Pinch," Oxford sighed. "All my life, I lived with the wealth and privilege of the court's inner circle, party to all manner of political machinations and international intrigue. I never knew that my life would take such sharp and precarious turns. I'm like a stone in a slingshot, flying far afield, only to hit on unfamiliar ground. Once I was a poet but now I'm a popular playwright, hiding behind a commoner."

"It must be so, my lord, or else you could not write."

"But sometimes I fear that my words betray me. You said so yourself moments ago. I write kings and queens extraordinarily well because I'm familiar with their ways, but not so with commoners. They're all clowns and fools in my plays because I know so little about them. Country people seem so simple and unschooled when they talk about things they don't understand. I've heard them in the pubs, with their odd accents and ridiculous word choices. Perhaps you could write their roles for me, to make the characters more believable."

"Oh, no, my lord. I could never do that. I couldn't put my words into someone else's mouth."

"Then do you think the groundlings will be offended by the shaggy-haired bumpkin in the play, the one being sent to jail?"

"Not if you give the role to a clever comedian. The lout isn't avoiding his taxes – he's simply avoiding the barber. I particularly liked the part where More and his servant trade clothes to fool the scholar Erasmus. I understand there's an actual historical reference to it."

"Truth be told, I took a few liberties with it," Oxford confessed. "The apocryphal story is that the learned Erasmus simply didn't recognize the noble More when he passed him on the street. That's not very exciting, so I embellished it. Mistaken identity is an old and trusted plot device in comedy."

"I would hardly call this play a comedy, my lord."

"It's not, but mistaken identity is very effective in tragedy, too. In *Julius Caesar,* when Cinna the poet is killed instead of Cinna the assassin, the audience is horrified. But More's precarious situation itself is the tragedy here. The scene you're talking about lets the audience know he's a flesh and blood man, and not a dry religious icon."

"Either way," Shaxper insisted, "I find it hard to believe that a servant could pose as his master without someone seeing through the disguise. More and his servant are from two different worlds; their manners are different, their speech is different. Everyone would know."

"Would you care to wager on that?"

"Wager? Oh, I think not, my lord."

"Why not? Don't you have the courage of your convictions?"

"I stand by my words, my lord, but not at the expense of my son."

"You have a son? Where is he? Why have you never spoken of him?"

"It's a sad story, my lord," Shaxper sighed. "I have a wife and three children back in Stratford, and I came to London to earn enough money to support them. Hamnet was always sickly, but his sister Judith is strong and robust. They are twins, you see, and my salary pays for Hamnet's medicine."

"In that case, perhaps you should have more money."

"I am grateful, my lord, but please don't feel obligated."

"It's a moral obligation," Oxford said, handing Shaxper a small purse. "My lady-wife the Countess has never recovered from the death of our infant boy, so you must do all you can to help your son. If it were not for our living children . . ."

Oxford thought of Anne's grief, and the sons he could not acknowledge.

"Thank you, my lord," Shaxper said. "I am your grateful and devoted servant."

"That will be all for today," Oxford said, turning towards the window. "Go and make the final changes for Tilney's perusal one more time."

Shaxper gently closed the door behind him. He tucked the purse inside his doublet and felt it rest snugly against his beating heart.

Lord Oxford bolted the door and returned to his desk. He dipped his pen in the inkwell and began a letter to the Queen.

Dear my love,

If only you had the desire to be honest with yourself! We both know that your life is not your own and that as Queen of England your private life is lived upon a very public stage. I know you have been ill of late, and you have confided in me that you fear Death is approaching. If that is the case, you should prepare for it by proclaiming your successor. Let all of the beauty that resides within you live on forever, regardless of the swirling tides of men's affairs. Then you will live on after death for all eternity, and everything that you have striven for in England's name will prosper. What manner of man or woman would let their house fall into disrepair, when any reasonably responsible person would protect it against the storms of winter and ravages of nature; yea, even against Death's eternal chill? No one would be so unwise, my love, except a wasteful and reckless soul. Dear Eliza, you had a father — let your son say so.

Yours E.ver,
Edward

He wept for the son he could not name, who did not know his true identity. Despondency devoured his heart, and he clenched his fists to his forehead. Fourteen years had passed since he had held his newborn son, and then the infant was whisked away and delivered into unknown hands. The Queen had refused to reveal his whereabouts, but with a few bribes and well-asked questions, he had been able to learn the truth.

Oxford had watched the boy from afar, displeased with his inferior education but unable to correct it. He had stood so close to Henry at the tournament - unable to speak to the sparkling echo, the fair youth, the hidden changeling for whom he so desperately yearned. He cried out until he was exhausted with grief.

He pushed his papers aside and wondered if a sonnet would melt the Queen's heart.

O, that you were yourself! but, love, you are
No longer yours than you yourself here live:
Against this coming end you should prepare,
And your sweet semblance to some other give.
So should that beauty which you hold in lease
Find no determination: then you were
Yourself again after yourself's decease,
When your sweet issue your sweet form should bear.
Who lets so fair a house fall to decay,
Which husbandry in honour might uphold
Against the stormy gusts of winter's day
And barren rage of death's eternal cold?
O, none but unthrifts! Dear my love, you know
You had a father: let your son say so.

He lit a few torches to prevent the twilight from descending upon him. He rubbed his aching hand and continued to write, protecting himself from the Queen's broken promises. She may have said that she was ready to name Henry as her successor, but she was equally capable of changing her mind.

Oxford gathered up his finished papers. Setting them aside, he took out a blank sheet and with clear and deliberate intent, he wrote a different letter to the Queen, suddenly realizing that nothing but an enforceable threat could hope to insure his safety.

Most Honored and Dread Majesty,

Blame me not, for it is with the boundless measure of my ardor that I swear to you this day, that if any infliction, mischief, danger or death befall me, the news of our sanctified secret marriage and our changeling child will be revealed to the world; that all may know him for your successor in this Majesty and know that you have forsworn our sacred and legal union without regard for the feelings of our son. Thus I do secure myself in the comfort and safety, to which, in the ameliorate times of our contentment you most lovingly and earnestly succored for me.

E.ver yours,

Edward, Earl of Oxenforde

He wrote late into the night, drafting his will and making a copy. He sealed the original inside his letter to the Queen, and placed the second one in the ebony box that bore his heraldic seal. He decided to make additional copies at a later date, to place in strategic locations, instructing certain honorable friends to reveal his will to the world in the event of his sudden and mysterious death.

He sealed the papers with his signet. In the morning, Shaxper would deliver them.

Fatigued and downcast, he noticed a royal dispatch discretely placed on the corner of his desk. He broke open the seal and held it up to the light. In it, his monarch commanded him to sail his ship, the *Edward Bonaventure,* to join Leicester and the other nobles in the battle against the Armada. Preparations had already been made.

The war with Spain had begun.

CHAPTER FIFTEEN

The Scene: Royal Palace
July 1588

"In thy orisons
Be all my sins remembered . . ."

– Hamlet

In looking through her private papers, the Queen came across Lord Oxford's angry letter. She read it again, and with great sadness, folded it and placed it deep inside her writing table. She expected Lord Burghley at any moment, and was sure the familiar sight of his son-in-law's handwriting would only have added injury to his heavy loss.

Dr. Lopez had assured them that Anne's death had been unavoidable. Her melancholia had evolved into full blown madness since Susan's birth one year earlier. That, coupled with the deaths of other children and her husband's hasty departure for the war unraveled the remains of her sanity. She slipped away from her caretakers in an unguarded moment, wandered over to the river and was swept downstream like a crumpled autumn leaf. Anne, Countess of Oxford, was buried in the Cecil family tomb at

Westminster Abbey, her drowning ruled an accident resulting from her pathetically troubled mind.

Feeling anxious, the Queen reached for her Bible. The gilded pages fell open to the prophet Nathan's parable, in which he chided King David about the slaughter of a poor man's only lamb. When the King ordered the thief punished, Nathan pointed an accusing finger at him and said that David was the guilty one, who had taken a man's wife and sent him to die in the war.

The Queen was sure the prophet's rebuke was also addressed to her. For years, she had come between Oxford and his wife, and he was the only man the poor girl had ever loved. Their star-crossed marriage was an epic tragedy that would make the boards in the playhouses weep, if it ever played upon the stage.

As a royal child, having suffered the degradation of being set aside as a bastard, she had imagined her father King Henry VIII as resembling King David - a red haired, warrior-monarch guilty of arrogance, gluttony and abuse of power. She was sure she had inherited his sinful propensities, and swore once more to atone for them. She carefully folded Oxford's Last Will and Testament and placed it between the pages of Nathan's parable, hoping to mute the flagrant reproaches of both poet and prophet.

She thought of Lord Burghley, so distraught at Anne's funeral, he could barely stand. He leaned on his staff of office, but lost his balance several times and his sons Robert and Thomas had to bear him up. The old man wept as if his heart would break when his daughter was laid to rest in the family tomb. Just steps away, seventeen years earlier, he had rejoiced at her wedding. The Earl of Oxford had been the love of her life, but her affection seemed unrequited. No one knew whether word of Anne's death had reached him at sea.

A herald announced Lord Burghley's arrival. The doors opened and the old man entered, relying on his staff to draw him forward. Robert

Cecil followed, keeping an awkward pace with his progenitor's hesitant footsteps. At twenty-five, Cecil was prepared to take his father's place as the Queen's advisor, but Her Majesty saw him as a shadow of his father's greatness. She distrusted him and frequently rebuffed him, nicknaming him Dwarf when he pompously asked for favors and advancement.

As a disciple of Sir Francis Walsingham, the nation's spy master, Cecil had learned how to apply interrogation and torture with consummate skill. To the Queen, who had known him since birth, his crooked body matched his devious intentions; and yet his dedication served the government well.

"Majesty, you have summoned me and I await your pleasure," Burghley wheezed, as he bowed before her.

"Don't stand idly by, fetch your father a chair," the Queen snapped. "He can speak to me while seated, without disrespect. You, Dwarf, are another matter. Stand aside. Leave us a while."

Robert bowed, brought a chair and scurried away while Burghley sat below the throne. He seemed weak with sorrow. Her Majesty's heart filled with compassion.

"How are you these days, good old man?"

"Sad to say, Majesty, my gout has worsened in the past few weeks. It's particularly bad on rainy mornings like this one."

"I know, the pain is as sharp as knives. My father suffered from it."

"He did indeed. You're fortunate to have been deprived of that particular aspect of his legacy."

"Has my physician called on you yet?"

"Yes, Dr. Lopez has altered my diet and offers me much encouragement."

"I'm glad to hear it. Make sure you heed his advice and hasten your recovery."

"I will, Majesty," Burghley said, bowing his head. "I humbly thank you for your kind attention to my welfare."

"You have always given kind attention to mine," she said, softly.

"I've tried my best."

"And you have succeeded brilliantly. Well, what news from the war?"

Robert stepped up and handed his father some papers. The Queen watched as Burghley clumsily unfolded them.

"According to these dispatches from the Earl of Leicester," he said, "the battle seems to be in the hands of God. At times a fierce wind blows the Spanish off course and the sea engulfs them; at others, their guns rain fire and brimstone on us and we suffer heavy losses. But Leicester assures me the Armada suffers far more grievously, and Howard seconds that opinion."

"Then the whole world knows that God is on our side."

"Indeed. The Almighty has turned his back on the evil doers."

"Amen!" the Queen said, her eyes cast up to heaven, her palms together in prayer. Her mood quickly changed. "God's blood, what is that dreadful noise in the hallway? Where are my guards? Dwarf, go and see the cause."

Before Cecil reached the door, a servant flung it open. He knelt breathlessly before the Queen.

"The Earl of Oxford is on his way here, Majesty, and he's in a terrible rage. The guards are trying to stop him."

The Queen glanced at Burghley. The old man withered at Oxford's name.

"Fear not, I'll put that bold Turk in his place," she said. "You, Cecil and you, herald – escort my Lord Burghley outside through the ante-chamber passage. He's too sick with grief to suffer this venomous bile."

"Permit me to stay, Majesty," Burghley said. "My son-in-law's out-bursts are nothing new. I've survived quite a few of them in my day. They always pass away like clouds."

"Nonsense! You're entitled to be spared at least one undignified onslaught. It's too soon after the tragedy and we must protect your bro-ken heart."

Cecil and the herald escorted Burghley away.

Seconds later, Lord Oxford pushed past the guards and burst into the room, his fine clothes drenched with rain. The Queen countered his rage by calmly ordering her guards to leave them. She would toy with the braggart, and show him no mercy.

"Your long arm has pulled me back from the war, Majesty," he bellowed, "but I have no idea why you've summoned me home like an errant child!"

"Good morning, my Lord of Oxenforde," she said pleasantly, just to irritate him. "It's not my fault you ventured out in the rain without your cloak."

"The almanac called for sunshine today."

"Sunshine, in England? Is that a joke? Your smile used to warm my heart. Come, kiss me, and let the brilliant rays of my countenance dry your storm-beaten face."

Oxford wiped off the rain and glared at her.

"Everyone on the battlefield is laughing at me. They say you sent for me to warm your bed!"

"I summoned you home on personal business. Haven't you heard the news?"

"What news? This 'personal business', is that what you call it nowadays? You've made me the laughingstock of my peers, but I won't tolerate it anymore. You've summoned me home and I've obeyed. I'm at your service, but this isn't the same service I used to perform for you in the old days, when you ordered me into your bed."

"Edward," the Queen said. "Didn't Leicester tell you why I've called you home?"

"No. Your pig-headed cousin has always taken a peculiar thrill in baiting me. Tell me then, why did you send for me?"

"To allow you time to mourn."

"Mourn for what, for the loss of your body? That works no hardship on me."

"Don't be cruel, Edward. I don't want to hurt you. I merely want to comfort you on your recent loss."

"What loss? Have my plays been destroyed in my absence? Where the devil is William Shaxper? He'll answer for it."

As the Queen drew her breath to speak, Robert Cecil stormed in and leapt at Oxford, throwing him to the floor.

"Wretched dog! Have you no shame, showing your face in England after causing my sister's death!"

"Majesty, this crooked little flyspeck is mad!" Oxford shouted. "I've done nothing to his sister. Anne and I have made amends, she's recovering from her illness."

"Liar!" Cecil roared. "My sister is dead, drowned, drowned – "

"Take . . . your . . . hands . . . off . . . my . . . throat!"

"Not until I send you to join her in the grave!"

"Cecil, stop!" the Queen shouted. "Release him, I command you, let him up!"

Cecil obeyed. The guards encircled the Queen for her protection as the two men stood facing each other.

"I treated you like a brother," Oxford said.

"But you treated my sister like a whore," Cecil cried, "and she was pure and innocent."

"I loved Anne. A battalion of brothers couldn't have loved her as much as I did."

"That's what you say now, but it's too late . . . too late."

"She deceived me. She took a lover while I was in Italy and gave birth to his child."

"For five years, you cut her out of your life!" Cecil hissed. "You were going to divorce her and marry Lady Vavasor, the Catholic whore who spawned the bastard that carries your name. You disgraced our entire family, and everybody knows it."

"That's not true!" Oxford said. "I gave Anne my estate at Wivenhoe. We reconciled and raised a family. I accepted her daughter. No girl should be bereft of a family name, unable to marry or maintain dignity in this world."

"And what will you do now?" Cecil bellowed. "Cry out to Anne's ghost in the night? Write penitential verses and hang them in the trees? It's too late. You killed a sweet and innocent girl and I warn you, you won't escape my revenge!"

"Silence!" the Queen shouted. She rose, trembling with fear and rage, remembering Oxford's letter. "I'll hold you personally responsible if any harm befalls Lord Oxford, Dwarf, regardless of what you consider to be a justifiable provocation for your act. You'll pay with your life if you harm him! Guards, take this wretched cripple to the Tower. Show him what happens when weak-minded inferiors threaten the great earls of our realm with violence."

Cecil was removed from her presence and the doors closed behind him.

Oxford sat on the steps of the dais and wept. The Queen rested her hand on his shoulder.

ACT III
CHAPTER SIXTEEN

The Scene: London
June 5, 1593

"Shall I not lie in publishing a truth?"
– Troilus and Cressida

A dense fog had enshrouded London since early morning, disguising familiar landmarks and casting a pall over the city. Church bells tolled for the dead, and a few brave souls ventured into the streets, risking their lives to earn some money from those who had escaped the contagion.

Summer had gone dark along with the playhouses. The wooden cockpits on the Thames stood empty, disease having closed them down where Puritan disapproval had failed. Because of the plague, there was no way of knowing when, or if, the theaters would reopen; but that was the least of London's worries. The stench-filled city was stifled by the large number of plague-ravaged corpses waiting to be burned. Not even a proper burial could insure that graves wouldn't be robbed by thieves unwittingly spreading infection by selling items stripped from pocky corpses.

Those who could afford to escape the city traveled to their country homes where the air was free of contagion. Clad in black, William Shaxper anxiously waited to join the Earl of Oxford at Hedingham Castle. His horse was groomed and waiting in the stables to begin the long journey, as soon as he finished his business with Richard Field.

They were meeting to discuss the publication of *Venus and Adonis,* the erotic poem Shaxper had submitted to the Stationers' Register a month earlier. At first, he wasn't sure he could convince his old friend that he'd written it. But Field was so stunned that the censor had approved it, he had little need to ponder its authorship. *Venus and Adonis* told the story of an older woman's seduction of a young boy. It steamed with sexual innuendos even the reprobate Ovid had not envisioned when he wrote his version of the ancient tale.

"Guaranteed to be a bestseller, Dickie," Shaxper winked. "Even I was surprised when the Queen ordered the Archbishop to approve it, but I suppose that shows how much I underestimate my talent. Either way, if you agree to publish *Venus and Adonis,* it will be the first work of its kind bearing my name - by me, William Shake-speare."

"But that's not your name," Richard said. "Look, it's hyphenated in the manuscript. What's that supposed to be, some kind of affectation?"

"I think the hyphen adds a touch of class, don't you? Like my earring."

"Foppish nonsense!" Richard sneered.

"It lends an air of mystery then."

"It certainly does. It suggests a pseudonym, as if the author has something to hide. You don't have anything to hide, do you, Willy?"

"Of course not. You said yourself the poem is piquant and saucy."

"But you showed no signs of literary talent when you were a boy. I must say, working with the Earl of Oxford certainly has changed you."

"Indeed it has," Shaxper said, impatiently. "Well, if you do publish the poem, you can drop the hyphen from my name. I don't care. So, do you want this valuable property or not?"

Field eyed the manuscript on the table and shook his head. "I don't think it's wise to print it with the romantic dedication you've given it."

"What's wrong with it?"

"You shouldn't flaunt your private passions in public. These effusive attentions will embarrass the Earl of Southampton."

"That's absurd!"

"You're making this very awkward for me, Willy, but I've got to ask. I know how ambitious you are, and I've heard rumors about lewd and perverted acts taking place in his household. You haven't gotten yourself involved in anything like that, have you?"

"Of course not!" Shaxper laughed. "The truth is, I've been earning some extra money doubling as his secretary too, but there's nothing indecent going on, believe me. It's just that Henry Wriothesley, Earl of Southampton, has an insatiable appetite for erotica, that's all, and I thought there'd be a big gratuity in it for me if I wrote him some, accompanied by a fawning dedication. So, here it is – take it or leave it."

"And he *paid* you for this?"

"Yes, quite well in fact."

Field wondered if pandering to the scandalous impulses of noblemen had reduced his old friend to trafficking in pornography.

For his part, Shaxper had no plans to tell his friend that Lord Oxford had written the poem and the dedication in honor of Southampton's twentieth birthday. He said nothing about Oxford's peculiar fondness for the young earl, or that he, Shaxper, would be allowed to keep the profits from *Venus and Adonis* to tide him over while the playhouses remained closed. It wasn't his fault that men of rank were forbidden to profit through commercial enterprise. After all, proceeds from the sale of the poem had to go somewhere; and if not into Oxford's coffers, what better cause than Shaxper's own enrichment?

"Frankly, I find the poem offensive," Field whispered. "Venus straddles Adonis and rides him like a succubus while he's flat on his back. That's sinful, an older woman forcing a young boy like that. No woman would behave that way."

"Wake up, Dickie! That's how my wife took me," Shaxper snorted. "Not all of us were lucky enough to marry widows who inherited their husband's print shops. Listen, our friendship goes all the way back to Stratford, and that's why I'm offering you the chance of a lifetime. Trust me, *Venus and Adonis* is going to be a huge success. I'd like to share that success with you, but if you turn me down, I won't hesitate to find another publisher."

Field studied his friend for a moment.

"I'll publish it," he said, shaking Shaxper's hand. "If the Queen and the Archbishop think it's fit to print, who am I to argue with them?"

"You won't regret it," Shaxper grinned. "And now I'm off to Hedingham Castle at the request of His Lordship. He and his new wife have taken their children there to escape the plague, and they've offered me lodging so we can continue our work. I pray that the plague passes over your house, Dickie."

"I'll pray for you as well. And we must all pray for poor Christopher Marlowe, God rest his soul, being stabbed to death over a tavern bill."

"Well, those who live by the sword, die by the sword," Shaxper shrugged.

"Surely you must have more sympathy than that," Field said. "Three young writers, all working with Lord Oxford, dead under mysterious circumstances within one year: Robert Greene, Thomas Watson and now, Marlowe. And from what I hear, Thomas Kyd was so gruesomely tortured, he could pass away at any time. He blames himself for Marlowe's murder, but a man will confess anything when he's broken on the rack."

Shaxper didn't tell his friend that he had seen the illegal pamphlets and bogus coins Marlowe had produced. Kyd's only mistake had been living under the same roof with him. Lord Oxford hadn't known about his clandestine activities, but his excitement over Marlowe's "mighty line" eclipsed any dangers that might have arisen from his shadowy practices.

So much for the nobleman's gullibility!

Shaxper tried to dispel the look of horror on Richard's face. "Oxford says it's the government's last-ditch attempt at literary censorship; and by 'last ditch' he means the grave. But I've been granted approval to publish *Venus and Adonis,* so not every writer in England is under suspicion."

"Be careful, Willy. Publication can be a double-edged sword."

"I look over my shoulder all the time, Dickie, believe me."

And that was an understatement.

"What a world," Field sighed. "If the plague doesn't kill you today, there's a rogue waiting around the corner to knife you tomorrow."

"And with that cold comfort, I shall take my leave," Shaxper said. He shook hands with his friend and exited the shop, relieved to be on his way. The tiny bell atop the door jingled after him.

A glow of street lanterns reflected against the fog. The air was dull and heavy. Shaxper could hardly wait to mount his horse and get out of London. He felt sick to his stomach as he walked past the homes of half-dead people writhing in agony as their loved ones wept and waited for Death to come, not as an avenging angel but as a peacemaker. He turned up his collar to protect his face from the hot breath of disease and rounded the corner towards the stables.

Suddenly he realized he was being followed.

Impersonating a man who thrived on living dangerously had made Shaxper sharply aware of his surroundings. He noticed the cadence of footsteps behind him, walking when he walked, stopping when he stopped. Taking a few more steps, he turned abruptly and caught the blur of someone ducking behind a fishmonger's stall to avoid being seen.

For an instant, he thought about confronting the stalker, but Dickie's farewell words echoed in his mind.

He began walking again, and the strident rhythm of boots reverberated behind him. He broke into a run and turned the corner at the end of the street, pressing flat against the doorway of a shop. He heard the stalker running towards him. He closed his eyes, held his breath and kept as still as he could, reliving the terror of his robbery outside Stratford.

His pursuer stopped at the corner. The rogue wheezed like a furnace, coughing and cursing the rancid air. He spat in the street and ran on. The sound of his steps disappeared in the distance.

Shaxper didn't move. He trembled at the thought of Marlowe's murder, and wondered if he had just escaped a similar fate. When he opened his eyes, the fog had lifted. He crossed the street, paid the hostler and mounted his horse, escaping the oppressiveness of London.

Robert Poley watched him as he rode out of town.

CHAPTER SEVENTEEN

The Scene: Hedingham Castle
June 7, 1593

"Hide fox and all after!"

– Hamlet

Countess Elizabeth, Lord Oxford's new wife, didn't know it, but the impostor had continued to receive his high salary despite his master's heavy losses on seafaring ventures. All things considered, Oxford's commitment to the theaters might have been a bit grandiose, but at least he had his family fortunes to support his predilection and the royal stipend to satisfy his impostor. He had liquidated fifty-four ancestral estates in twelve years to endow London's playhouses and sponsor elaborate productions for the Queen. Shaxper could scarcely believe the large sums of money that changed hands to pay tailors, carpenters, wig makers, actors, scribes, musicians and all of the other production costs a good play required. Because he kept the theatrical account books, he was aware of every penny.

Beyond that, he had observed Oxford's restless ambivalence in trading his courtier's doublet for a jester's motley coat. He occasionally complained that he might have made a mistake in retiring from Court and abandoning the noble obligations entrusted to him at birth. He and the Countess were planning to make King's Place their main residence after the plague lifted and it was safe to return to London. The secretive house was the most distant mansion from Court, yet it was close enough for the Earl to arrive quickly whenever the Queen summoned him to attend on her.

Unfortunately, such summons rarely came anymore. Masking sixty years of lust under layers of wax makeup, the aging Queen had taken another young lover. Thirty-three years her junior, the Earl of Essex wooed her with vain compliments and insincere flatteries that yielded him special favors and advancement.

Since matters of the heart never escaped a servant's notice and he now served two formidable masters, Shaxper was aware that Southampton also yearned to receive favors in the Queen's bed. At nineteen, the fair youth fancied himself handsomer and more favorable in demeanor than his friend Essex, and yet the Queen rebuffed all of his overtures. Southampton had been driven to tears over it; the Queen had always treated him like a son, but now she suddenly and inexplicably cut him out of her company altogether. His self-destructive behavior grew even worse when he and Essex became lovers. Essex taunted him with stories of his royal lovemaking, even demonstrating some of Her Majesty's maneuvers on the young Earl himself.

When invited to join their pillow talk, Shaxper awkwardly acquiesced and continued to keep their secrets, acting as a voyeur during their encounters.

But oh, the stories he'd be able to tell if the time was ever right!

He wondered what Oxford would think of Southampton's extraordinary lust for his monarch, and couldn't even begin to imagine what the

Countess would say about such matters. On his way upstairs, he passed by the front room and saw the new mother cradling her infant son in her arms. Countess Elizabeth was still new to the household and hadn't yet confided in him, but Shaxper would soon prove his trustworthiness. He would craft some special flattery to win her confidence. One never knew when wifely opinions might prove valuable.

After glancing into the nursery only briefly, Shaxper bounded upstairs to Oxford's study. As he prepared to knock, he was surprised to hear childish laughter on the other side of the door.

He hadn't heard sounds like that in years, not since his last visit home. He was suddenly struck with an incredible longing to see his own children. How long had it been? He was ashamed to admit he didn't know. How old was Susanna now, and the twins, Hamnet and Judith? He tried to recall their tender little faces, confident that Time had surely matured them. He wasn't certain he'd recognize them, even if he passed them on Henley Street.

He hoped they appreciated his money. His wife had never bothered to ask Hamnet Sadler to write and thank him for it. Anne and his daughters couldn't read or write, and his son Hamnet had been too ill to attend school. Unless his health improved, the boy would never receive an education and have the chance to forge a better life for himself.

The sound of Ben Jonson's husky laugh cut into his thoughts like a knife.

What on earth was *he* doing here?

Jealousy overpowering propriety, Shaxper burst into the room. He hadn't expected to see the Earl of Oxford sitting at his writing table, watching as his five-year old daughter and his brick-headed associate played a game of Hoodman Blind. Ben Jonson wore a burlap hood, and Shaxper thought he looked ridiculous, stumbling around the room with his beefy, outstretched arms flailing away, pretending he couldn't find the little girl giggling at his feet.

"Ah, Shaxper, you've arrived," Oxford said. "Just in time."

Jonson pulled off his hood. He knelt down with open arms as Susan ran into his embrace. He scooped her into the air and set her on his broad shoulders. She hugged his neck as they bounced around the room.

"I came from London as quickly as I could, my lord," Shaxper said.

"I'm sure you did. I'll wager you didn't expect to find us playing games, did you now?"

"No, my lord, I didn't. It seems Jonson here has lost his head."

"Relax," Jonson growled. "The executioner hasn't taken it yet. It's still right here, where it belongs."

"I thought you'd lost it to Susan," Oxford laughed.

"If so, my head is in good company – she already has my heart."

Susan squealed with delight as Jonson playfully bobbed up and down.

"My lord," Shaxper said, irritably. "This child's game is all very well and good, but I have some important matters to discuss with you."

Oxford told Jonson to take Susan outside. When they were gone, Shaxper spoke.

"How long has Jonson been here?"

"About a week," the Earl replied. "Thomas Nashe came with him. Marlowe's murder sent them running for their lives. They came here to finish *The Isle of Dogs*."

"Do you think it's wise to let them work on it here? It's a questionable play, and if it's shown that you were involved in something treasonous–"

"You needn't worry. The Queen will protect me, and that same protection also applies to you."

"I wish I could believe that. Her Majesty hasn't done much to safeguard anyone else lately. They say the dagger pierced Marlowe's eye and tore straight into his brain. The killers were arrested and immediately released."

"Marlowe's killers got their start with Walsingham before they entered Lord Burghley's service," Oxford said, "and now it seems the old man has handed them down to his son. Can you imagine such a legacy on paper? 'In the name of God, to my son Sir Robert Cecil I hereby bequeath: Item: Nicholas Skeres, bloodthirsty cut-throat; Item: Ingram Frizer, notorious assassin; and Item: Robert Poley, infamous butcher.'"

"I was followed out of the city, my lord," Shaxper said, nervously, "by a man who could have been an assassin. We're in terrible danger. You must do something."

"I am. Ben and I are doing all we can to keep Marlowe's plays alive. The Queen has assured me that she'll reopen the playhouses when the plague is over."

"That's not important now. Our play factory is under attack. How will you save it?"

"By disbanding it," Oxford sighed.

"You mean close it down completely?"

"Yes, sadly. I need to avoid the appearance of a conspiracy against the government."

"If that protects us, I approve," Shaxper said. "But why are you sad about it?"

"After all these years, you still don't understand my role at the writers' table, do you?" Oxford said, as he rose from his chair and paced the room. "Permit me to enlighten you. Even if Greene, Marlowe, Kyd, Watson and all the others were steeped in heinous evil from head to toe, I would still grieve for them because they were talented literary men. I guided them in the art of playwriting, and they were eager and capable followers. We passed our manuscripts back and forth until we crafted words so sublime it was as if they fell from Heaven onto the page in the unfolding of some Divine Plan. But now the play factory has outlived its purpose. My students are either dead or they've deserted me. Once we were charged by the Crown to produce history plays in fast succession to inspire our nation to defend itself, and we produced those plays. But now that need is past. The very same Crown that nurtured our work has become terrified of our influence in the playhouses. I was right, you see – 'the play *is* the thing.' So it seems I must bury my play factory, and continue writing plays on my own."

"Does that mean you won't be requiring my services?"

"God's blood! We are shackled together as Shake-speare for the rest of our lives. I'll continue to write the shocking and unabridged truth about anyone I please," Oxford said. "And you will continue to stand in for me. You'll smile like a thief, puff on your pipe, ignore all questions about your work and let everyone think you conveniently made it all up in your head: all those warlike kings, tormented queens, uncouth princes, greedy noblemen, hired assassins, evil conspirators . . ."

"Will they believe it?"

"You'll *make* them believe it. That's why I'm paying you to be England's greatest actor!"

"Then you'll continue to protect my safety?"

"Upon my honor, yes, for as long as I live, if you continue to protect mine."

"Oh, my lord, I will."

"Swear it. Swear it upon this Bible."

Shaxper, a Catholic, hesitated a moment before placing his hand on Lord Oxford's Geneva Bible.

"I swear to keep your secrets until the day I die, my lord," he said. "Thank you for allowing me to remain in your service."

The Earl of Oxford locked eyes with his impostor.

"I cannot be Shake-speare without you, cousin."

CHAPTER EIGHTEEN

The Scene: London
January 15, 1601

"In time the savage bull doth bear the yoke."
– Much Ado About Nothing

With a feeling of satisfaction, Sir Robert Cecil relaxed comfortably into the coach for his long ride back to England. His audience with King James VI of Scotland had been a success, and had even exceeded his expectations in carving out a place for himself in their newly conceived government. Over the past two years, their intermittent meetings had been long and drawn out, but he was pleased that this one had been quick and to the point. Their final negotiation for the throne of England had been more relaxed than any of their previous encounters, perhaps because Time was now conspiring to speed them towards their goal.

As the carriage raced down the road, Cecil recalled the hectic ride three years earlier on his way to his father's deathbed. Sadly, Fate had intervened by breaking the carriage's axle that night, causing a delay in his arrival. By the time he had reached the house, Lord Burghley was dead and the instructions he had hoped for regarding the royal succession had become undeliverable. His father had taken the unfinished business to his grave, leaving the specters of civil war and national chaos looming over his son's head.

It was so unlike his father to have died with the successor's name unspoken and undocumented when he had so carefully recorded and scripted every other aspect of Elizabeth Tudor's reign. Lord Burghley had elevated her from the reviled spawn of Anne Boleyn and Henry VIII to Gloriana, the Virgin Queen, polishing every aspect of her reign until it shone like a jewel against her sister Mary's infamous and bloody rule. He could scarcely believe there wasn't a piece of paper somewhere in Lord Burghley's hand that anticipated Elizabeth's choice for royal heir.

But he could find no such paper, and only in that regard did his pedantic father leave him nothing.

The Queen still refused to name her successor, but these days Cecil found her silence convenient. It enabled him to act in his own self-interest, supporting a monarch who would reward him for placing the crown within his reach. He had already preyed upon the Queen's guilty conscience to send James £3000 a year, supposedly as reparations for the execution of his mother. Naturally, James was grateful for this generosity – not to the murderous monarch who had signed Mary of Scotland's death warrant, but to the hunchbacked counselor who had paved his way towards England's throne.

At sixty-eight and in poor health, Elizabeth Tudor's once-reasonable mind had become clouded. She suffered intense emotional outbursts and looked mournfully pallid. Her eyes were thick with tears and her hair had become gray and sparse. Not even the skills of her ladies in applying auburn wigs and wax makeup could hide the ravages of infirmity and age.

The Queen had become even more embroiled in the power struggles of her courtiers. She was devastated by the betrayal of her beloved Essex, who had turned against her while commanding the troops in Ireland. Because of his popularity with the commoners, he had convinced himself that he could organize their support in deposing her. For her part, the Queen seemed more concerned about his corruptive influence on the Earl of Southampton than she did with her own safety, making it difficult for her to deal effectively with the traitors.

As a result, Cecil had asked his cousin Sir Francis Bacon to spy on Essex. The promise of advancement made it easy for him to turn on his old friend, set his trap and wait. Bacon quickly informed Cecil that Essex had paid forty shillings to finance a revival of Shakespeare's *Richard II* as a way of rallying the popular support of the commoners to join in his revolt, and that Southampton had selected the date and time for the play intended to catapult Essex onto the throne.

Six years earlier, Cecil had seen *Richard II* at the home of a friend and even then had found it troubling. He had been astonished when the Queen had turned to him and said that *she* was Richard II, the failing monarch cozened out of his throne and deposed by traitors. This unusual display of weakness made him realize that her days as a monarch were numbered.

After all, his father was dead. Lord Burghley had established Elizabeth Tudor's rule, and like all things mortal, it was drawing to an end. Now his son's star was on the ascendant. It was time for Sir Robert Cecil to play the role of king-maker and support James of Scotland, whose ambition for England's crown was not unlike that of Richard's nemesis, the usurper Bullingbrook.

But unlike Bullingbrook, James didn't want any blood on his hands. He and Cecil were simply waiting for the Queen to die of old age. Essex, not James, was the butcher seeking her destruction. It seemed odd to think that a single performance of an old play like *Richard II* could touch off civic violence. While it was true that *Sir Thomas More* had once caused similar fears, years ago the censor had purged both plays of all incendiary material that might cause political unrest.

But what if Shakespeare had been paid to add a few incendiary lines? In his plays Lord Oxford had frequently done so, at no cost to anyone but his victims. The upstart crow from Stratford had probably learned that brand of treachery at his table. By virtue of this upcoming performance, Shaxper, Shaksper, Shakespeare (or however he signed his name) was clearly part of the conspiracy, which made it essential that Robert Poley continue to follow him.

Suddenly, Cecil's coach hit a bump in the road and he was roughly tossed to the floor. He struggled to climb back onto the seat but his deformity made it difficult. After much effort, the little man regained his place and pounded on the roof with his walking stick, warning the driver to slow down. He quickly covered his mouth with a handkerchief to keep from losing his breakfast.

Making matters worse was the complex mix of generations of royal and noble intermarriages, which had yielded fourteen people who had credible claims to the throne. Most of them were probably prepared to do battle over it. Add to that the thousands of commoners seeking riches, ready to choose up sides in the hope of backing the victor, and a bloody civil war seemed inevitable.

Cecil had to summon every ounce of his political skill to prevent that calamity. James was already an experienced monarch in his own right, and would unify the nation. As a great-great grandson of Henry VII, James had a strong (albeit distant) claim to the throne, and was a staunch Protestant. The only strike against him was that he was a foreigner. England's commoners were vehemently opposed to being ruled by outsiders. Still, Cecil believed that the guaranty of stability James conveyed would pacify the most obstreperous of his countrymen.

And yet the possibility troubled him that a single Shakespeare play could undermine all of his well laid plans.

Having spent his life taking control of events that lesser men had deemed uncontrollable, Cecil left nothing to chance. Missing his father's last moments had strengthened his resolve to be alone with the Queen when her time came; and when she drew her last breath to choose her successor, only one name would resonate for all to hear. The election would light on James of Scotland.

As to any conspirators, all of those spoiled sons of wealthy noblemen who presumed to challenge the divine right of kings would be plucked up like weeds to make way for the new regime.

James VI of Scotland would become James I of England.

The coach steadied and began to pick up speed.

CHAPTER NINETEEN

The Scene: London
January 15, 1601

"Look to the Queen!"

– Hamlet

Alone in her private chamber, the senescent Queen broke with tradition and gazed into her mirror. Despite her velvet gown and layers of jewels, she searched in vain for the remnants of her beauty, but found no trace of them in her reflection. Time had forced her into the strange and unfamiliar mask of an old woman. Regardless of her efforts to revive the natural blush of youth, she recognized that it was irretrievably gone.

These days, she felt as if she wasn't fooling anyone. In the eyes of the world she was an old crone, like those burned at the stake in the superstitious villages to the north. Men had no respect for such haggard creatures. Even though she still ruled a powerful nation, she was no different from any other wretched woman who had suffered the indignities of Time. In men, old age symbolized wisdom; but in women, it meant decay. Age had rallied her enemies against her and made her more vulnerable to destruction.

Tonight she barred all attendants from her door. Alone and unobserved, she removed her wig and ran her fingers through her wispy gray hair. She tried to recall the face of her mother, the beauteous Anne Boleyn. But so many years had passed; she had been only three at the time of her mother's execution, and the memory refused to answer her summons. At least her unfortunate mother hadn't been forced to endure the agony of outliving her beauty.

Indeed, Elizabeth Tudor had survived long enough to have gained wisdom, the essential quality Lord Burghley had assured her was required by a successful monarch. But now she wondered if it was better for a female monarch to die young and at the peak of perfection – like her mother, bereft of the head whose face would one day betray her in the mirror. Wisdom was a fine quality, though perhaps overrated; for when it came down to a universal truth in a world governed by men, women without a trace of sensual beauty were powerless to control events in their favor.

She dipped a small towel into the bowl of rosewater and wrung it out. She closed her eyes and spread the linen across her face, feeling her tears merge into its warmth. After a few moments, she removed the cloth and gently began peeling away the layers of wax that covered her face, just as her ladies had routinely done under strict orders of absolute silence. When finished, the mask of her royal persona lay in pieces on the table.

In the glass, she saw the reflection of an ordinary woman who had governed in extraordinary times. The Earl of Oxford would have understood her ambivalence at this cruel unmasking, for he had often described his emotions after a performance, when the illusions he had created were stripped away, yielding a harsh reality that slowly emerged from the fading mists of glamor.

She twisted the ring on her finger. She had worn it all these years to mark their secret marriage, even while they had engaged in passionate affairs with others. When she had boasted to the world that she was married to England, Oxford had been the true embodiment of that phrase.

They had conceived a child together. Perhaps if they had been commoners, this act would have bonded them as it did the most humble peasants; but her rank demanded strict adherence to dignity, and Oxford's devil-may-care antics in the playhouses made that dignity impossible.

First and foremost she was Queen of England, secured by the myth of her virginity. Oxford's damning papers threatened to unravel that mythology. If only she could remember where she had placed those papers. There was never any safety in allowing Oxford or any husband to be named as her King Consort, when a male presence so close to the throne would only incite her enemies against her. She needed to look no farther than Scotland to see how her cousin Mary had fared in turning lovers into husbands and giving birth to a son, allowing men closer access to her throne.

A thousand of her darkest fears had built a protective wall around Henry. She wondered if practicality would ever have allowed her to proclaim him as her heir. Historically, kings were considered far preferable to queens as rulers of great nations, and he could easily have been used to supplant her as regents had used the infant James to replace his mother as the ruler of Scotland.

No one could have predicted that Henry would have valued his love for Essex more than his love for her. Ironically, his best protection, the ignorance of his true parentage, had also sown the seeds of his destruction.

And then there was Essex, the last in the long line of her lovers. Oh, how she missed him in her bed, with his strong arms and powerful thighs. But he had never truly loved her; in anger, she had slapped his face for his peevish behavior on the battlefields of Ireland, and he had grabbed his sword as if he would strike her. His foul expression said he wanted her dead, and that he would steal her throne.

Henry had been such a fool to follow him.

She closed her eyes and prayed for her son's repentance. Against Cecil's advice, she was prepared to wait until the last possible moment before making any arrests in the treason conspiracy, in case her lover Essex had a sudden change of heart or Henry was smitten with a guilty conscience.

She opened her eyes and saw that her reflection had no patience for a woman's tears.

If Henry failed to repent, she had already followed Cecil's proposal to secure an alliance with King James of Scotland. She had toyed with him numerous times over the matter of her succession and sent him large sums of money. When James finally insisted that she legalize her intentions in Parliament, she declared that her word alone was sufficient. Of course he knew it wasn't, but at least he was waiting patiently for Time to take its toll, if only to settle the score on behalf of his mother.

She wiped her eyes and realized that upon her death, all of the world's leaders (including the Pope) would understand how well she had protected herself from the domineering men who had sought to undermine her rule from the moment of her coronation. Her propensity for making hasty promises and quickly revoking them had kept everyone off guard, especially King James of Scotland.

Elizabeth Tudor smiled. Lord Oxford had been right about one thing – beneath a mask, it was possible to deceive an entire world.

ACT IV
CHAPTER TWENTY

The Scene: The Globe Theater
February 4, 1601

"Old Adam's likeness, set to dress this garden."
— Richard II

C ostumed as the Gardener in *Richard II*, William Browne used a long rake as his walking stick to draw him across the stage. Two actors clad as his assistants followed him on; and to them, he addressed his metaphoric lines about England.

> *Gardener.* Go bind thou up young dangling apricocks,
> Which like unruly children make their sire
> Stoop with oppression of their prodigal weight;
> Give some supportance to the bending twigs.
> Go thou, and like an executioner
> Cut off the heads of too fast growing sprays,

That look too lofty in their commonwealth:
All must be even in our government.
You thus employed, I will go root away
The noisome weeds which without profit suck
The soil's fertility from wholesome flowers.
Man. Why should we in the compass of a pale
Keep law and form and due proportion,
Showing as in a model our firm estate,
When our sea-walled garden, the whole land,
Is full of weeds, her fairest flowers choked up,
Her fruit trees all unpruned, her hedges ruined,
Her knots disordered, and her wholesome herbs
Swarming with caterpillars?
Gardener. Hold thy peace.
He that hath suffered this disordered spring
Hath now himself met with the fall of leaf.
The weeds which his broad-spreading leaves did shelter
That seem'd in eating him to hold him up
Are plucked up root and all by Bullingbrook,
I mean the Earl of Wiltshire, Bushy, Green.
Man. What, are they dead?
Gardener. Depressed is he already, and deposed
'Tis doubt he will be –

He continued his speech as Southampton angrily stalked into The Globe and threw his cloak down on the bench where the Earl of Essex and William Shaxper were watching the rehearsal.

"What is it, my lord? What's the matter?" Shaxper whispered anxiously to Southampton.

"What in God's name is wrong with you, Henry?" Essex snorted. "If you could only see yourself, frothing at the mouth like a mad dog."

"Mad dog indeed. I daresay you'd be frothing at the mouth, if you'd been treated like a mongrel cur! That royal bitch has done it to me again."

"There, there. What has Her Majesty done to you now?"

"She ejected me from her bedchamber and refused my offer of love. I'll never speak to her again."

"You said that yesterday," Essex laughed.

"Quiet!" Lord Oxford shouted. "Quiet in the house!"

Disguised as Browne to portray the Gardener, he broke character and strode to the edge of the stage, glaring like a father at his spoiled children. "We're trying to rehearse a play here, if you don't mind, so kindly keep quiet."

"Well, I've never been so insulted!"

"And by a rude mechanical," Essex sneered. "Perhaps we should withdraw our support and take our production elsewhere."

"Perhaps we should," Southampton agreed.

Shaxper winced. Oxford quickly realized he'd overstepped his authority as a mere actor, and essayed a fawning apology as Browne.

"Forgive my outburst, Your Lordships. Let me explain. The Lord Chamberlain's Men always welcome patrons to watch our rehearsals, especially when they sponsor a play as generously as you've sponsored this one. But it's been several years since any of us have spoken these old lines. Augustine Phillips, our Richard, must capture every nuance of his very moving scenes. We require strict concentration, and so I beg you not to take offense when I ask you to talk outdoors and not in the theater while we are working. After all, you've paid a bonus for this play, and we open in three days. We beg your indulgence as we rehearse it a little while longer."

Browne crossed his arms over his chest and offered an affected Italian bow.

"Get on with your work," Essex grumbled, as he headed towards the door. Southampton followed like a puppy. At the end of the aisle, Essex turned and shouted.

"Well, playwright? Are you coming with us?"

It took a moment for Shaxper to realize that Essex was talking to him.

"My lord," he stammered, "I thought I'd stay and see if my play needed any last minute changes."

"Nonsense, it's perfect, especially with the old Deposition Scene added back in. That'll certainly strike a blow in our favor. The old crone on the throne won't know what's happened until it's too late. Don't waste your time here any longer. There's more work to be done."

"That's right," Southampton added. "Just follow along. You're one of us now."

Shaxper waited for Lord Oxford to say something that would require him to stay, but the Earl held his ridiculous pose, hoping to annoy Essex. Caught in the midst of their peevish nonsense, Shaxper shook his head, put on his cloak and followed the young noblemen outside.

A short distance away, Robert Poley covered his face to avoid being seen. He leaned against the fence behind The Globe and watched as the irate men entered the tiring house. He hurried to the door and listened.

"Who does that ill-mannered busker think he is?" Essex roared, pounding his first on the table. "Imagine, a common player taking the liberty to insult courtiers with such impunity!"

"Browne is a very strange fellow," Southampton said.

Essex waved the air to indicate that the subject was of no further interest to him.

"I'd withdraw my backing from your play this very instant, Shakespeare, if my whole plan did not depend on using it to arouse the commoners to support us."

"In what way, my lord? I don't understand."

"It sounds like my friend Southampton has failed to explain our plan. You are helping us choose the next King of England."

"The next king!" Shaxper gasped. "What are you saying, my lord? The Queen still lives! God save the Queen!"

"Let God save her then – *we* have no intention of doing it."

"Keep your voices down," Essex whispered, as he grabbed Shaxper by the arm. "You don't understand, do you, being a commoner from the country. Some of us nobles are a little frightened, that's all, about what will happen to England if the old Queen dies without an heir."

"Without an heir? There are plenty of nobles ready and able to rule England when the time comes," Shaxper said.

"That's exactly the problem," Southampton explained. "Only one person can be king, and he should never be challenged or there will be a huge civil war. Lord Essex will be the next monarch, and we will see to it that no one dares to challenge him. For example, you know our friends, the Earl of Rutland and Sir Charles Danvers?"

"Are they involved?"

"Lots of us are involved," Essex said. "It's no secret that the Queen could die at any time, whether we're allowed to speak of it or not, she being mortal like the rest of us. So we've banded together to help her choose her successor. But don't worry. No one will be harmed. Our sole purpose is to persuade the Queen to appoint me as her successor when she dies. No one will be hurt to make that happen; but if it doesn't happen, many will be hurt, and the England that we know and love may suddenly be destroyed."

"Now wait a minute," Shaxper said, pulling away from Essex. "I may be a country commoner, but even I know it's not your job to help her make that decision. Kings rule by Divine Right and according to God's Will."

"We *are* doing God's Will by helping the Queen – "

"Go to her grave in peace," Southampton muttered. "How can our country be at peace without a named successor? She's had a long run, but the curtain is closing. We have a man to enact the part of king."

"Who's that?"

"Don't be such a simpleton, Shakespeare," Essex growled, thumping his chest. "*I'm* the man!"

"This is madness," Shaxper insisted. "Do you realize what you're saying, my lord? This is open rebellion!"

"Of course it is, and we have *you* to thank for it."

"*Me*? What did *I* do?"

"You wrote the play that started it all," Southampton said, as he clapped Shaxper on the back. "That's what I meant when I said you're one of us now."

"Remember, we want you on our side," Essex said. "I'm depending on you, Shakespeare, and the great power of your mind, to teach my subjects how to live together in peace. You'll do it with your wonderful plays. You know English history; think of me as Bullingbrook. *Richard II* will set the crown of England on my head. And when I'm king, you can write me whole plays to insure that I retain my sovereignty. I've seen your magic in the playhouses. You've inspired the commoners to cheer me in the streets, like the other military heroes in your plays – and they absolutely adore me because of your influence! Those are *your* audiences, Shakespeare. The same people who love me also love you."

"And who can blame them?" Southampton said, as he preened in the mirror.

"Your plays will offer me a unique service," Essex added. "What were those ennobling words you used in this one? 'This sceptered isle, this earth of majesty, this seat of Mars, this realm, this England.' It stirs my blood to think of how you'll write about me when I am England. Naturally, I'll reward you for your work, and whatever the Queen is paying you for your Court masques, I'll double it."

For the first time in his life, the thought of accepting money made Shaxper sick. He was about to speak when William Browne entered. His sudden appearance made Essex and Southampton start guiltily towards the door.

"My lords," the actor said, bowing again. "I apologize. I didn't realize you were still here. I would have thought our tiring house would prove too tiresome for you."

"Not as tiresome as you are. We were just leaving."

"Indeed. I'd have thought the delights at The Golden Lion would have taken you away by now."

"That's a splendid idea. Are you coming with us, Shakespeare?"

"No, I'd better stay and w-work with the actors, my lord."

"As you wish," Essex said. "But don't tell anyone what I've told you."

"And beware of the caterpillars in your apricocks," Southampton said, as he stepped outside.

Robert Poley heard them coming and flattened himself against the wall. At first, he wondered whether to follow the two noblemen, but then he heard the door lock and quickly sensed that the most important secrets were still inside the tiring house. He pressed his ear against the door.

"You're as pale as a ghost," Oxford said to his impostor. "Are you ill, or did Essex pour some of his poison into your ear?"

Shaxper slid a bench across the floor and sat down next to his master.

"We're in terrible danger, my lord."

"Danger?" Oxford laughed. "What, from those two popinjays? What harm could they possibly hatch?"

Shaxper whispered into his master's ear the deadly word that had remained unspoken.

"Treason?" Oxford gasped. "Are you sure?"

"Essex is planning to incite a rebellion. He means to use the plot of *Richard II* to disparage the Queen in public and equate himself with the victorious usurper Bullingbrook."

"He told you this?"

"Because he thinks I'm Shakespeare," the impostor said. "And he wants me to write more plays promoting his authority, after he proclaims himself king."

"He must be out of his mind. Did you give him any encouragement?"

"I said nothing. That's when you came in and found us here."

"What about Southampton? Is he involved?"

"He believes Essex would make an excellent king. He's willing to die for him, if need be."

Oxford sighed as if his life's breath were escaping.

"Are you all right, my lord?" Shaxper asked.

"Yes, yes, I'm all right. How widespread is this misguided sacrifice?"

"I don't know, but Essex thinks his rebellion has the support of the entire nation, or at least of anyone who has ever seen a Shakespeare play."

"Cecil must be aware of it, but I can't be sure," Oxford said, as he secured his dagger. "I must warn the Queen."

"You'd better hurry, my lord. Don't you think we should cancel the performance?"

"No. Trust me, the only danger inherent in this play is in the deluded minds of the conspirators."

"But they think I'm the playwright."

"Everyone in England thinks so, too. Consider it a tribute to your acting skills. But the Queen is aware of the truth. She knows my loyalty, and I'll convince her of yours. You'll just have to mew up your manhood and take your bows with the rest of us on Saturday. I'll be there with Augustine Phillips, Richard Burbage, Hemminge, Condell and the rest of the Lord Chamberlain's Men. It's said that Shakespeare has never missed a performance. I haven't missed one yet, have I? And neither have you."

"But my lord, surely the danger –"

"There's always been an element of danger in our ruse, cousin. You knew that, every time you carried my plays or poetry to the Stationers'

Register and passed them off as your own. You strutted like a peacock, puffed on your pipe and put on airs like an inscrutable buffoon. You abused my kindness with your occasional extortions. Don't misunderstand me – I needed an impostor so I could write whatever I pleased, and I'll rely on you again when this crisis is over. I've always met your demands, whatever the cost; but it seems to me you reveled in your Shakespeare persona so often, you came to believe it yourself. That's why I wrote that provocative induction to *The Taming Of The Shrew*: 'For all your writers do consent that *ipse* is he; now you are not *ipse*, for I am he.' I'm the nobleman playwright," Oxford laughed. "There, I've said it myself."

"Forgive me, my lord," Shaxper said, falling to his knees. "Please tell me what to do. You promised you'd protect me!"

"After the performance, you'd better ride to Stratford as quickly as possible. Stay there until I can get word to you that it's safe to return. No doubt there'll be an extensive search for conspirators, and you must not be found among them."

"And what will you do, my lord?"

"I'll attend to the Queen," Oxford said. "At such a precarious time, she's going to need the comfort of an old friend. And we do have a few longstanding matters to discuss."

"Please, my lord, when you see her, tell her I'm innocent. I beg you, ask her to protect me."

"I will," Lord Oxford said, as he exited by way of the stage. He stopped for a moment to whisper something to Augustine Phillips and was quickly on his way.

Shaxper nervously fumbled with the door to the yard. When it finally opened, he leapt out of the playhouse as if it were on fire.

He didn't see Robert Poley lurking in the alley.

CHAPTER TWENTY-ONE

The Scene: Royal Palace
February 25, 1601
the execution of the Earl of Essex

"If any plague hang over us, 'tis he."
— Henry IV, Part I

The Queen had never played the virginal so beautifully, interlacing "Robin Is To The Greenwood Gone" with the wistful "Bonny Sweet Boy," her fingers moving across the keyboard like spiders. Her somber rendition confirmed that she was thinking of her beloved son. Not far away at the Tower, the egotistical traitor Essex, who had conspired her death, knelt down to face the executioner's ax. He was not the first of her lovers to have broken her heart, Lord Oxford mused, but in this wintry season of finales, he was certainly the last.

When the Queen had summoned him, Oxford had hurried to her side. The dismal irony wasn't lost on him, that as her oldest surviving lover, he had been invited to sit with her as her youngest paramour prepared to die. He wondered whether she would sentence their son Henry to the same fate for his role in the conspiracy. In the weeks since their trials, the Queen had said nothing about her intentions for Henry, while Cecil had insisted on death for every traitor involved.

The clock ticked off the minutes without mercy. Oxford watched as the Queen grew more agitated and poured her sorrow onto the keys of the virginal.

Throughout her reign, political necessity had forced her to severely punish all traitors. Although she hated bloodshed, she had executed her cousin, Mary of Scotland and Oxford's kinsman, the Duke of Norfolk, because they had conspired against her. Crimes against the heart also necessitated punishment. Oxford had feared for his life while imprisoned in the Tower, since the Queen had considered his affair with Lady Vavasor a treasonous betrayal of her affections.

But in spite of his reckless behavior, Eliza had always forgiven him. She had fostered his literary work as Shakespeare and had allowed him to inspire others to become playwrights. For these indulgences, he was truly grateful.

Still, she hadn't always granted him everything. With Henry in danger and Cecil demanding blood, he wasn't sure if the Queen had the power to protect him.

Both Southampton and Essex had been found guilty at their trials. Their bombastic performance of *Richard II* had failed to rally the hoards of cheering commoners Essex had anticipated to advance his cause. The irony wasn't lost on Oxford that more people had gathered to applaud his execution than had joined in his rebellion.

The Queen heard the cheers, too. She knew it meant that her lover's head was being held aloft as an example of death befitting a traitor. She had gone out of her way to give him a merciful execution, compared to the harsh penalties of burning and disemboweling usually enacted upon those who plotted treason. Her heart filled with grief. Her fingers stiffened on the keyboard as if she were screaming through it.

A messenger entered and bowed hastily, confirming that Essex was dead. Without much thought, he added that it had taken three sharp blows of the ax to sever his head.

"Get out!" she cried, "or by God in Heaven, your head will be next!"

The terrified messenger bowed anxiously and fled.

"This is all your fault!" the Queen shouted to Lord Oxford, her face drenched in tears. "You, and all the men like you who sought favors in my bed. I'm too old for this distasteful business. And now my dear Essex is dead, and I must sign my own son's death warrant. I never should have agreed to Burghley's wicked scheme. I must have been insane to let him talk me into conceiving *your* child! What else could a son of yours be, but a mercurial rascal and a dissembler? All these years I've suffered heartache over him. I've worried about Henry day and night, ever since he was born. Perhaps I should have told him who he was. Perhaps I should have raised him as my heir, for all the world to see. But I was terrified of being deposed by a gang of bloodthirsty regents who would make my infant son their king! The same thing happened to Mary when James was only one year old. And these regents often murder the very boy-kings they've sworn to protect, the way they poisoned my brother. They run rampant whenever there's a crown at stake."

"What will happen to Henry now?"

"Every day Sir Robert Cecil thrusts his death warrant in my face, demanding that I sign it. I can't delay any longer. He doesn't know Henry is my son."

"And mine, too."

"I have that letter you wrote me years ago, threatening to expose him. What would you have me do with it now, Edward? I can't believe you want to see our Henry dead."

"For all practical purposes, he *is* dead to us, Eliza. Neither of us can confess our parentage of him."

The Queen wept. Oxford gently placed his hands on her shoulders.

"Not even Lord Burghley could have imagined this," he said softly. "This shipwreck of events – that a royal heir would unwittingly revolt and lose the crown that should have been his."

"What am I to do about him? What am I to do?" the Queen cried, wringing her hands.

"He was raised as Henry Wriothesley, Earl of Southampton. I think he should continue in that role."

"Continue in that role?" the Queen roared. "There's a warrant demanding his life."

"Let me bargain with you for it then," Lord Oxford said. "I'll rescind my stale threat if you change his death sentence into one of life imprisonment. You were right when you said that he is just like me – a rascal with quicksilver in his blood. You could lodge him in the Tower indefinitely, to watch over him and keep him safe, like a liquid prisoner pent in walls of glass, to resolve his mercurial nature. If you command it, Cecil will be compelled to obey."

"Any mother would choose life for her son," she said. "Then you agree to destroy that menacing letter and those damned copies of your will that you threatened me with?"

"I've already destroyed them," he said. "I had to write a new will when my lady-wife the Countess gave birth to our son ten years ago."

The Queen sighed and held his hand.

"As long as Henry receives a harsh punishment, Cecil will be appeased," she said. "God's will be done, as far as Henry is concerned."

"By Heaven, it appears to me that our earthbound wills are meaningless," Oxford said. "Someday Henry might win his freedom, after you and I are dead and gone, and our mortal afflictions no longer matter. For now, we'll bury these secrets in our graves."

"So be it. It is a shame that the vows we made on Henry's behalf a lifetime ago have come to naught."

"We were actors, playing the roles that were written for us," Oxford said.

"Do you really believe that, Shakespeare?"

"Yes, Gloriana. I do."

"I think it's time we released each other from the ancient vows we made under the flag of St. George. Here is the pearl you gave me to symbolize our union," she said, as she took off her ring and gently folded it into his hand.

"And here is the ring you gave me that night at Lambeth," he said. He kissed it and placed it in the palm of her hand. "That seals our bargain for Henry's sake."

Together they watched the sunset through the casement.

"It's evening," she whispered. "Essex is dead."

"Night has fallen on the old players. Burghley, Leicester, Hatton . . . "

"Promise you'll outlive me, Edward. Don't die and leave me all alone on this dreary orb. The rest of my friends and lovers are dead. I'm an old woman. I haven't the strength to endure it anymore."

"Now, Eliza," he said lovingly, "you mustn't speak of death when I'm about to present you with eternal life. I have good news for you. The monument you requested will soon be ready."

The Queen's eyes lit up like stars.

"You mean that play you promised me? The one you wrote so long ago and wanted to revise into greatness?"

"Yes. I think it parallels *The Famous Victories of Henry the Fifth* very nicely. I've decided to call it *The Famous History of the Life of Henry the Eighth*. Both of these works represent the alpha and the omega of my history plays. What do you think?"

The Queen was overjoyed.

"I want it to be the most elegant production ever presented in the theater," she said, "the richest and most sparkling jewel in the Tudor crown. Oh, but I am sure it is! Your words will spring forth like a fountain of youth and grant me immortality. It will be the greatest play you have ever written, and also be a monument to our love."

She looked deep into his eyes and whispered, "As I have given you your immortality, so you have given me mine."

After a moment of silence, she continued, "Lord Burghley would have approved this great telling of history."

"Oh. Perhaps I should reconsider it then."

"Fie! Don't toy with me, Edward," she laughed. "When can we see this play on the stage?"

"That depends on you, Eliza."

"Are you asking me for money?"

"No, for something infinitely more valuable. I need access to my servant, William Shaxper of Stratford, who has gone into hiding for fear of his life."

"Oh, yes, the impostor. Cecil wants to question him for his involvement in the Essex Rebellion, but so far all attempts to locate him have failed."

"I know where he is, but he's innocent of any wrongdoing. Essex named him as a conspirator. You might want to save Cecil some trouble, if he plans on pursuing the bogus playwright to the ends of the earth. Shaxper is an innocent minion whose only crime – if you can call it that – was in accepting forty shillings to produce a play he knew nothing about, and then wallowing in praise for it."

"Then perhaps I should punish you. *Richard II* is a very dangerous play."

"I'd agree with you, Eliza – if we had performed the original version – the one you saw six years ago. But we didn't. I revised everything, including the Deposition Scene. But Essex didn't know that, and neither did William Shaxper. They put on the wrong play. When I wrote the first version, I was angry and had sworn to take my revenge against you in the playhouses. But when I realized the impact my words had on the audience, I knew I had to make Richard a more sympathetic character for your sake, as well as for England's."

"I love my people, but they're so easily cozened," she said. "They seldom understand the intrigue our enemies use against us ."

"Political machinations are not part of their world," he replied.

"You must know that Cecil has questioned your actor, Augustine Phillips. He was found to be an honest man and was released very quickly."

"Augustine is honest and very perceptive. He played Richard with grace and sensitivity, as an openhearted and sympathetic king."

"Hopefully, the audience sees the same qualities in me."

"Anyone seeing his performance would never have supported a brutish lout like Essex."

The Queen studied Oxford to make up her mind about the truthfulness of his words.

"I'll speak to Cecil," she said. "Augustine Phillips will be rewarded for his loyalty."

"And what about Shaxper? I can't finish your monument without his help."

"I'll ensure his protection, and in return I'll expect a glorious play. But what about the rest of the Lord Chamberlain's Men? Have I no enemies among them?"

"Not one," Oxford said. "They look upon you as sacred to the Muses. You allowed the English theater to flourish and fostered every aspect of their art. For all of that, you have the allegiance of every actor and playwright in the world."

"That's a monument to both of us," she said.

Gloriana leaned over and kissed Shakespeare for the last time.

CHAPTER TWENTY-TWO

The Scene: Theobalds, Home of Sir Robert Cecil
April 26, 1603
One month after the Queen's death

"Shipwrack'd upon a kingdom, where
No pity, no friends, no hope, no kindred weep
For me . . ."

– Henry VIII

obert Cecil sipped his wine in the privacy of his library and contemplated the Queen's final hours. In a scene worthy of Shake-speare, the defiant monarch had refused to lie down, granting Death a special audience as if it were a foreign ambassador. Propped up and strapped against a mattress, Elizabeth Tudor sucked her thumb, lost in the oblivion of second childhood.

A month ago when it happened, Cecil had done everything right. He had planted himself by her bedside, watching every move and calculating each breath as she lapsed in and out of consciousness. At just the right moment, he had sent the Archbishop away on an official errand.

He wasn't going to take any chances. He had to be alone with the Queen so he could prompt her into naming her successor, and he had to do it without the meddlesome interference of morality to contradict his plans.

For Cecil's part, there was only one man she could choose, but for obvious reasons the name uttered by a senile old woman in the throes of dementia couldn't be trusted. His brain-sick sister Anne had reviled their goodly father with shocking accusations before she died, and thus being mad, nothing she said was dependable. He was determined to prevent any royal rantings from challenging James' impending sovereignty, which he had tirelessly promoted.

His thoughts strayed back to his father. While Death had caused him to forget the pedantic timbre of Lord Burghley's voice, he remembered every aspect of his laudable advice: that powerful men engineered significant events behind the scenes, and that it was best to do so without witnesses. In the early days of his career when the late Queen's bid for the monarchy was endangered by pretenders, Burghley had used that principle to win her the crown.

But since his death, a new age had dawned. Robert Cecil now maneuvered his own political machine using King James as the lever. He had secretly negotiated James' succession in return for lucrative rewards and it was only a matter of time before he could collect. Not even the Queen in the waning hours of her life could subvert his plans. If she said nothing or her words were unintelligible, Cecil would interpret to the world the foregone conclusion.

The more Cecil drank, the more he reveled in his tidy retrospective. He was proud to have surpassed his father by crafting his own special niche. From the moment of the Queen's death until James was notified, if only for a short time, he was in control of England. The poor little hunchback who had accidentally been dropped down the stairs by a careless nurse, and who was scorned and reviled by his enemies, had excelled beyond his father's accomplishments. That was no small achievement. History would memorialize Lord Burghley as a great elder-statesman, but he had edited that history to favor Protestantism and trumpet his own deeds while consigning the efforts of other men to unmarked graves.

Cecil had been asleep in a chair by her bed when the Queen awakened and murmured, "I cannot have that rascal on the throne."

"What rascal, Majesty?" he asked, pressing closer.

"That rascal's son. I cannot have him on the throne."

"What rascal? Tell me his name."

The Queen waved him away as if he were an annoying fly. When she fell silent, he whispered something in her ear about the large annuity she had been paying James to ease her conscience at having executed his mother so long ago.

With the Archbishop out of the room, he asked her the fateful question.

"Majesty, do you plan on naming James as your successor?"

The Queen sucked her thumb and shook her head no.

With his hot breath against her cheek, he rephrased the question.

"Majesty, do you want your Scottish cousin?"

Taking Mary of Scotland's hand at Heaven's Gate, and with her thumb still in her mouth, the Queen nodded yes.

With that, she died.

Cecil let a few moments pass before he let in the Archbishop and the rest of the Queen's counselors. He wanted those few moments alone to savor his triumph. Then, when all were assembled, everyone knelt in prayer as the church bells tolled. While the nation went into mourning, a rider hastened to notify King James, and Cecil circulated his official letter enjoining England's nobles to pledge their allegiance to the Protestant King. A number of Catholics would refuse, he thought, but the rebels would be dealt with accordingly.

The scene had played out with well-timed precision, as if they had been actors on the stage. After that, Cecil's most daunting task involved reviewing the late Queen's documents. In the same orderly manner he had used to scrutinize Walsingham's papers after his death a decade earlier, Cecil arranged for some illiterate servants to collect the late Queen's correspondence and bring it to Theobalds. As James' advisor, he was compelled to sort through every scrap of paper so that no state secrets would fall into the wrong hands. Cecil would decide which letters were personal and which were of significant historical value. Some might even contain current political strategies while others would be candidates for the fire.

At least for now, his most decisive challenge was to finish his wine.

He sighed wearily when he saw the unopened letter at his elbow. On recognizing the handwriting, he found no desire to read it. It had been a busy month, juggling complex responsibilities: first, in securing James' transition, and second, in collecting on the promises James had made him in carving out his place at Court. The last thing he needed was another plaintive letter from Lord Oxford, begging for his intervention on the reversion of an old estate or for granting a coat-of-arms to the aging father of some petty underling.

It rankled Cecil that his former brother-in-law had no idea how lucky he was, living in the peaceful seclusion of the country. If only he would stay there! Oxford was an infirm relic who'd been absent from the Court for so long, he'd forgotten its pernicious back-stabbing. But by virtue of his lineage, his bold defense of James' embattled mother, and his reputation for arranging performances of the Shake-speare plays, James had given him preferment and renewed his mysterious stipend.

Almost instantly, the King and the Earl had become great friends. They shared a taste for music, art and literature that left Cecil cold. The King's new right hand man really wasn't interested in such trivialities.

When he heard that James adored the Shake-speare plays, Oxford firmly cinched their bond by arranging a Court performance of *Robin Goodfellow*. Cecil felt like the dust swept behind the door in the epilogue.

He highly resented being made to feel like a common drone, devoid of the sparkle of popular entertainment.

This new friendship made it much easier for Oxford to re-insert himself into official proceedings. As Lord Great Chamberlain, he was required to serve at the coronation, but since he had so few household servants to number as his attendants, Cecil was sure it would be a humiliating impossibility. Then the Earl made the outrageous move of selecting actors to play those ceremonial parts. Cecil thought it scandalous, but the King was highly amused, especially when he learned how quickly Oxford's secretary had ordered the crimson cloth for their liveries.

Worse yet, the King had instantly accepted Oxford's invitation to stay at his estate in Bath prior to the ceremony, to protect him from the plague that was ravaging London. The monarch's safety had always been a part of Cecil's plan, but he hadn't factored in the stopover at Bath and was furious that the King had been so crudely commandeered.

Cecil wasn't about to relinquish his authority, but he worried that James was already complicating matters by adamantly insisting on bringing his male lovers to Court. They were nothing but a flaming coven of effeminate whores. And worst of all, the traitor Southampton was among the first to receive one of the flurry of pardons with which the new King was littering the countryside. Cecil had to act quickly. His first order of business was to make himself indispensable to the new King and shepherd him through the subtle cultural complexities of England, which were quite different from those in Scotland. James risked inflaming public disapproval by casting himself in the role of usurper (among other defamations). Many were already disgruntled at the mere thought of having a foreigner as their king.

With all of these concerns Cecil had so much to do that it made his head spin. And then there was the letter from his former brother-in-law, who always seemed to re-enter the family whenever he needed a favor.

Cecil wondered what it was this time. He decided to read the melodramatic missive as if it were an entertaining diversion, and so he poured himself more wine, opened the letter and settled back into his chair.

The letter began with Oxford's usual fawning praise, thanking him for his abundant kindnesses and courtesies. Cecil snickered, hard-pressed to know exactly what these were. Despite his brother Thomas' ardent support of Lord Oxford, Robert had successfully barred him from ever receiving the Royal Order of the Garter, a nobleman's highest honor, and he had reveled in that disappointment.

The letter continued:

> *Because of my infirmity, I cannot come among you as often as I wish, and my house is not so near. The other day, I received a letter at nine o'clock telling me not to fail to be at Whitehall at eight the same morning! This being impossible, I hastened to Ludgate to join the royal procession, but through the press of people and horses I could not reach your company as I desired, but followed as I might.*

Why didn't Oxford take the hint? How credulous of him, not to figure out that the letter about Whitehall had been delayed on purpose!

Cecil grimaced every time Oxford mentioned his cursed infirmity caused by the knife wound in his leg because it drew his attention to Cecil's own deformity. Oxford's limp was the consequence of a crime of passion, whereas Cecil's injured back resulted from an accident in infancy. Really, the Earl of Oxford had become a tedious antique.

Cecil sat bolt upright when he came to Lord Oxford's eulogy for the Queen.

> *I am greatly grieved in remembering the mistress we have lost, under whose care you and I from our greenest years were in a manner brought up – and although it has pleased God after an earthly kingdom to take her up into a more permanent and*

heavenly state (wherein I do not doubt that she is crowned with glory) and to give us a Prince that is wise, learned, and enriched with all virtues – yet considering the long time which we spent in her service, we cannot look for so much left of our days as to bestow so much upon another. Neither (as denied by the infirmity of age and common course of reason) are we ever to expect from another Prince the long acquaintance and kind familiarities wherewith she did use us.

In this common shipwreck, mine is above all the rest, who, least regarded (though often comforted) of all her followers, she has left to try my fortune among the alterations of time and chance – without either sail whereby to take the advantage of any prosperous gale, or anchor to ride till the storm be overpast. Therefore, there is nothing left to comfort me but the excellent virtues and deep wisdom wherewith God has endowed our new master and sovereign lord – who does not come among us as a stranger but as a natural Prince, succeeding by right of blood and inheritance, not as a conqueror, but as a true shepherd of Christ's flock to cherish and comfort them.

Wherefore, I most earnestly desire of you this favor, as I have written before, that I may be informed from you concerning those points I earlier mentioned, as to time and place. And thus recommending myself to you, I take my leave, your assured friend and unfortunate brother-in-law,

E. Oxenforde

Grudgingly admitting that Oxford's words had moved him, Cecil looked up and saw the Queen's documents and other belongings filling half of his cellar, awaiting his perusal.

CHAPTER TWENTY-THREE

The Scene: Shaxper's Apartment

May 8, 1603

"Life's but a walking shadow, a poor player."

– Macbeth

S haxper entered his apartment and slammed the door behind him. He tossed his cloak on the bed and ran his fingers through his hair in a gesture of frustration. He walked over to his washbasin and glanced in the mirror. Bruised and battered, he looked like something the landlady's cat had half devoured.

Ben Jonson had infuriated him for the last time. He was never going drinking with him again. He had no further wish to waste his time sitting in the Boar's Head watching a curmudgeonly pack of writers and actors knock back drinks while he paid the bill.

Those boorish bastards had tricked him. Jonson had it all figured out, when he had leapt onto the table, waved his arms and shouted at the top of his voice, "Gentlemen, I have a demand. Since our inscrutable Master Shake-scene is now the most highly-paid playwright in England

and several of his comedies have already been published, it's high time the upstart crow rewarded us for our friendship by buying drinks for everyone in the house!"

Customers banged on the tables and catcalled their approval.

"He can afford it," Philip Henslowe said. "He's a proper businessman now, owns ten percent of The Globe, and his plays are in constant repertory. I know, I keep very detailed records." The theater manager proudly waved his ledger as proof.

"And he owns several homes in Stratford," Drayton shouted, "not bad for an entrepreneur who sells loads of grain back home."

"He sold 'em a load of something," Jonson muttered.

"Maybe he'll show some civic pride and pay his delinquent taxes," writer Thomas Dekker called out. "And let's not forget his unpaid tithes."

"*He* seems to have forgotten 'em!" Jonson bellowed.

"I like his jewelry," William Slye said, reprising his foppish role as Osric in *Hamlet*. Comedians Robert Armin and William Kemp linked arms and danced after him. The pub erupted into laughter.

William Shaxper rubbed his head and wondered what he was doing surrounded by these lowlifes.

"Well?" Dekker asked. "Are you buying us drinks or not?"

The crowd grew silent. Everyone stared at Shaxper, including Augustine Phillips, now a fellow shareholder in The Globe, who had no idea what the ruckus was about. Ben Jonson wore a supercilious grin that Shaxper desperately wanted to knock off his face. The impostor clenched his fists and struggled to control his temper. He had no choice but to buy drinks for everyone, now that he'd been called out. He tossed a purse to the barkeep as the crowd cheered.

Disgusted with the extortion, Shaxper sat down in a shadowy corner of the pub. When he got his wine, he proceeded to water it down. He was angry at the whole wretched lot, and wished that between player and playwright, they'd all drop dead on the spot. He didn't like being challenged in the light of day, which had happened recently when the students at Cambridge parodied him in their Parnassus plays. The young writers and actors had been merciless in their satire of him as an inarticulate fool who stole his words from a true poet.

Perhaps he'd played the impostor for so long, his role had become transparent.

"Gentlemen," Jonson bellowed, from a bench this time. "Let's raise a tankard to our new King James in gratitude for his love of the theater."

Tankards collided as everyone stood and chorused the toast.

"And," he said reverently, "let's toast our late beloved Queen who fostered the plays and playwrights as if she were our mother. And to the Old Player, who fathered England's great passion for the stage."

"To our late beloved Queen . . . and to the Old Player . . . mother and father of England's playhouses."

Everyone toasted, except Shaxper.

"What's the matter with you?" Jonson asked angrily, walking over to confront his rival. "You're supposed to be England's greatest playwright and you haven't written one single word of tribute to our late departed Queen, who made all of your success possible."

"Yes, why haven't you written her a tribute?" Drayton echoed. "It's the least you could do, since she's favored your work so highly."

"I – I don't know how to put my gratitude into words," Shaxper said.

"God's blood!" Henslowe laughed, slamming down his tankard. "I have a whole diary of the plays you've written. Don't tell me you're at a loss for words."

"Well, I am, at the moment anyway. I feel somewhat ill. I must be getting home."

"What's your next play going to be?" Augustine Phillips innocently asked. Everyone leaned forward. Shaxper felt his tongue stick to the roof of his mouth.

"Yes," Jonson asked, with a wicked grin. "What is your next play going to be, Shaxper? Some saucy little comedy, or a woefully incontinent tragedy? Or perhaps you've got one where the protagonist dies as a pretender, impaled on his master's pen?"

"I've had no thoughts --"

"What? The great bard with no thoughts? Tell me, how is that possible?"

"I don't know what my next play will be. I shall have to think about it."

"You'll have to do more than *think* about it. You'll actually have to put something down on paper – unless, of course, you pay someone else to write plays for you."

Everyone laughed. Jonson smirked and started to walk away.

"That's enough!" Shaxper shouted, jumping to his feet. He grabbed the hefty playwright by the arm, and to everyone's surprise, spun him around. "I don't normally lose my temper in public places like this, but you've pushed me too far!"

"Aw, are you going to strike me, you dainty little milquetoast? Fie, I'll break you in half!"

"I'm warning you, Jonson, stop spreading rumors about me!"

"What rumors? It's all true. I served as your errand boy, remember? I know all your dirty little secrets, you bloody opportunist!"

"I'm performing a valuable service —"

"That's just what the whore said to the constable."

"Shut up! You don't know what you're talking about. You're causing a public scandal and endangering the life of a man who's actually very dear to your heart. You don't know the truth."

"Truth tells me you're not a playwright," Jonson growled. "You might be able to fool the groundlings, but every man-jack in this room knows what you really are."

The impostor's fist sent Jonson reeling. Benches scraped across the floor as men cleared out of the way. Jonson lunged at Shaxper and the fight continued on the floorboards.

Shaxper wasn't exactly sure when the Earl of Oxford had arrived. Henslowe, Drayton and several others broke up the fight, and within minutes, the impostor and Jonson found themselves nursing their wounds at the shadowy table. Except for the barkeep, Oxford and the stranger sitting next to him, the others had disappeared into the night.

"Don't expect me to pay damages this time," Oxford warned. "Which one of you started it?"

"Shaxper did," Jonson said, as he cupped his injured jaw. Oxford turned to his scribe, whose bruised face and torn doublet spoke of his desperation.

"Is that true, Will? Did you strike the first blow?"

"Not without right," Shaxper said, his head throbbing. "He threatened me."

"I'll call an end to our association here and now, Ben, if you don't stop humiliating Will in public," Oxford said. "He has committed no wrong against me nor harmed me in any way. My word on that should be enough to convince you."

"It is, my lord. I'm sorry. It won't happen again."

"And Will, you seem to have forgotten everything I've taught you. Don't let yourself be antagonized into a common brawl. You can't afford to lose your temper. You never know who's watching."

"Yes, my lord."

"Besides, what would George Bucke think, if the poet and playwright came to blows?"

"Who the hell is George Bucke and why should we care?" Jonson asked.

"Gentlemen," Oxford said, "and I use that word with great hope for the future, this is my friend George Bucke from Hedingham. I know you're going to care very much what he thinks because King James has appointed him Master of the Revels, in charge of all performances."

"Master of the Revels," Jonson whispered, reverently.

"It's a pleasure, sir," Shaxper said, regaining his composure.

"I'm afraid I've got some bad news about *Sejanus,*" Bucke told Jonson. "The official censor is deeply concerned about your play and you can expect to be called in for questioning by the Privy Council within the next few days."

"God help me, I don't want to go to prison over another play, my lord," Jonson moaned.

"My friendship with the King will keep you out of prison," Oxford said. "His Majesty generally likes your plays but he doesn't know you yet. I can arrange an introduction, but in the meantime, your testimony before the Privy Council cannot be avoided. Remember that if anyone else is implicated in the authorship, it may become impossible to protect you."

"Who else could be implicated?" Shaxper asked, wondering what secrets Oxford and Jonson shared.

"*Sejanus* is a very intense play," Bucke continued. "You've written very forcefully about political corruption, but as far as the King is concerned, your timing is dreadful. You must tread softly before this new regime, sir, and remember that royal support can be shaped to serve you quite well."

"We can't afford trouble right now," Oxford said. "Remember what happened with *Richard II.* Our actors were pursued all over England with warrants for their arrests and the entire company was in danger. The political implications of that deposition scene were obvious. Anyone with a brain could have seen them, except for Essex and that rascal Southampton. It's the perfect example of why a man can't serve two masters at once."

"Henslowe must be careful, too," Bucke advised Shaxper. "If he's unsure of any play you give him, tell him to return it. I'll remove any details that could be considered treasonous."

"Bucke is doing this as a favor to me," Oxford said. "I wish I could have offered such protection to Kyd, Marlowe, Greene and Watson."

"So I'm the sacrificial lamb to be roasted before the Privy Council," Jonson sighed. "I'm sure I'll prove quite leathery for their tastes."

Shaxper considered the double meaning, and wondered how he himself would be served.

It had been a night of gross humiliation. Shaxper vowed he would never let himself be put in the position of repeating it. Back home in his private rooms, he dabbed his wounds with a wet cloth. He carried the towel to bed with him and fell asleep.

In the morning, a hazy inspiration filled his mind. He sat down at his writing desk and dipped his quill in the inkwell. After all, he was posing as England's greatest playwright, and it was high time he published a tender tribute to the late Queen who had furthered his career, without so much as speaking to him or looking in his direction.

For several years now, he'd been paid to write epitaphs for some of the better tombstones around Warwickshire. He had turned this morbid versifying into a petty sideline. John Coombes had paid in advance, and it made sense for his customers to do so. Still, though he'd never see a penny from writing anything for the late Queen, it seemed she deserved a decent but modest eulogy, and everyone expected it from him. And so he began.

> *This Queen, who lived and died, judge not,*
> *Her bones within the earth do rot —*

No, not right. The image of moldering bones, could that possibly be a bit treasonous? He didn't know. He blotted the line and tried again.

> *This Queen, who lived and died, judge not,*
> *For she shall never be forgot*

Yes, of course, because no one likes to be forgotten, even a Queen . . .

This Queen, who lived and died, judge not,
For she shall never be forgot
While we her subjects memory have,
For she did sometimes mourn and sometimes laugh,

That was terrible! He crossed out the last line but it still wasn't right. He stood up, rolled up his sleeves and began pacing nervously, muttering the poem to himself as if it were a plea to the Muses. Surely they were laughing at him! He rewrote the last sentence three times before deciding to keep it, for lack of anything better.

This Queen, who lived and died, judge not,
For she shall never be forgot
While we her subjects memory have,
For she did sometimes mourn and sometimes laugh,
Thus she did reap her memory to be good
As God, he knows, 'twas well she should.

Damn, something still wasn't right. Where was the divine quintessence? Where was that ethereal spark that spawned poetry in the human soul? He couldn't find it anywhere. Inspiration eluded him. Why was it that Lord Oxford could touch the face of God, but Shaxper's reach wasn't long enough? He tried again.

This Queen, who lived and died, judge not,
For she shall never be forgot
While we her subjects memory have,
For she did sometimes mourn and sometimes laugh,
Thus she did reap her memory to be good
As God, he knows, 'twas well she should.
Our wretched Queen is gone away
How much our lamentations say!

In the name of God, all say amen
And ne'er her like we'll see again.

Shaxper read the epitaph several times and shook his head. Something was missing, but he didn't know what it was. Could a poem be filled with pathos and also be pathetic at the same time? He didn't think so, but this one certainly seemed as if it could. He ran through his alphabet of rhymes as if rummaging through his poetic wardrobe, but nothing seemed to fit. Furious with his fumbling thoughts, he crumpled the paper, tossed it aside and went back to bed.

CHAPTER TWENTY-FOUR

The Scene: Robert Cecil's estate at Theobalds

June 24, 1604

"They smile at me who shortly shall be dead."

– Richard III

ecil discovered the poems by accident among the late Queen's personal effects. Her most intimate trophies were a cache of romantic sonnets written by the Earl of Oxford, collected over an astonishing period of forty years.

He lingered over the verses like a voyeur at a keyhole and was amazed to learn that their stormy liaison had spanned the course of his sister's marriage. When Cecil realized that his father had turned a blind eye to the affair and had even encouraged it, he felt the depths of Anne's sorrow mingling with his own.

Cecil also found a curious stack of personal letters concerning young Henry Wriothesley, Earl of Southampton, covering everything from his education as a royal ward to his marriage prospects. He read with keen interest. He had always argued for Southampton's execution because of his role in the Essex Rebellion, but the late Queen had refused to listen. He couldn't understand why she spared a man who meant nothing to her while beheading her young paramour Essex. After the Queen's death, Southampton had been reprieved, and he had joined the assortment of male lovers that inhabited King James' bedchamber. He was usually given the honor of escorting Queen Anne at various official occasions. To Cecil, the fact that Southampton had escaped execution seemed nothing short of miraculous luck.

On the bottom of the stack, Cecil found a dog-eared unsigned letter. The handwriting looked familiar, but he couldn't quite place whose it was. Still, the message drew him to his feet.

> Blame me not, for it is with the boundless measure of my ardor that I swear to you this day, that if any infliction, mischief, danger or death befall me, the news of our sanctified secret marriage and our changeling child will be revealed to the world; that all may know him for your successor in this Majesty and know that you have forsworn our sacred and legal union without regard for the feelings of our son. Thus I do secure myself in the comfort and safety, to which, in the ameliorate times of our contentment you most lovingly and earnestly succored for me.

His heart beat wildly at this scandalous threat. If it was true, somewhere in England lurked the Queen's living heir, the man with the closest claim to the throne, and most likely he would be amassing an army to overthrow James' weaker claim. And if the new King fell, king-maker Cecil would fall with him.

Cecil needed an immediate answer. His father had always found answers in random quotations from the Bible, and from across the room, the Queen's gilded volume of the Holy Scriptures seemed to beckon him.

Cecil stood in front of it and placed his hands on the cover. He closed his eyes and reverently posed his question to the oracle of God. Slowly he opened the tome, and the pages readily parted. Tucked beside Nathan's parable about King David's theft of the poor man's beloved lamb was the Last Will and Testament of the Earl of Oxford, written in his unmistakable hand.

Cecil shoved the document aside as meaningless. Again he closed the Bible and anxiously rephrased his query. Three more times, God mocked his burgeoning fear by showing him irrelevant phrases. He nervously glanced around the room and his eyes distractedly fell on the will lying beside his clenched fist. In a flash of insight, he recognized the handwriting and saw that it matched the unsigned letter. Unfolding Lord Oxford's will, Cecil perused it quickly and a familiar name caught his attention.

He felt faint when he read that Henry Wriothesley, Earl of Southampton, was Oxford's son delivered of Elizabeth Tudor, the late Queen, and was stunned to learn that they had entered into a secret marriage for the purpose of breeding a legitimate royal heir.

Cecil instantly felt his father's calculating mind in that scheme. For a moment, he also wondered if the efficacious old man could engineer events from the grave. Lord Burghley had never imagined that his son Robert might one day secure the throne for James. Thus, thirty years earlier, he had contrived to breed a successor while preserving the Queen's virgin image. No wonder she had refused every suitor with the excuse that she was married to England! The immorality of the scheme outlined in the seditious document showed a clear belief that the end justified the means, another of his father's guiding principles.

The idea of Southampton ruling England made Cecil sick to his stomach. Oxford and his unholy spawn were dangerous threats to his plans. One could indeed smile and smile and be a villain. Suppose they smiled like crocodiles while planning to kill King James, and staged a revolution like those in Shake-speare's plays where audiences could see that bloody battles over the crown were standard practice in England's history. If Oxford used the playhouses to spread his message and promote his son's claim, he could easily sway public opinion and urge the commoners to fight for his cause, just as he had urged them to rally and fight against Spain.

Southampton had tried to use *Richard II* for that same purpose during the Essex Rebellion, hoping to arouse the commoners with that evil play and its treasonous Deposition Scene.

Sir Robert Cecil had to find Oxford's own copy of his Last Will and Testament immediately or face the terrible consequences of governmental insurrection. Knowing Oxford as well as he did, he realized he would have to take it by force.

CHAPTER TWENTY-FIVE

The Scene: Oxford's home at King's Place

June 24, 1604

"Such novel scenes as draw the eye to flow we now present."

— Henry VIII

S ince 1470, Lord Oxford's house at King's Place had kept a watchful eye on strangers, protecting its owners behind conspiratorial walls that framed an inner courtyard. Secret doors and hidden passages designed by its earliest builders led to tunnels that terminated in the distant fields. As it happened, Lord Oxford's friend and fellow poet Lord Vaux, the previous owner, had used the underground avenues to help persecuted Jesuits escape the clutches of fanatical Protestant reformers.

Keenly aware of protecting his own secrets, the Earl of Oxford lay in bed with his leg painfully throbbing, and his mind filled with unfinished verses. He energized his hands by rubbing his palms together and remembered the first time he had ever held a pen. He had used a quill as a childhood toy, spiraling his inky thoughts on paper long before he had been schooled in language and literature. These days, his head swam with words and he found it impossible for his hands to keep pace with the rapid fire of his thoughts.

Scattered on his bed lay several scenes from the revision of *Henry VIII* he had promised the Queen before she died. He was in the middle of dictating it to Shaxper. He no longer left the house very often, except to go to the theaters or visit the King when summoned, but today his aching leg forced him to stay in bed even though he resented being shut in on a beautiful mid-summer afternoon. Shaxper had been expected hours ago to help him continue revising the play that he wanted to fashion into his greatest work, but for some reason he was late again. Unfortunately, this was becoming a tedious habit.

Ever since the name Shake-speare had come to signify quality in the minds of theater-going audiences, their working relationship had deteriorated. Oxford had noticed the condescending way Shaxper regarded his audiences, as if he were performing a public service by nodding in their direction. He mimicked the same haughty condescension the late Queen had shown him, as if that was proper etiquette for all social situations. Shaxper always had a problem that stemmed from confusing illusion with reality, perhaps the very quality that made him such a good impostor.

Beyond that, since the theaters demanded a steady supply of plays, Shaxper had become the master under the terms of their ruse. Oxford had evolved into *his* obedient servant, and he could do nothing to change the bitter arrangement.

He cast his anger aside when his eyes fell on a sonnet lying on his bed linen. He picked it up and remembered having written it to his royal mistress shortly after her death.

> *The dear repose for limbs with travel tired,*
> *But then begins a journey in my head*
> *To work my mind, when body's work's expired;*

For there my thoughts (from far where I abide)
Intend a zealous pilgrimage to thee,
And keep my drooping eyelids open wide,
Looking on darkness which the blind do see;
Save that my soul's imaginary sight
Presents thy shadow to my sightless view,
Which, like a jewel hung in ghastly night,
Makes black night beauteous, and her old face new.
Lo, thus by day my limbs, by night my mind
For thee, and for myself, no quiet find.

Since the Queen's death, he hadn't sought peace or quiet, but those qualities had found him in the gentle rhythms of country life and the calm serenity of his second marriage. He cherished his devoted wife Elizabeth, who had nurtured him and his work when so many others, many of them his family and closest friends, had abandoned him. Some of their exits had been so gradual that he had barely noticed them. Others, like the untimely deaths of Marlowe, Greene, Kyd and Watson had been excruciatingly painful.

For a moment he wondered if *he* had abandoned others, including his children, by closeting himself to write impassioned speeches that the Queen had forbidden him to claim. They would never know or understand the true nature of his words and actions, or why he had spent his fortune seeing other men's lands, showing them to others in the wooden cockpits of the playhouses.

The Queen had abandoned him in death, but with all his senses he longed for her again: the regal countenance, the long, tapered fingers, the fragrant scent of roses in her hair, the passionate taste of her lips, the lilting laughter that was so often overshadowed by the dark tones of her discontent. He had known her since childhood and had fallen prey to her seduction, only to be scorned as her husband and the father of their son. He recounted the secrets they shared that lay buried with her, and felt that his own pockets would be so heavily laden with them that upon his death, his coffin would be a difficult burden for his pallbearers.

Like a character in one of his plays, he realized that the time and setting of his life had changed. New actors had taken the stage now that the Queen was dead and King James of Scotland was her successor. Commoners had overtaken the nobility, forging new riches and titles for themselves while the older and more illustrious families endured the fading of their fortunes. Lord Oxford was no longer summoned to Court on matters of national importance, even though King James held him in the highest regard.

Lord Oxford's secret service to the state had also ended. The incessant and harrowing demands for his history plays and the gallant speeches that had inspired audiences in the days of war had passed. While the provocative histories were less often produced in the public playhouses to avoid inflaming audiences against the new King (whom many considered to be a foreign usurper) Shaxper made sure that the more popular comedies were regularly shown. Over the years, Lord Oxford had watched the keen entrepreneur grow into the role of Shake-speare. He still supplied him with plays, now that writing was no longer a matter of life and death.

And just the other day, King James had requested Lord Oxford's notable talent as a translator in assisting with a new English version of the Bible.

Lord Oxford sighed deeply, and considered the one thing about his life that he would ask God to change, if such an editing miracle were possible. He would show more mercy and less arrogance towards his first wife Anne, the silent victim of unimaginable cruelty.

A servant knocked on the door and timidly poked his head into the room.

"Master Shaxper has arrived, my lord," he announced. "He says to tell you that he regrets his lateness and wonders if you still wish to see him."

"Of course I wish to see him," Oxford said, infuriated by the impostor's need to send this grandiloquent announcement through one of the servants. "Tell him to come in. We've got lots of work ahead of us."

The man nodded, and within seconds Shaxper appeared with his secretarial portfolio, blustering as if he'd gone to great lengths to attend this meeting.

"It's about time you came, peacock," Oxford said. "You were supposed to have been here hours ago. What happened?"

"I was detained at the theater. Henslowe needed help with some discrepancies in the accounts."

Oxford waited for an apology. Shaxper seemed casually unwilling to offer one. After eighteen years, he felt too secure in his position to bother, and chose instead to remind the poet about his poor health.

"I trust your leg feels better today, my lord."

"It doesn't. But everything will improve as soon as you move that bottle of sack closer and pour me some. Has Henslowe given the play to the actors?"

"Yes," Shaxper said, pouring the drink. "He's assembled a fine cast for *Henry VIII*. He's even promised me a part, but you haven't written it yet."

"Really? How would he cast you?"

"As Cardinal Wolsey's executioner. Henslowe said he thought it would be a rather considerable part, since the play is about Henry VIII."

"You should have consulted your history book," Oxford laughed. "Wolsey was never beheaded. He died on the way to the block and cheated the executioner."

"Is that true?"

"Yes. Henslowe must have been jesting."

"But you could write in a headsman, my lord. It wouldn't be the first time you've stretched historical truth to fit theatrical purposes."

"I've never stretched the truth *that* far," Oxford snarled. "Still, I suppose I could write a few lines about a headsman mourning the loss of a head he's been cheated of chopping off. But let's get to work. Pull up a chair and we'll start with Wolsey's soliloquy."

Shaxper opened his portfolio and arranged his pen, ink and papers on the table, ready to take dictation. Lord Oxford closed his eyes and offered the speech as it would play on stage.

WOLSEY

So farewell to the little good you bear me.
Farewell? A long farewell to all my greatness!
This is the state of man: today he puts forth
The tender leaves of hopes; tomorrow blossoms
And bears his blushing honors thick upon him;
The third day comes a frost, a killing frost,
And when he thinks, good easy man, full surely
His greatness is a-ripening, nips his root,
And then he falls as I do. I have ventured,
Like little wanton boys that swim on bladders,
This many summers in a sea of glory,
But far beyond my depth. My high-blown pride
At length broke under me, and now has left me,
Weary and old with service, to the mercy
Of a rude stream that must forever hide me.
Vain pomp and glory of this world, I hate ye!
I feel my heart new opened. O, how wretched
Is that poor man that hangs on princes' favors!
There is betwixt that smile we would aspire to,
That sweet aspect of princes, and their ruin,
More pangs and fears than wars or women have;

And when he falls, he falls like Lucifer,
Never to hope again.

"And then the stage directions should say that Shaxper enters, stand-ing amazed."

"Pardon, my lord. That can't be correct. You've made an error."

"Did I? What error?"

Oxford snatched the soliloquy from the table. In the speech, he had paraphrased the tribute Giles Fletcher had once written to him: *Thy valor puts forth leaves and begins to bear early fruit, and glory already ripens in thy earliest deeds.* So much for brave deeds of the past that were long ago forgotten.

"Where's the error? I can't find it. Show me where it is," he said impatiently, thrusting the papers at the scribe.

"It's in the stage directions," Shaxper said, calmly pointing to the mis-take. "I believe you intended for Cromwell to enter, but you said my name."

Oxford reread the papers and handed them back to the scribe.

"The entrance is Cromwell's," he agreed, "but make sure you say he stands amazed."

"Done," Shaxper said, blotting the line.

They worked for several hours until Oxford fell asleep. As Shaxper continued on his own to create a fair copy of the new material, a cool breeze blew in from the window, calling his attention outside to Countess Elizabeth, who was gathering flowers in the garden. He set down his pen and watched her. He had never seen a woman with such beautiful hair, the color of luminescent honey. She was graceful and very sophisticated, a complete contrast to Oxford's first wife, who had never outgrown her childish awkwardness.

From the first day she had entered his life after her marriage to Lord Oxford, Shaxper realized that he also loved her. That made him wish his role as an impostor included conjugal rights. Whenever he came to the house, he listened for her voice; and whenever she spoke his name, his heart flew into his throat. He decided it wasn't a good idea to arrive late for work anymore, since it deprived him of these secret stolen moments. Countess Elizabeth had no idea how he felt. He had to be careful not to betray his feelings to anyone. It wouldn't do to arouse Lord Oxford's notorious temper. Maybe the Earl wasn't as ill as he looked. Maybe he was strong enough to stab someone to death, just for having impure thoughts about his wife.

Still, Shaxper wondered what his life would have been like if he had wed such a fine lady as Countess Elizabeth instead of that bovine peasant to whom he was hopelessly tied.

"What are you staring at?" Oxford snapped on awakening.

"N-nothing. I just thought I'd get some fresh air," the scribe said, nervously apologetic as he moved away from the window.

"You don't look well. Your face is flushed."

"Is it?"

"Yes. Look in the glass. You're as red-faced as Bardolph."

Shaxper looked in the mirror and turned his head from side to side.

"I don't see anything," he said.

"That's not good. Perhaps you've lost *your* head."

"Very funny, my lord, a little humor at my expense." Shaxper glanced out the window again, but the Countess had gone. His heart sank.

"Tell me, what do you think of poor Cardinal Wolsey?" Oxford asked.

"What should I think of him?"

"Pity him, for God's sake. He dies simply because he fell out of favor with the King. Aren't you afraid of that?"

"Why should I be? My position as a playwright is very secure."

"That's what Marlowe used to say. And so did the others."

"Well, thank God I have you to protect me, my lord."

"Don't thank the Almighty yet. Lord Strange was poisoned for writing plays and the same thing could happen to me."

"What are you saying? That if we fall out of favor in the new regime, we could be murdered?"

"It's possible, especially with Cecil's passion for keeping score. Take it from me, I've lived in the shadow of the executioner's axe all my life. Meanwhile, the tides have changed and we're no longer in safe waters. It's essential for you to beware of hidden dangers."

"God's blood! Are we to be next?"

"I don't know. But ever since the Queen's death, I've felt as if the world holds nothing more for me," he sighed. "And that's a dangerous sentiment."

"Now wait just a minute," Shaxper said. "This world is all I have. It suits me, and I'll fiercely defend my right to stay in it."

"You may well need to do that. I'm only trying to warn you, in case we become separated for some reason and you find yourself on your own."

"Thank you, my lord, but I have no intention of separating from you."

"Spoken like a true parasite."

"Shall we finish now, my lord?" Shaxper said, with an edge in his voice.

As Oxford was about to speak, there was a gentle knock on the door and Countess Elizabeth entered with a vase of flowers. She placed it on the writing table and sat down on her husband's bed. Shaxper stepped back into the corner.

"Good evening, Master Shaxper," she said. "And how are you feeling tonight, my dear husband?"

"Better," the Earl said. "But I won't be dancing any time soon."

"There's plenty of time for dancing once you've recovered. But if you're going to be a wallflower, I'll plant myself by your side."

"I'll just step out into the hall and leave you two alone," Shaxper muttered.

"Don't go too far," Oxford cautioned. "We still have to finish your headsman scene. But whatever you do, don't linger at the keyhole!"

Shaxper blushed and closed the door.

"Try to be more patient with him, Edward," the Countess said. "He's a simple man with good intentions."

"Nonsense, he's an ass! He's worked so hard all these years to convince everyone that he's Shake-speare, and now he's come to believe it himself. And do you know what? Sometimes, I'm not so sure he isn't!"

"It sounds like you deserve each other," the Countess laughed.

"He's got his eyes on you, and he thinks I don't know it."

"Well, he can put his eyes right back in his head. I only have one subscriber this season, and it's you. *Amans uxor inviolata semper amanda* – a loving wife that never violated her faith is always to be beloved."

"You are my beloved treasure," he said, taking her in his arms.

In the hallway, Shaxper grumbled. For a few minutes, he couldn't hear a thing until the Countess broke the silence.

"Master Shaxper arrived quite late again this afternoon, didn't he?"

"Yes. He's arriving later all the time."

Again, Shaxper resolved to be more punctual.

"I think it might be a good idea for him to stay the night, now that he's here," the Countess suggested. "That way you could begin early tomorrow. And if you have only a little to do, you can finish and send him away early after dinner."

"That's a splendid idea."

"Shall I make the invitation?"

"No," Oxford said, firmly. "The way he feels about you, he'll take it the wrong way. It'll sound more businesslike coming from me."

"Very well, dear," the Countess said. "But when you finish, you'll put this play behind you and we'll go to the house in Bath, just as you promised."

"Yes. Just as I promised."

Shaxper bowed as the Countess walked by, and when she was gone, he entered the room. He gathered up his papers and awaited Lord Oxford's generous invitation.

CHAPTER TWENTY-SIX

The Scene: King's Place
June 24, 1604 a few hours later

Whoever hath her wish, thou hast thy 'Will'
— Sonnet 135

haxper was awakened from his dream by a distant noise. He lay
in bed, listening to the dull thud of horse's hooves pounding
against the dusty road. He stumbled to the window and saw a
cloud of dust hovering in the night air. Beneath the full moon, he saw
royal soldiers in uniform riding towards King's Place.

There was no time for anyone in Oxford's household to react. The
soldiers leapt off their horses and pounded on the heavy oak door. They
forced their way inside with a battering ram, shouting and waving
torches as they rummaged through the house.

At the top of the hallway, Shaxper cowered behind his bedroom
door. Cracking it open, he saw the captain confront Countess Elizabeth
downstairs. He grabbed her by the wrist and she slapped him in the
face. The captain stiffened angrily, surprised by her boldness. One of

the servants rushed forward to rescue her, but he was beaten to the floor.

Shaxper wanted to run to her defense, but he could not move. The shouts of the soldiers grew louder as they ransacked the house, overturning furniture, slicing tapestries and scattering the books in Lord Oxford's library.

Shaxper saw the Countess struggle free from her attacker.

"This is an outrage!" she cried. "We've done nothing wrong."

"We've been ordered to seize your husband's private papers. Where is His Lordship?"

"Upstairs. He's in bed. I pray you, don't disturb him. His health is not good."

"It will save your house a great deal of wreckage if you tell us where to find his papers. We've been ordered in the name of King James to seize them."

Shaxper did not hear the Countess' reply. The captain pushed her aside and ordered his men to search upstairs. Shaxper hurried into Oxford's room. The Earl was awake and sitting up in bed.

"What is this riot?" he asked. "Has the King declared war?"

"He's declared war on *you*, my lord," Shaxper said, breathlessly. "They've come for your papers."

"I'll take care of that. You mustn't be found here, Will. Get out, while you can!"

Before Shaxper realized what was happening, Oxford shoved him through a secret panel in the wall. Suddenly, he found himself engulfed in darkness. In all his years with Oxford, Shaxper had never known this passageway existed, most likely the legacy of Lord Vaux.

He heard the sound of heavy boots on the stairs. Shaxper fumbled and leaned forward in the direction of the noise, touching his palms gently to the wall and parting it slightly.

Through the crack, he saw Lord Oxford quickly place the ebony box with his papers behind a panel across the room. He armed himself with a dagger and slid back into bed.

Suddenly, the soldiers burst into the room. They ignored Oxford's protests and began opening doors and rummaging through closets and trunks. They scattered his clothing and papers, and ripped apart the manuscript he and Shaxper had been working on that afternoon.

With a fierce cry, Lord Oxford leapt from the bed with his dagger poised to strike. His eyes blazed, the need for self-defense overruling the pain in his leg.

A young soldier wrenched the dagger from Lord Oxford's hand. It crashed to the floor as he was forced back onto the bed. A second soldier grabbed Oxford's injured leg until the Earl howled like a wounded animal. Still fighting, Oxford rolled onto his back, and with his good leg, kicked one of the soldiers against the opposite wall. The man struck a second hidden panel and the wall opened slowly with a casual ironic squeak. A soldier seized the ebony box that Oxford had hidden and handed it to the captain.

"Get out of my house!" Oxford roared. "Do you know who I am?"

"We know who you *were*, Lord Oxford," said the captain, in a low, threatening voice. He proclaimed that the papers were now the property of King James; and with a sinister glance, he removed a slender vial from his pocket and said it was a gift from Sir Robert Cecil.

Two soldiers held Lord Oxford while the captain poured the poison down his throat. With ghoulish fascination, they all stepped back and watched as Oxford coughed and sputtered. His breath stalled as his eyes grew wide and glazed over. As he stopped moving, an eerie stillness filled the room. Shaxper heard the empty vial roll across the floor.

"Won't the coroner call it murder?" someone asked.

"The official word is that Lord Oxford has died of the plague," the captain replied.

Covered in the darkness, Shaxper continued to listen until he heard the soldiers ride away. After what seemed an eternity, he crept out from behind the wall and walked over to the bed. Lord Oxford's unfocused gaze fell upon him. He reached up, said a prayer and gently closed his master's eyes.

His attention was suddenly drawn to Countess Elizabeth. She was downstairs, weeping, which made him think that she too had been hurt. He moved towards the door, but then stopped and surveyed Oxford's room. He didn't know how to tell the Countess that her beloved husband had been murdered in his own bed. He wanted to take her in his arms and comfort her with stories of her husband's final bravery; but he knew she would only ask him why he had cowered behind the wall and done nothing.

He had no good answer.

A shaft of moonlight broke through the window, drawing his attention to the manuscripts strewn across the floor.

His thoughts of consolation were eclipsed by his need to run. He greedily gathered up the papers, setting aside his concern for Countess Elizabeth. His mind was overwhelmed, swarming with calculations of the precise monetary value of the plays, particularly *Henry VIII,* even though the headsman's scene was still unwritten. With all his heart, he longed to play that role.

Then it struck him that there would be no more Shakespeare plays. How would he earn his living now? Could he return to Stratford and carry on as if nothing had happened?

Perhaps *he* could hire someone to write plays. He knew many playwrights, but none of them particularly liked him. And when the news of Lord Oxford's death spread, they would all write tributes to him as the great Shakespeare. Shaxper would become a non-entity, reduced to the impostor that Ben Jonson had ridiculed.

He quickly reminded himself that he was a businessman, owning a ten percent share in The Globe. He was sure that the theater owners and publishers wouldn't care *who* finished the plays, as long as Shakespeare's name appeared on them. In that case, he could still collect his share of the receipts and his stock in the remaining plays for the future. He could copy out the plays and sell them as his own, just like before; or better yet, hire a lean and hungry youth to do it and sell the fair copies at a tidy profit.

Inspired by this vision, he returned to his room and gathered up the fair copy. Then he went to his master's chamber and stuffed his portfolio with whatever papers he could find. He glanced at Lord Oxford for the last time. A final peace had descended upon the Earl, a calm he had never known in life. Shaxper crossed himself and said another prayer.

Then he slipped down the back staircase and out the door. He caught sight of Countess Elizabeth through the window, holding a candle as she entered her husband's bedchamber.

The moon exited behind a cloud.

CHAPTER TWENTY-SEVEN

The Scenes: Theobalds, The Royal Palace and The Tower
Early morning June 25, 1604

"A king, but by fair sequence and succession?"
— Richard II

Cecil listened stoically to the reports of Lord Oxford's death. He dismissed his soldiers and turned his attention to his former brother-in-law's personal papers.

At first, the boar-shaped lock on the ebony box resisted his attempts to open it. He used his dagger to pry it apart, and when the lid finally yielded, he rummaged through the miscellany in search of the treasonous document.

He found the Earl's last will among several love poems written by Lady Vavasor and plaintive, placating letters from his sister Anne, Oxford's first wife. A gold ring inlaid with ivory and onyx rested on the bottom of the box wrapped in silk, enclosed with a note from the Queen. Cecil quickly pocketed the ring.

With wanton disregard, he broke the seal and read the will. He found its terms very clear. On Oxford's death, his eleven-year old son Henry became 18th Earl of Oxford, inheriting all the titles, lands and rights appertaining thereunto. Countess Elizabeth received a generous share for herself and a special portion towards their son's education. A tidy sum went to Oxford's illegitimate son Edward, and equal portions were divided among the Earl's daughters Elizabeth, Bridget and Susan. Small sums were left to family members, servants and retainers. Oxford's extensive library was parceled out to friends, and a unique bequest of £50 was left to "my dumb man," whose name was known only to Oxford's executors.

Struck by the document's sheer irrelevance, Cecil turned it over and searched frantically for at least one reference to Henry Wriothesley, Earl of Southampton. He dug through the papers like a hound, looking for a forgotten codicil or a brief note stating his intentions. Instead, he was mocked by the sentimental letters composed by Oxford's women, his daft sister's maudlin poems among them.

He slammed the box on the table. Clearly, Oxford had written a will to supersede the older one, and he could find no evidence Southampton had any place in it or knew anything about it.

Suddenly, the weight of his violent raid on Oxford's household struck him. In killing Lord Oxford, Cecil had also killed Shakespeare. He had murdered the father of his beloved nieces, the girls he'd been charged to protect. Susan, the youngest, was still in his care and Cecil had yet to arrange a suitable marriage for her. How would she react if she learned that her uncle had ordered her father's assassination?

And how, Cecil wondered, could he possibly explain to King James that he had ordered his friend's assassination, when Oxford was the author of the Shake-speare plays the King loved so dearly?

As for Southampton, he had already received a number of pardons, one of them granted by the Queen he had tried to depose. It was the special mercy only a mother could grant, but obviously, Southampton didn't know she was his mother, or he wouldn't have risked his life conspiring with the treasonous Earl of Essex to steal a crown he would have inherited by right of blood.

Worse yet, Southampton had become one of the King's intimates, allowing him close proximity to the throne. If the idea of assassination ever entered his head inspired by the knowledge of his royal birth, King James would be in immediate danger.

Whatever the case, Cecil needed to interrogate Southampton immediately, and he had to create a plausible story for the King.

Angry at being awakened, King James was slow to arise. His attendants washed his face and helped him into his robe as Robert Cecil entered the room. The Earl of Southampton dashed past him, half-naked and wrapped in a sheet. Clearly, he had been the King's companion for the night.

"You'd better have a good reason for waking me at this hour, Little Beagle," the King growled.

"I strongly advise you to arrest Southampton, Majesty. He's an enemy of the state."

"What, arrest my dear sweet Henry? He's already apologized for stepping on my wife's toes at the dance. What more does Queen Anne want? Is this some kind of joke?"

"I don't jest at this hour, Majesty, especially where the government is concerned. Southampton's treasonous doings have just now come to light."

"You had better have a good reason for these accusations."

"It's all in here, Majesty," Cecil said, handing him the ebony box. "Peruse the papers and you'll see what I mean."

"What's this? It looks like a Last Will and Testament."

"It's the Last Will and Testament of Edward de Vere, 17th Earl of Oxford."

"Where did you find it?"

"Inside the late Queen's Bible. Read it and you'll see my concern."

The King yawned and stared blankly at Cecil for a moment. But as he read the will, he trembled with rage.

"Are you implying that Henry stands to inherit my kingdom? Why have there been no whispers about his birth after all this time, after so many years?"

"I knew nothing about it until this evening, Majesty," Cecil said, adopting his most unctuous manner as the King nervously paced the room.

"The Great Virgin Queen!" James bellowed. "Mother of a bastard, and after she castigated my own mother for her love affairs and murdered her. God's blood, what a mockery!"

"Apparently, she kept her pregnancy a secret by dropping out of sight for nine months," Cecil said. "Oxford was forced to be silent on the matter, or so he says in the document."

"You should have known about this, Cecil. It's your business to know about such things."

"I know about it now, and that's why you must arrest Southampton and do what needs to be done, regardless of your love for him. Remember, a monarch has no true friends. You must burn this God-forsaken document immediately and consign it to the ashes."

"But Lord Oxford is still alive. He'll merely draft another will."

"You needn't worry about that, Majesty. The Earl of Oxford is dead."

"Dead? By what means?"

"The plague," Cecil said, casting his eyes to the floor. "It came upon him quite suddenly."

"But there's no danger of the plague in England now. That evil has passed."

"Alas, we have a plague of traitors among us, Majesty, and Lord Oxford was its chief contagion."

"I find that hard to believe. He's a very witty man, a fine scholar, clever, entertaining and always fashionable."

"But his unholy spawn Southampton is a danger to you."

"Henry is so dear. And he's very tender with my wife."

"He'll kiss you 'ere he kills you," Cecil whispered. King James' generosity vanished.

"Can you by dint of questioning and without suspicion find out what he knows?"

"You can depend on me, Majesty. I'll perform a very thorough interrogation."

"Be quick about it," James said. "This matter must be settled before sunrise. I'll order guards to protect me and my family, especially my son. Meanwhile, arrest Southampton and his retinue and confine them to the Tower. Use torture if necessary, but find out what he knows and if you feel it's the only recourse, you have my order to silence him forever."

Cecil bowed and took his leave.

When he was gone, King James walked over to the window. As he clutched Lord Oxford's box to his heart, his mind teemed with memories of his literary friend. Only last month, they had enjoyed a charming and exhilarating dinner at the Earl's estate in Bath. And not long before, they'd spent a few days together at Wilton House. Oxford had seemed very anxious to protect him from the plague; surely he had meant James no harm. And now, alas, Oxford had fallen victim to the plague, and there would be no more sparkling dinner conversations and no more Shakespeare plays. It was a tragic loss made even sadder, now that Oxford's fine poetic style would be missing from King James' new English translation of the Bible.

The King closed his eyes and said a prayer, pardoning his friend's unintentional transgressions. Then he tossed the box into the fire and watched as the flames snapped and curled around it. Within minutes, only the boar's head lock glowed fiendishly from among the ashes.

Southampton trembled as the door to his cell slammed shut. Absent from his face was the youthful glow described in Shake-speare's Sonnets. The fair countenance King James loved so much was sick and pale with grief, distorted by panic.

As one of his first official acts, King James had granted him a pardon. While it was true that he had committed treason back then, this time Southampton had no idea why he had been arrested. Somehow, he had jeopardized his preferment with the King, whose bed he had warmed the night before. He was innocent of any wrongdoing. Perhaps his rival Buckingham had aroused the King's jealousies.

Within minutes, Cecil entered. Southampton tried to remain calm, but his voice cracked and his hands shook.

"Why have you arrested me?" he asked. "I've done nothing wrong. I love the King and he knows it. I've honored all our agreements."

"As I shall honor mine," Cecil said, sitting on the cell's only stool.

"You violated our agreement," Southampton cried. "Not once have I broken the terms of my release. I demand that you tell me what crime I'm charged with, and if you have no cause for this arrest, you must release me."

"The King has sent me to make some inquiries."

"Inquiries can be made outside the Tower. Where are your spies, Cecil? Where are your ruffians? You always have an audience when you stage these inquisitions."

"Accept my assurance that we're alone this time. It wouldn't serve either of us to be overheard in this exchange."

"I have nothing to hide. I demand my freedom."

"I'll set the terms for this interrogation. Of course, if you'd prefer to stay in this hellhole," he said, getting up from the stool.

"Wait, don't go," Southampton pleaded. "I'll answer your questions. What does the King want to know?"

"Your mother was a good lady, was she not?"

"Yes, very good."

"She suffered mightily from your father's cruelty, isn't that so?"

"Yes. Theirs was a bitter divorce and everyone knew it."

"She never recovered from it, did she?"

"No, but she put on a cheerful face. That was her nature."

"So I've heard. And what of your father?"

"My father was a vicious monster. He used to beat her cruelly."

"Would his beatings have enticed her to pay him voluntary conjugal visits while he was imprisoned in the Tower?"

"I wouldn't know about that."

"Oh, wouldn't you?"

"No. I wasn't born then. How would I know any of this?"

"Maybe your father wasn't always cruel. Maybe he was occasionally kind."

"I wouldn't know about that either."

"Did she ever speak of him as a loving husband?"

"No."

"Did she ever say that his beatings intensified with the difficulties of giving birth, and that their one struggle was in conceiving you?"

"Conceiving me? What, is my birth the crime for which I've been imprisoned?"

"I said no such thing," Cecil cooed, in a mocking tone. "But were you aware that your father was confined to this Tower in January of the year you were born, and that he was unable to have intercourse with your mother, unless she chose to visit him of her own accord?"

"I remember that when he spoke of his freedom, he used to call it his autumnal homecoming. That's because he was released in October."

"On the contrary, the record shows he was released in May. But perhaps he had lost track of time in his lonely cell. So many minds go to jelly inside these walls."

"I was told I was conceived on his return home."

"'It is a wise child that knows his own father,'" Cecil sighed. "That's a quote from Shake-speare, and I believe I have it right."

"No, you have it wrong," Southampton laughed. "The actual quote is 'it is a wise father that knows his own child.' And my father knew me."

"And yet he knew not your mother, at least not in the Biblical sense. He wasn't home to conceive you. Someone else had that pleasure and coupled with your mother in an adulterous bed."

"That's a lie!" Southampton shouted. "Are you calling my mother a whore?"

"Your mother wasn't married to your father until after you were born – as you yourself have pointed out."

"My mother was an honest and virtuous woman. Everyone has always said that."

"Yes, that was the general opinion. But I have it on good authority that while your father was imprisoned, your mother took a lover and you were their issue."

Southampton lunged at Cecil. The inquisitor leapt up, overturning the stool.

"My mother was no whore!" the prisoner cried. "You can do what you want to me, but don't malign her memory. She was everything to me and when my father died, they took me away from her and made me a royal ward and I barely saw her after that. Take back your insults! She was a good and virtuous woman!"

"Calm yourself or I'll summon the guards."

Southampton sat on the floor and wept. Cecil stood over him and waited a few moments before resuming his inquiry.

"How do you think your father impregnated your mother from the Tower?" he whispered. "Did he copulate from a distance and send his seed flying through the air?"

"He must have been home at the time of my conception."

"But the records show he was not released when you say he was."

"How would I know? Maybe he escaped this dreadful place. Some men are lucky."

"Not usually, and certainly not in your father's case. The records show he was in the Tower when you were conceived."

"Oh, why does it matter? Why do you torment me with these infernal questions?"

"You love your mother very much, and you'd do anything to protect her memory, wouldn't you?"

"Any man would do the same."

"How true it is," Cecil said. "Such is the loyalty a son bears towards his mother. I feel that way towards my own dear mother. The mother is the queen of the family, is she not? As you say, your mother was an honest lady throughout her long life. A veritable queen. A queen among women. Was she not a queen?"

Southampton didn't flinch. He wiped his tears on his sleeve.

"She was a great lady," he said, mournfully.

"A great lady," Cecil echoed, waiting for a telltale revelation. "I speak as honestly as I can and now I see that I must dispel the terrible rumors against her good name."

"What rumors?"

"That you were a bastard, a changeling of undetermined issue, and that the Earl and Countess of Southampton were not your true parents."

"That's madness!" Southampton shouted. "Who dares to make such a claim?"

"A dead earl, who lived under the illusion that you were his first-born."

"I've never heard of such a thing. Who was it?"

"Edward de Vere, the late Earl of Oxford."

"What, is Oxford dead? I saw him last week. He was recovering his health. What happened?"

"It seems he suffered an attack in the night."

Southampton raised a curious eyebrow.

"Now why on earth would the Earl of Oxford say such things about me?" he asked. "When I became friends with his son Henry, Oxford treated me like a son, too."

"Like a son?"

"Yes. He treated all aspiring playwrights and poets that way."

"That's true," Cecil said. "I must say, I always found him to be a singularly odd man."

"He must have been mad with fever to say such things about me."

"Probably. At least you know the true identity of your parents, and that's all that matters now. Someone must have dropped Lord Oxford's poisonous gossip into the King's ear, but I'll cure him of it."

"Why should the King care so much about my parents?"

Cecil didn't answer. He strode towards the door and pounded for the keeper to unlock it.

"You've answered all my questions, and I promise to speak in your favor to His Majesty in regards to your freedom."

"Thank you!" Southampton cried. He fell on his knees and kissed Cecil's hand. For an instant, he gazed affectionately into his captor's eyes, as if willing to go further.

"Speaking in your favor is the very least I can do, for one who enjoys the pleasurable delights of the King's bedchamber," Cecil said, turning away in disgust. "But before I leave, tell me again the names of your parents; their full Christian names and titles."

"My father was Henry Wriothesley, 2nd Earl of Southampton, and my mother Mary Wriothesley, Countess of Southampton, nee Browne."

"Any relation to William Browne, the actor?"

"I don't believe so. Why?"

"I suppose it was before your time, but I once saw William Browne play the role of Banquo in that Scottish play, *Macbeth*. He was an excellent ghost, very silent and accusatory--"

"I pray you, Cecil," Southampton pleaded, "speak to the King about my freedom immediately and tell him I love him more than ever, with all my heart."

"Most certainly," the interrogator replied.

The jailer unlocked the door. Cecil stepped into the hallway and spoke through the bars. "I promise to do whatever I can to encourage your speedy release."

Several hours later, Southampton was set free.

CHAPTER TWENTY-EIGHT

The Scene: Oxford's home, King's Place, Hackney
December 1612

"The weight of this sad time we must obey,
Speak what we feel, not what we ought to say."
– King Lear

The letter summoning him to her bedside came into his hands in Stratford on a rainy Monday morning. Shaxper dropped everything and left his nephew in charge of the family businesses. Ignoring his wife's tirade about the foolhardy expense, he hired a carriage and driver for the long journey to King's Place. He packed a change of clothes in his satchel, knowing he would need to stop at an inn for one night or possibly longer, depending on the weather.

Countess Elizabeth was dying. He wondered if she was the victim of his neglect since he hadn't seen her after that terrible night at King's Place. Although he had traveled to London frequently to collect on his shares as a stockholder in The Globe, he had never been able to bring himself to visit the home at Hackney. The memories of that day made it impossible for him to pray at Lord Oxford's grave or inquire about his widow.

Consumed with self-reproach, he couldn't think what he would say to her now. Perhaps he should invent a series of plausible lies to white-wash the horrible ordeal eight years ago. Even in ill health, she was sure to question him about the grotesque piece of unfinished business. There were still moments when he felt emotionally trapped behind the wall in the house, with the soldiers advancing, hell-bent on murder.

He had never meant to stay away from Countess Elizabeth for so long. With his new wealth and coat-of-arms, perhaps he might have had a chance with her. In retrospect, as the days had passed in rapid succession, he'd lost track of them. He'd been busy brokering her late husband's plays, raking in the money and cashing in on their longtime partnership as Shakespeare.

With the grinding of the carriage wheels, his mind raced back to Countess Elizabeth. He couldn't imagine what the sweet lady would be like, now that she was so close to death. It seemed horribly unjust for God to take such a kind soul when thieves and murderers lived to ripe old age.

Raising a headstrong son like Henry de Vere all by herself could not have been easy. After Lord Oxford's death, he had grown up surrounded by men of base inclinations. The Earl of Southampton was one of them. During his perilous stint as Southampton's secretary, Shaxper recalled having been forced to witness various acts of perversion by members of the household that made him run to his room, bolt the door and vomit into a chamber pot.

Southampton had been a terrible influence on young Henry de Vere. When the latter came of age, the two carried on like savages in the pub-lic houses, drinking, whoring and raising hell all over London. They called themselves sworn brothers and behaved like animals. And yet when called upon to attend royal ceremonies at Court, they sobered up and presented themselves in the most genteel fashion, perfumed to the hilt, dressed in posh garments, prim and highly respectable. Shaxper often marveled at what chameleons members of the nobility could be. They were never trustworthy and reliable, like working people.

It was a sad commentary on the times that young Henry de Vere had never been accorded the glittering honors that were due him as the noble descendant of his lineage. With the upward social rise of Protestant commoners, the Elizabethan age had dulled the ancient Catholic family escutcheons. While Shaxper had profited by the new opportunities and kept his religious beliefs to himself, he was saddened to see the splendor of England's ancient nobility fade into history. His master had often spoken of its lamentable disappearance. Perhaps it was best that he hadn't lived to see the lackluster honors grudgingly offered his son.

After two days on the road, Shaxper arrived at King's Place. The immense house hadn't changed much, except that many of the items broken or destroyed that night had been repaired or replaced. Only its great human treasure had been obliterated beyond redemption. It was true that he and the Countess had survived – but they would never be the same. Even the house seemed resigned to accepting its tragic losses.

The Countess' gentlewoman led him into the conservatory located in the mansion's inner courtyard, an unusual innovation for its time. The warm temperature and heady fragrances of the flowers delighted his senses and almost made him forget the sad reason for his visit. The gentlewoman pointed to a chaise where her mistress rested, surrounded by the flowers she loved. Then she smiled and left them alone.

Shaxper walked in quietly. When he saw that the Countess was asleep, he pulled up a bench, sat down and waited for her to awaken.

Her honeyed hair had turned silver, but her serene smile and fine complexion made her beautiful, even in her illness.

She must have sensed his loving thoughts, for she awoke and turned towards him with her petal-soft blue eyes.

"Edward," she whispered. "My dearest husband, is that you?"

The irony wasn't lost on him.

"No, my lady," he said, as he kissed her hand. "It is I, Will Shaxper of Stratford, your husband's scribe."

"Oh, how good of you to come. How many years has it been?"

"Eight, my lady. Eight very busy and productive years."

"And have you been well?"

"Yes, my lady, very well. And you?"

"Most unwell," she said.

"That's what brought me here. Oh, I wish I could do something to ease your suffering, my lady. Please tell me, what can I do for you?"

"Just stay with me, Master Shaxper, and talk for a while. What are you doing these days to earn your living?"

"Oh, I do some occasional acting and once in a while I sell a few plays to the London theaters. But you know how it is: times change and audiences change and tastes change; and lately, other men have taken over the playwriting business, so I don't get much call for plays anymore. And thanks to His Lordship's extreme generosity, I own shares in The Globe and Blackfriars, so trust me, I'm not starving. Far from it, I'm doing quite well."

"I'm so glad to hear it. My husband always said that no one else could have carried off the authorship ruse as cleverly as you did. I understand you don't spend much time in London anymore. How is life back in Stratford? I was sad to hear of young Hamnet's death. How are your wife and dear little family managing?"

"My wife is the same, my lady," Shaxper said. "Hamnet's death was a terrible blow, but I've managed to marry off one of my daughters to a very respectable doctor. But how did you know I was living in Stratford?"

"Ben Jonson told me. When I asked him about you, he knew exactly where to find you."

"Oh, did he?"

The Countess read his uncertainty. She held his hand.

"I told him it was urgent. I wanted to tell you personally that I'm leaving you a bequest in my will."

"My lady," he said with astonishment. "I'm not worthy of such consideration."

"Of course you are. You enabled my husband to become England's great bard. He couldn't have written the plays without you to pass them on to the playhouses and stand behind them as your own."

"I was only doing the job he hired me to do."

"And you did it well. Never regret a job well done."

"Thank you, my lady. I'm proud to have been of service."

"I'm telling you about my bequest because you aren't mentioned by name in the will," she continued. "I did that to protect you, should there be any more political danger associated with the plays or my husband's name and service to the state. It's not likely, since most of the play factory are dead. I suppose I'm to be next."

"Don't say that, my lady. You'll live and be well for years to come."

"That's a lovely sentiment, but the doctors have pronounced otherwise."

Again he felt like an idiot.

"My executor knows your name and where to find you," she said, "but I wanted you to be aware of the bequest, in case something happened and you were compelled to come forward quietly and ask for it."

"Thank you, my lady, for your kind remembrance."

She waved away his gratitude.

"You said you wanted to do something to ease my suffering. I do believe there is something you can do for me, Master Shaxper."

"What might that be, my lady?"

"Surely you must know what happened eight years ago, the night this household was ransacked and violated. You were with my husband when he died. Tell me what happened. I believe you saw the whole thing."

Shaxper cast his eyes to the floor. Countess Elizabeth touched his sleeve.

"Why won't you speak? You have it in your power to calm the mind of a dying woman. Please don't refuse me this wish. If you know what happened to my husband, tell me. You owe me that much. Don't let me go to my grave with this mystery gnawing at my heart."

Even in old age, her eyes were like bluebells.

"I'll never forget that night," he said. "His Lordship died of a weakened heart."

"A broken heart, more like."

"He had been in bed all day. He told me himself his heart felt very weak."

"I don't remember it that way. He spent the day in bed because of his sore leg."

Shaxper couldn't frame the words to tell the Countess about her husband's murder. She looked so frail and delicate, and the truth was so despicable, he could not inflict it on her.

"My lady, I do believe that in the midst of the terrifying invasion, it was his heart that worked against him."

"Did you know that they officially listed his cause of death as the plague?" she asked.

"No," Shaxper responded. It was as if he could still hear the empty vial of poison rolling across the floor.

"It's quite remarkable, that story about the plague," she said. "You served as one of my husband's attendants at the coronation. You must remember the plague was still rampant back then, and that King James was terrified of it."

"Yes, I remember."

"A year before my husband died, he paid a long visit to King James after the coronation. I was terrified he'd catch the plague while traveling, but when he came home, he was fine. He laughed at me for worrying, but I worried nonetheless."

"As any good wife would do."

"It doesn't take a year to die of the plague. No one in our household had it. None of our servants were ill, and they all came in close contact with His Lordship. You and I were both in and out of his bedchamber all the time, and we never caught it."

"Perhaps we were lucky."

"Good luck doesn't accompany the plague. It was a terrifying night; perhaps his heart gave out on him after all."

"Perhaps," Shaxper whispered.

Weary from their talk, Countess Elizabeth closed her eyes and sighed deeply.

Guilt consumed him. This beautiful lady, the only woman he had ever truly loved since Anne Whatley of Temple Grafton, was fading before his eyes. Why had he abandoned her? Perhaps he could have stepped into her dead husband's shoes, like the impostor he was, and eased her burdensome sorrows. Perhaps he could have protected young Henry de Vere the way Richard Field's father had once protected him.

And then he looked at her, slim, poised and imperial, and recognized that in all ways she was a true lady, superior to him by her high birth and aristocratic nature.

She would never have accepted him.

The Countess stirred and slowly opened her eyes.

"My husband wanted you to have that oak trunk in the corner. You're to take it with you when you go. Have one of the servants load it onto your carriage."

He said nothing and looked over at the trunk. It would make an excellent place to store the plays.

"I'm to be buried beside my husband in the churchyard. Please attend my funeral and pray for me."

"I'll pray every day with all my heart. You were always so kind to me, my lady."

"Read me one of his sonnets, would you? His book is on the table."

"I see it, my lady. Which one would you like?"

"You choose," she sighed, touching his arm. "They're all very dear to me."

The scribe opened the book at random and read aloud. The Countess closed her eyes.

> *Who will believe my verse in time to come,*
> *If it were fill'd with your most high deserts?*
> *Though yet heaven knows it is but as a tomb*
> *Which hides your life, and shows not half your parts.*
> *If I could write the beauty of your eyes,*
> *And in fresh numbers number all your graces,*
> *The age to come would say, "This poet lies,*
> *Such heavenly touches ne'er touch'd earthly faces."*
> *So should my papers (yellowed with the age)*
> *Be scorn'd, like old men of less truth than tongue,*
> *And your true rights be term'd a poet's rage,*
> *And stretchéd meter of an antique song:*
> *But were some child of yours alive that time,*
> *You should live twice, in it and in my rhyme.*

William Shaxper finished reading. Countess Elizabeth's hand slipped gently from his arm.

CHAPTER TWENTY-NINE

The Scene: Royal Palace
January 1613

"Murder cannot be hid long."
– *The Merchant of Venice*

King James re-read Robert Cecil's final letter with trepidation. The hunchbacked king-maker, who prided himself on his great logistical dexterity, had ended his days with a sadly muddled mind. In spite of this, his letter offered a credible warning about a gentleman named William Shaxper, an actor and shareholder in The Globe, who had once served as secretary to both Lord Oxford and the Earl of Southampton.

That was explosive alchemy. Secretaries were more than just competent note-takers and letter-writers. They were faithful confidantes, sworn to secrecy on a variety of intimate matters and backstage business. That meant Shaxper probably knew all of Oxford's darkest secrets, including his paternity of the royal heir.

To make matters worse, Southampton had sponsored that treasonous play *Richard II.* Apparently, William Shaxper had had something to do with it, but he had gone unpunished. In this bit of unfinished business, the late Robert Cecil warned that if Shaxper ever tried to use the play-houses again to raise public sentiment in favor of Southampton's claim to the throne, the King's life would be in danger.

Grateful for the dead man's advice, the King had sent for Robert Poley, one of Cecil's best operatives. When he was shown into the throne room, he knelt before the King to receive his orders.

"I want you to follow this actor, William Shaxper of Stratford. Find out where he lives and where he stays when he's in London. Don't let him out of your sight."

"Yes, Majesty. And what do you want me to do with him when I find him?"

"Nothing, for now," the King said, disgusted by the filthy wretch with the long scar. "Just keep an eye on him. Watch out for the kinds of plays he puts on. Make sure none of them are dangerous. You'll know what to do when the time is right. If he mouths a word of treason, silence him."

"The way we silenced Marlowe?"

"Yes, I've heard about that. Make it look like an accident. We'll publish our findings at the inquest and acquit you of everything, just as they did for you then."

"I've been watching Shaxper for a while already. He doesn't drink, so we can't very well dispose of him in a tavern brawl."

"I don't care what you do. Use your imagination, as long as you make it look like an accident."

"I understand, Majesty. We'll arrange a little mishap for him in one of his barns, or perhaps in the back of one of the theaters. A few of us, when we used to work for Sir Thomas Knyvet back in the old days, would lie in wait for Lord Oxford and his men to come out of a theater or a brothel or a pub, and then we'd start a brawl and knife as many of 'em as we could. We nearly killed the old Earl outside of Blackfriars. For a blue-blooded nobleman, his blood was as red as anyone else's —"

"Enough about Oxford!" The King rose from his chair.

"Yes, Majesty," Poley said. "As you say, Your Majesty."

"If Cecil were still alive, I'd ask him to arrange things. But as it is, I'm forced to deal with you gutter rats directly."

"You can pay us directly, too," Poley said, smiling as he held out his unwashed hand.

King James tossed a purse onto the floor. With great disgust, he hurried from the room.

Poley's eyes never left him as he stooped to pick it up.

CHAPTER THIRTY

The Scene: The Globe Theater
June 29, 1613

"They told me I was everything: 'Tis a lie, I am not ague proof."
– King Lear

With the balance of his rent paid in full, William Shaxper locked the door of his apartment for the last time. He told his landlady that he would be heading to Stratford after his farewell speech at The Globe at the conclusion of *All is True*. Mrs. Mountjoy cooed and thanked him for always having paid his rent in a timely manner. She tucked the key into her bodice and wished him a safe journey.

She wouldn't have cared that Lord Oxford's trunk was also on its way to Stratford, stuffed with manuscripts Shaxper intended to sell. He was confident that the theater owners would seek him out, willing to pay for the use of the Shake-speare name.

As he walked towards the theater, he tried to understand the bitter unfriendliness he felt from the new generation of playwrights. Hiring them to fill in a few scenes every now and then was an extravagance he thoroughly enjoyed, and yet know-it-alls like Ben Jonson, Thomas Middleton, Francis Beaumont and John Fletcher kept whining about things like denouement, dramatic flow, symbolism, and something called catharsis that belonged in a chamber pot. They assumed that he had all the answers to their questions, especially with the large number of successful revivals the Shake-speare plays were enjoying. But since he wasn't a writer, Shaxper had nothing to say to them, and he could no longer put them off by looking inscrutable and puffing on his pipe.

Beyond the need to protect himself, he felt the extreme importance of his farewell address to the London stage. His partnership with Lord Oxford had been Heavenly Ordained, and it was time to express his gratitude for the many gifts he had received. It had been hard work: all those hours of dictation and transcription, of meeting the demand for the history plays, of reading lines out loud for dramatic effect, of risking life and limb every time he delivered a play to the Stationers' Register. In the early days, his lust for advancement had propelled him forward. He had never imagined the exhilaration of working with a literary genius and then, pretending to be one.

It had been a bizarre arrangement, and it had worked well until Lord Oxford's murder almost nine years ago to the day. No one had ever been punished for the crime, and Shaxper had never told anyone what he had witnessed. Using the Shake-speare name, he had sold several of the manuscripts he had carried off that night. He had asked John Fletcher to finish *The Two Noble Kinsmen* and *Henry VIII*, although the playwright had balked at writing a scene for the executioner, the one Shaxper him-self had hoped to play.

Still, it was a relief to be working with real playwrights again, much better than buying foul papers from obscure authors, copying them, and sticking the Shake-speare name on them. In doing that, he faced the risk of having other writers notice his changing style, whereas any play bearing the Shake-speare name could be sold for several times more than what it cost him to buy it from a lesser known playwright.

As he turned the corner, he thought about how quickly he had started his own play factory, signing his illustrious pseudonym to other people's work. While Fletcher had cobbled together a cohesive version of *The Two Noble Kinsmen,* Middleton, completely unaware of the authorship ruse, had traded Shaxper *The Second Maiden's Tragedy* based on Cervantes' *Don Quixote* in exchange for a few personal belongings.

The scribe-turned-impostor promised to see what he could do with the script. He handed it to Fletcher, who exchanged it for his newly completed play, *Cardenio.* While Fletcher made a small number of revisions in *The Second Maiden's Tragedy*, Shaxper clapped his name on *Cardenio* and sold it to The King's Men at a tremendous profit.

Billed as a Shake-speare play, *Cardenio* saw only one performance. Audiences were sorely disappointed by its stiff and inferior quality, and from then on, the script was relegated to a dusty shelf in the tiring house next to *The Second Maiden's Tragedy,* which also never was performed.

Shaxper knew that if Middleton and Fletcher had ever sat down to discuss it, they would have discovered that they had collaborated on both plays, and that Shaxper had nothing more to do with either of them than signing his famous pen name to the title pages and absconding with the fees from the theater owners.

But when it came right down to it, Fletcher and Middleton had nothing to complain about. At least their theatrical reputations were still intact. Possessed with no literary talent whatsoever, Shaxper's career was over. Too many of the plays he had commissioned from other writers failed in performance, to the point where the Shake-speare name had lost some of its luster.

That was why he had decided to confess the truth. In his mind he rehearsed his farewell speech, to be delivered after the epilogue of *All is True.*

I stand before you, ladies and gents, at the expense of the epilogue, which our author hath writ for performance today. With God's grace, in lieu of the author, I have come here to announce in this wooden O news of great importance to myself and the author.

Author I have claimed to be, but author am I not. I have represented myself to be one, but for shame, I am no author at all, but a mere copyist of these plays.

The true author is a man whose name is truth, or Vere, which means truth in Latin, derived from veritas. "Vero nihil veritas" is his motto – "Nothing is truer than the truth." And now, I can no longer be false to you.

De Vere is the great nobleman who wrote your favorite plays: <u>Hamlet, King Lear, Henry V, As You Like It, Titus Andronicus, Pericles</u> and others, to which we appended the name Shakespeare, not altogether different from my own.

For the truth is that I was merely the author's secretary and his distant cousin. I have penned these plays from de Vere's foul papers and affixed my name to his fair copies.

Why? Because the true author was a nobleman, who by virtue of his high rank, could not publicly lay claim to his work. He has been dead for more than nine years. It is no longer proper for me to prostitute his name onto works that have none of his divine spark. Audiences have discerned the difference.

I have entitled this play <u>All is True</u> for two reasons. First, it represents history; secondly, the author's name de Vere means truth, and it is my way of telling you the plays were his, not mine. Nothing is truer than <u>that</u> truth.

Ladies and Gentlemen, I take my leave of you to return to Stratford. I give you these great plays in memory of their true author, Edward de Vere, Earl of Oxford, the true Shakespeare. So farewell from Shaxper of Stratford, the devoted scribe and impostor. Give me your hands in tribute to our author.

Once he gave the speech, he knew there would be no turning back.

Robert Poley watched as William Shaxper checked with the boy to be sure his horse would be ready for his departure. He smiled as the demure playwright walked right by him without a word. He didn't recognize Poley from The Golden Lion the night before, when Shaxper had failed to water down his drinks and had clumsily announced to everyone to expect his farewell speech at The Globe.

That was all Poley needed to hear. He made his plans.

He watched Shaxper enter The Globe through the back door and signaled his accomplices to take their places. When the play was over and the crowd had dispersed, they would encircle him with flattery like charmed admirers before he had a chance to take his leave, and run him through with a dagger. Later they would dispose of the body in the Thames.

Poley sauntered over to the throng gathering to pay admission. When he reached the head of the line, he put his three pennies in the box like the rest of them, although he had a rather different kind of entertainment in mind. He squeezed past the horde of groundlings to stand as close as he could to the stage.

For more than a year he had shadowed the unassuming playwright, staying a few steps behind him on the street or a few tables away in a tavern. He never betrayed his presence. He took pride in his ability to become a nondescript face in the crowd. After all, in his younger days he'd been personally trained by Spymaster Walsingham and thus had become a precious commodity, handed down from Walsingham to Burghley to Robert Cecil and ultimately into the personal service of the great King himself.

He spotted the pseudo playwright sitting on the stage among the noblemen. Shaxper seemed a bit nervous. He kept looking up at the roof as if anticipating something. Poley followed his gaze and turned to look behind him. He was startled to see a cannon in the highest balcony, tended by two lumpish stagehands who were being nervously hounded by Burbage with last minute advice.

In all the time he'd been trailing Shaxper to and from the theater, Poley had never seen a cannon there before. It looked ridiculously out of place, but he knew there had to be a practical reason for its presence. Obviously, it had something to do with the play because Burbage was a stickler for detail and theatrical verisimilitude. Poley had overheard the writers using jargon like that in the pub, and suddenly realized how quickly he'd caught on to it. If he ever wanted to change careers, it would be easy for him to promote himself from assassin to theater critic.

He turned back towards the stage and studied his victim more closely. He cursed under his breath when he realized that Shaxper hadn't worn his infamous flashy jewelry. He felt cheated because it would have been so easy to cut off his ear or his fingers and collect the spoils right off the corpse, as sweet as eating apples from the tree.

From his special seat on the stage, Shaxper cast his eyes idly around the crowd. He remembered his first visit to London, when John Lyly had tossed him into the cockpit for sitting with the noblemen where he didn't belong. Taking that empty seat had been an honest though brazen mistake, and he'd been publicly humiliated for doing it. How the audience had mocked him then. But now he was the object of applause.

As he surveyed their faces, he noticed that most of them were strangers to him. Almost all of the original patrons who had occupied the balconies had been replaced by a wealthier and younger class of theatergoers with more sophisticated tastes. At that moment, he realized that he had become a stranger to these new times.

Then he noticed a squinting man in a broad-brimmed hat, smiling and nodding at him. Shaxper politely nodded back, wondering how he knew this man with the long scar and where he'd seen him before. He couldn't quite place him. He might have seen him on a crowded street or in a dimly lit tavern, or even at one of the plays; but he had the vague impression of seeing only his partially covered face and furtive eyes. He brought to mind the cur that had stolen his money years ago, near Stratford. He resembled one of the assassins accused of killing Marlowe in the tavern brawl. By the grace of God, could it be the same man?

The hautboys trumpeted the start of the show and the audience grew silent as the Prologue stepped forward to deliver his lines.

> *I come no more to make you laugh; things now*
> *That bear a weighty and a serious brow,*
> *Sad, high, and working, full of state and woe:*
> *Such noble scenes as draw the eye to flow,*
> *We now present.*

Twenty-seven years ago almost to the day, the Queen had commissioned the history plays from the Earl of Oxford. *Henry VIII* was one of the first history plays that Shaxper had helped Oxford prepare, but his lordship was not pleased with it and had long planned to rewrite it. After his death, a patched-together version of it had been performed twice. But this production of the long forgotten play had been newly retitled *All is True,* and had been billed as the most elaborate production

The Globe had ever mounted. Burbage had spent several months fussing over the historical validity of the costumes, and it had been his idea to fire the cannon on the Act One entrance of John Lowin, who was playing King Henry VIII.

Shaxper looked nervously up at the cannon. He didn't like the idea of such a heavy weapon firing over the heads of so many paying customers, but being a minority shareholder, he was outvoted by his partners. Still, as the first act progressed, it captured his attention and he began to relax.

Each scene proved more dazzling than the one before it. Shaxper was pleased at the audience's reaction, even though he desperately wanted to go outside and relieve himself. The actors' words resounded in his ears and he leaned forward to watch a scene that had proven difficult in rehearsals.

They were approaching scene four, the entrance of King Henry VIII. Burbage had argued that Lord Oxford would have enjoyed the rousing burst of cannon fire, and that audiences would be impressed with its real life grandeur. That, he said, would make the revival of *All is True* well worth the high price of admission, at least in their minds; and future ticket sales would soar. Shaxper couldn't argue with the fact that those sales would indeed line his pockets with huge profits.

The audience had no idea what was to come. Shaxper saw Burbage stand back and instruct the stagehands to light the fuse. He covered his ears, and Shaxper did the same.

The audience screamed at the sudden violent explosion. The theater rocked on its foundation, and a mild panic ensued until the smoke cleared and everyone saw that the fiery salute had been part of the show. The audience applauded and cheered wildly. Burbage was overjoyed at their response. He winked at Shaxper as if to confirm this meant good money.

No one noticed the tiny spark that ignited the thatched roof of The Globe. It smoldered while the audience watched the play, completely spellbound. The flames crept around the dry roof until the ceiling caved in and the theater erupted into a conflagration. Screams pierced the air. The audience panicked as people pushed towards the exits, scrambling for safety. Wealthier patrons crammed the tight staircases, trying to escape. The surging crowd engulfed the exits at the street level and people were shoved and trampled in the chaos.

Flames encircled the wooden O like witches dancing in a coven. Burbage, having barely escaped with his life, ran back and forth begging for people to help him put out the fire, but the theater was rapidly becoming a holocaust. Several Puritans watched with delight at this Act of Divine Retribution and praised God for the demise of Satan's house of worship, the unfortunate Globe.

Shaxper leapt to his feet. The back door where the prompter normally stood seemed like his closest avenue of escape. He pushed through the crowd and found himself in the tiring house, engulfed by smoke and trapped against a wall of flames.

He coughed, squinted and covered his eyes with his arm. Smoke filled his lungs. Through his clouded vision, he saw a man in a monk's robe, his face partially covered with a hood, reach out and grab him by the collar.

Terrified, Shaxper fought him off. He struggled to breathe and his heart beat wildly. He thought of Lord Oxford's warning, and knew that death had finally come for him. Smoke and heat overwhelmed his senses, and in his mind, he traveled the road back to Stratford where his wife and children would be waiting for him. Then he closed his eyes and prepared to concede to Death's summons.

Two strong hands lifted him up. Within seconds, he felt himself flying through the air, propelled backwards. He saw nothing but blackness until he hit the ground; and then, stars.

Suddenly, the air was clean. He inhaled deeply and coughed and sputtered. He opened his eyes to see that The Globe was being devoured by the flames. Burbage and his actors sat in the lane, weeping like children bereft of their home.

And then Shaxper knew there would be no final speech to credit the true author of the plays. The theater was burning to the ground, along with his chance at redemption.

The hooded figure silently brushed past him. Shaxper opened his mouth to speak, but the smoke had injured his throat so badly, he was rendered temporarily mute. He reached up and tried to catch the monk by the hem of his cloak, but the stranger pulled away and strode towards a pillar of smoke. He turned and drew back his hood.

The warlike apparition of Edward de Vere, the 17th Earl of Oxford, looked at him for a moment and then quickly dissolved into the inferno.

Shaxper trembled. He struggled to his feet and staggered over to his horse, which was tethered a safe distance away by the river. He didn't see the stranger with the long scar until he stepped out from behind the animal and handed him the reins.

Poley used his dagger to point the way to Stratford.

ACT V
CHAPTER THIRTY-ONE

The Scene: New Place, Stratford-on-Avon
April 22, 1616

"When sorrows come, they come not single-spies, but in battalions."
– Hamlet

A red-faced youth accosted Michael Drayton as he tied his horse to the fence post outside New Place.

"Stop, sir!"

"What is it, boy?"

"You can't leave your horse tied up in the street like that."

"Why not? I'm visiting the man who lives in this house."

"We may be a small town, sir, but we have laws in Stratford protecting the cleanliness of our common areas. You'll have to put your horse in the village stable. I'll take him there for you and save you the trouble of a hefty fine. I'll only charge you a penny and I'll see he's well cared for."

"You should be a lawyer, with your 'stop, sir' and your hot pursuit of money," Drayton grumbled, as he rummaged through his pockets and paid the youth.

"Thank you, sir. I'll consider the opportunity, if it ever presents itself. I'm always in favor of improving my lot."

"The man I've come to see first improved his lot by bringing plays from London all the way out here."

"That must have been before my time, sir."

"Do you know him? His name is William Shaxper."

"Oh, yes. He's a bit of a recluse these days."

"Is he famous around Stratford?"

"Infamous would be a better word. He abandoned his wife and children to work for an earl in London."

"So he could become a writer?"

"He was already a writer. He wrote usurious bills for grain while the rest of us were starving."

"Is he a famous playwright?"

"We have plenty of wheelwrights in Stratford, but no playwrights," the boy laughed. "Wait! Come to think of it, we do have a playwright stopping here now, and he is rather well known. Perhaps you've heard of him. His name is Ben Jonson and he's visiting the very man you've come to see."

"Jonson's here?"

"Yes," the boy answered. "He left his horse tied up here overnight, and when I confronted him about it, he had to pay me a whole lot more than a penny for cleaning up the mess."

"I'm glad you stopped me. You've proven very helpful, my boy."

"It's all in a day's work, sir. When you're ready to leave, come to the stable and fetch your horse. He'll be brushed and watered and ready."

Drayton nodded and walked towards the front door. He knocked, and when no one answered, let himself in. The sound of his boots echoed in the empty hall.

"Hello, is anybody home? William Shaxper? Are you here?"

Drayton and Shaxper were roughly the same age, bonded by the geographical fate of having been born in Warwickshire County. When practically everyone in London began talking about Shaxper's illness, Drayton felt obligated to go and see him. While he was lucky to be in good health, he felt sorry for the scribe, whose old acquaintances were betting on how long it would take him to die. No one seemed the least bit interested in paying him a call.

And that wasn't altogether unexpected. For years, the writers had watched as Shaxper hid under his famous pseudonym and gorged on applause he didn't deserve. They couldn't understand why the Earl of Oxford had been so generous with him, when he was so inflated and unworthy. Shaxper had feathered his nest with the profits from Lord Oxford's scavenged works, like an upstart crow stealing objects that glittered. Robert Greene had accused him of that by using the term "upstart crow" when he called him a tiger's heart wrapped in a player's hide. New Place itself was evidence that his greed had worked in his favor.

"Anyone home? It's Michael Drayton. I've come to visit you, William."

Ben Jonson bolted down the stairs. "Drayton! Well, I'll be damned! You horse's arse! What the devil brings you here?"

The two men pounded on each other like a couple of high-spirited tavern rowdies.

"I've come to pay my respects to Shaxper," Drayton said.

"Aw, there's no need for that. He's always been paid more respect than he deserves. Don't wake him up. He's sleeping in the next room."

"Yes," Drayton whispered, "but I've heard that he's dying . . ."

"What's the big deal? It's not as if he invented Death, although he might try to take credit for that too, the way he's taken credit for everything else. Sit down and have a drink. It's not my liquor, so help yourself and be sure to drink as much as you'd like."

"Always the perfect host, generous to a fault with another man's liquor."

Stools scraped across the floor as the men sat in the kitchen and filled their goblets.

"Of all things," Jonson said. "I never thought I'd see you here."

"Nor I, you. I can't believe our old friend is dying. Did you come to cheer him up?"

"Are you crazy? I came to cheer him *on*! But never mind that. Is it true, what I've heard about you?"

"Bless you, that all depends on what you've heard."

"That you've just published thirty-thousand lines of poetry on the feminine pulchritude of English geography! Do you think it's nearly long enough?"

"Actually," Drayton blushed, "I do plan on revising *Polyolbion* . . ."

"You haven't changed a bit," Jonson laughed.

"I can't say the same for you. You seem to be everywhere these days. I know you didn't come here to counsel the scribe on the fate of his immortal soul."

"You know I'd be lying if I said I cared one whit about that immortal jackass. Actually, I'm editing a folio of Shake-speare plays and I'm trying to collect the missing manuscripts. I thought I'd start here."

"A reasonable choice."

"Don't be so sure. I haven't found anything yet."

"I assume you think the scribe knows where they are."

"If he knows, he's not telling. He just talks rubbish and plays the part of a senile old man."

"What did you expect? You've ridiculed him for years. I'd be surprised if he talked to you at all."

"Right. Maybe now that you're here, you can pry the information out of him."

"I could try loosening his tongue with this," Drayton said, waving the bottle of sack they'd helped themselves to.

"You've forgotten. Shaxper doesn't drink sack. Only small beer."

"Well, if he's senile, chances are he's forgotten that, too."

"Very funny. But it won't work."

"I happen to know that tomorrow is his birthday. That's why I'm here. The talk around London is that it might be his last. So what's wrong with pouring him a sacred libation as he crosses the Stygian Lake on the way to Hades?"

"Nothing, I suppose, as long as he drinks religiously. I don't want to waste any more time with that old fool."

"I promise, you won't. I'll get him to tell me where the manuscripts are. That's the least I can do for a friend."

"Thank you, Michael. And by way of our friendship, I'd like to invite you to compose a poem for the folio, something touching Lord Oxford's literary talent and bountiful patronage. You write it and I'll publish it, however long."

"I'd be honored, Jonson."

"Of course I'm writing something too, as are several associates of the de Vere family. There's Thomas Freeman, half-brother of Oxford's son with Lady Vavasor, William Barkstead and Hugh Holland, former boy actors from Oxford's troupe at St. Paul's, William Basse, retainer to the Earl's daughter Bridget, and his old friends James Mabbe, Leonard Digges, John Marston and some others."

"I'll write something, as long as your folio doesn't perpetuate the authorship hoax. That's gone on long enough."

"I quite agree."

"I don't," an elderly voice called out from the other room. "What are you two talking about in there? It doesn't matter what you say, Ben Jonson. I can hear every word, you wretched scoundrel, and don't deny it! You're plotting against me, all of you. Well, I won't have it, do you hear me? Don't think I'm a mayfly. I wasn't born yesterday . . ."

"Who in the hell is that?" Drayton asked.

"That's the scribe. He's hallucinating again – happens every hour or so when he wakes up from a long nap. It doesn't mean anything. Ignore it."

"Ignore it? How can you ignore it?"

"Michael Drayton, is that you? I know that voice as if it were my own. Come in here. Pay no attention to that pismire who calls himself a playwright."

Drayton rose to his feet.

"Sit down," Jonson grumbled. "It's not a call to arms."

"He knows I'm here. I've got to go see him."

"Why? Isn't hearing him bad enough?"

"Michael Draaaaaaaaayton . . ."

"Just tell me where to find him and I'll get it over with."

"He's in there, on the couch over by the window. Well, what are you waiting for? Go and see him; but I warn you, it's not pretty. And don't forget this." He handed Drayton the bottle of sack. The poet took it and left.

Shaxper didn't look at all as Drayton remembered him. Ill health had changed every aspect of his body. In his heyday, he had always shown an apish devotion to style, having adopted foppish gestures to flaunt his gaudy jewelry. He had taken up smoking, a useful affectation that kept his admirers at a distance. As a member of the Lord Chamberlain's Men, he had strutted like a peacock, giving the actors bad advice. In his yellowing nightgown, he looked small and frail.

"Hello, William," Drayton said softly. "It's me, Michael."

"Michael, how good of you to come and see me."

"That's the least I can do, since we're practically neighbors. How are you feeling?"

"It won't be long before I meet my Maker."

"You shouldn't talk like that."

"But it's true, and you can't fight God's truth."

"I suppose not," Drayton sighed.

"Because nothing is truer than truth. That was Lord Oxford's heraldic motto," Shaxper asserted.

"I remember."

"My family's motto is on that wall. Can you see it? It says 'Non Sans Droict.' That means 'Not Without Right.'"

"Yes, I know, but not so loud. You know how Jonson feels about it. 'Non, Sans Droict' is the same wording that's used to reject a claim for undeserved heraldry. It means 'No, Not Right.'"

"He thinks I bought this coat-of-arms for ready money. Well, I don't care what that pillock thinks," he shouted so Jonson could hear him. "I earned that coat-of-arms the hard way, keeping Lord Oxford out of trouble. You have no idea what that was like."

"I remember Lord Oxford quite well. I'm sure it wasn't easy."

"So many times I risked my life for him. Sit down, Michael."

"No thanks, I don't want to overstay my welcome."

"Nonsense. Slide that stool closer to me."

Drayton obeyed and set the bottle down on the floor. Shaxper moved into a more comfortable position.

"Has the Crown burned any more of your books lately?"

"You remember that? It was twenty-nine years ago," Drayton said.

"I remember it like it was yesterday. It was a terrifying experience. I'd never seen a book burning before, flames shooting straight up from hell and devouring all reason and common sense. Your book was called *The Harmony of the Church.* Isn't that right?"

"I'm flattered that you remember it."

"You're much too modest, Michael. A little vanity would suit you. How could I ever forget that day? Only forty copies of your book were spared the torch and the Archbishop kept every single one of them for himself. I could never understand why he burned your sublime and godly masterpiece. There wasn't a threatening word in it."

"Not one," Drayton said.

"Not like that trash Marlowe and Kyd and Greene and Chettle used to write. Very inflammatory, most of it downright treasonous. And that poor poet. You know, the innocent man wrongly arrested and tortured to death."

"You mean Thomas Watson."

"Yes. *The Passionate Century of Love.* It's a pity, having a common name and being mistakenly killed like that. But all of us were doomed when the monarchy had finished with our little play factory."

"Don't upset yourself with talk of the past."

"I'm not upset. I need to purge my mind of these nightmares. Strange, how Anthony Munday has survived all the other writers."

"Maybe he's just lucky."

"That's very naive, Michael. It's a miracle I've survived this long. I was so sure the government would come after me, once they'd disposed of Lord Oxford."

Hoping to avoid that subject, Drayton picked up the bottle at his feet.

"Would you care for a drink, William? I can water it down for you. I remember how you like it."

"Yes, I could use a drink, but don't bother to water it down. My son-in-law's medical opinion is that liquor is bad for me, but lately I've found it comforting."

"I never thought I'd hear you say that."

"Neither did I," Shaxper chuckled, as Drayton poured the sack.

Jonson was surprised, too. He stood in the doorway and watched as Shaxper downed his drink.

"Aaaahhhh," the scribe grinned, as he lay back on the couch and closed his eyes. "That's much better. I'd never realized until I got sick how drafty this house is. My wife used to complain about it, but frankly, I never noticed it, not spending too much time here over the years and being mostly in London and all, and I . . . I hope you don't mind, but I think I'd like to sleep for a while. Please don't go, stay until I wake up, Michael, and then we'll continue our visit."

"Very well. While you're resting, I'll have a few words with Jonson."

"Choice words, I hope! And don't bother to clean them up!"

Drayton nodded. He covered his host with a blanket, put the stool back in the corner and tiptoed into the next room.

"Christ!" he said, as he bent down to warm his hands by the fire. "I had no idea he was so far gone and pathetic."

"It's just an act," Jonson said. "He's milking you for sympathy, that's all. Here, have another drink."

Drayton quickly drained his goblet. Jonson poured him another and drank one himself.

"What's wrong with you, Michael? You're shivering."

"Shaxper is right," Drayton said. "This house does have a dreadful chill."

"Really? I don't feel a thing. But you look pale, as if someone had stepped on your grave."

"It's not *my* grave that's been stepped on. Oh, you wouldn't believe it if I told you," he said, as he finished his drink in one long series of gulps.

"Told me what? Stop being so inscrutable. What's the matter?"

"Sit down, Ben, and pour us both another drink. Keep your voice low. I don't want the scribe to wake up and hear us."

"So what if he does?"

"He's so close to death himself, it wouldn't be right for him to hear what I have to say. I don't want to upset him."

"Oh, I see. You can spare him the bad news, but you have no trouble telling me, is that it?"

"This is no joke, Ben. What I have to say isn't funny at all, and I wish to God I'd never heard about it."

"All right, don't get so upset. Sit down and tell me what's troubling you."

The two sat in front of the hearth. Jonson fixed his eyes on Drayton. The visitor took a deep breath and exhaled, as if forcing his words from the depths of his soul.

"The Earl of Oxford's tomb at Hackney has been desecrated again."

"Oh, God!"

"Shh! And this time, the thieves stole the brass plaque that memorialized him as Shake-speare. But that's not the worst part."

"What on earth could be worse than that?"

"Someone dug up his grave, pried open his casket and scattered his remains in the churchyard."

"Oh, no!"

"It was a ghoulish scene, with the sexton and the gravedigger chasing away stray dogs while they hastily gathered his bones —"

"What monstrous adversary would do such a thing?"

"No one knows, no one knows . . ."

"First his statue, then his obelisk, then his plaque and now his bones? Is the Earl of Oxford to have no resting place?"

"Someone doesn't want that, even twelve years after his death. Who would do such a heinous thing? Could it be thieves looking for treasure?"

"What treasure could they find in Shakespeare's tomb, unless they think his manuscripts were buried with him? Remember how his sonnets were stolen from his wife? They turned up a year later, published as *Shake-speare's Sonnets*. Someone profited by that delicate piracy. Even Shaxper tried to sell some old manuscripts until Thomas Middleton caught him in the act. God, this is terrible, just terrible! What will the family do?"

"They're going to bury him in an unmarked grave, somewhere."

"So his name *will* be buried where his body is. I can't believe it. It's not right. He wrote those words himself. It's as if he knew what was going to happen!"

"What else can they do?"

"Offer a quiet ceremony with those of us who were his friends."

"What friends? You and I are the only ones left, plus that scribe in the other room. The family needs to find a secret place where no one will disturb his bones."

"Disturb his bones?" Shaxper cried out. "Who's going to disturb my bones?"

"Good gracious, he's heard us!" Drayton exclaimed.

"I'll fix that blathering baby," Jonson said angrily, as he grabbed his goblet and stormed out of the room. "Somehow or other, this is all his fault! I'll send him to his eternal sleep once and for all."

"Ben, don't!" Drayton shouted. "You're upset! What happened isn't his fault. He didn't dig up the grave and scatter his remains —"

"Scatter the remains?" Shaxper said, trembling as he struggled to sit up. "Is that what they did to Lord Oxford, they dug him up and scattered his remains?"

"Shut up!" Jonson roared. "You're an insult to hardworking writers, you mealy-mouthed impostor, you litigious grain hoarder, you crud-soaked deer poacher!"

"Ben, don't, he's much too frail —"

"Take this, impostor! And I'm not going to water it down for you!"

He tossed his drink in the scribe's face and threw his empty goblet to the floor. Shaxper coughed uncontrollably. Drayton rushed to his assistance.

"William, are you all right?"

"I'm all right, but I won't talk to him anymore," Shaxper said. "He'll never find out where the plays are now. My lips are sealed, and not even his bullying fists will be able to open them!"

Doctor Hall, who appeared at the door at that moment, rushed into the room and straight to his father-in-law's side.

"What are you doing? I leave you on your honor to treat my father-in-law kindly, and you ruthlessly attack him! I warned you, he isn't well. He doesn't need this commotion. It'll send him into a fit of apoplexy. What is it, Father? Tell me what happened. What have they done to you?"

"It was Ben Jonson. He struck me, and he put his hands around my neck and tried to strangle me."

"That's not true; I did nothing of the kind."

"And then he threw poison in my face."

"That's not poison, you idiot, it's wine. But of course, a bumbling milksop like you wouldn't even know the difference."

"Ben, please," Drayton said. "You're not doing yourself any good."

Shaxper grabbed his son-in-law's sleeve.

"John, someone dug up Lord Oxford's bones, John," he said, tearfully. "Someone dug up his grave and left his bones to the dogs! Please, John, please don't let them do that to me, don't let them shovel me out of my grave when I'm dead, please, please —"

"Easy, Father. I promise no one will do that to you. Calm yourself. Lie down now while I show these men the door."

Shaxper put his head in his hands and wept.

"I must say, Drayton, I never expected this kind of behavior from you," Hall said, when they were outside. "You were my patient for a long time, and I was proud to doctor you when my services were needed, but don't come here to see me anymore. Find yourself another doctor."

"But Doctor Hall, I —"

"And you, Jonson. My father-in-law warned me about your criminal behavior. I don't know what on earth possessed me to let you in here to talk to him about those manuscripts in the first place. Frankly, this whole folio project is ridiculous, since you don't have one single play in your possession. But your little game is over. You had your chance to make things right with my father-in-law, and now you've ruined everything. Get out of this house, off our property and don't come back to Stratford, ever."

"I'm sorry, Doctor Hall," Jonson said. "I know my actions were irrational, but in light of the terrible news I was given, I – well, please forgive me and let me stay and finish my work."

"Let you stay? Are you crazy? You've done enough. You're not welcome in this house ever again."

"Please, Doctor Hall," Drayton pleaded. "You're the best physician in Warwickshire; please don't make me go somewhere else."

"Is that all you can say, Michael? Get out of here, both of you, and don't ever even show your faces in this town again!"

Doctor Hall slammed the door. A long silence followed.

"You were right, Michael," Jonson said. "I didn't do myself any good at all."

Drayton shook his head and walked off towards the stables.

CHAPTER THIRTY-TWO

The Scene: New Place, Stratford-on-Avon

April 23, 1616

"Come, sweet Audrey; we must be married or we must live in bawdry."

– As You Like It

E arly in the morning, Michael Drayton found Ben Jonson asleep in the hen house behind Shaxper's barn. He gently kicked the playwright until he rolled over and woke up. Jonson growled like an ill-natured bear.

"You never give up, do you?" Drayton chuckled. "In case you don't remember anything from last night, Dr. Hall threw us out and told us never to come back."

"What's wrong with you?" Jonson yawned. "I know that, and I've obeyed his every word. But since I never really *left* the premises, I haven't actually come back, have I?"

"Only you could devise logic like that."

"It's the curse of a brilliant mind. Where the hell did you spend last night?"

"At The Peacock, just down the road."

"Well, you might have come back to fetch me. I'd have preferred a nice warm bed to sleeping with these damned chickens."

"What, and offend Doctor Hall even further? Not on your life. Good physicians are hard to find. It's not as if they grow on trees."

"That's right – they usually bury their patients under them. Say, if you were so intimidated by the good doctor, why did you come back?"

"Because my visit with the scribe wasn't the honorable farewell I intended. I need another chance to make my peace with him before . . . well, you know, before he dies."

"That ham actor never did know how to make an exit," Jonson said, as he stood up and dusted himself off. "I don't know what I'm going to do now. They've probably locked me out of the house, and I'll never get a chance to coax that old impostor into telling me where the plays are."

"I might be able to get you inside for a price."

Drayton paused for a moment to let the offer sink in.

"Speak up," Jonson said, impatiently. "I'll pay your price, whatever it is. Well, stop looking like the cat that ate the cuckoo and tell me, how do we get back in the house?"

Drayton was interrupted by a lady calling from the yard.

"Oh, Michael. Michael Drayton, where did you go, my love?"

"Who the hell is that?" Jonson whispered hoarsely. "Did some whore follow you all the way back from The Peacock to collect her fee? What an ass you were, giving her your real name!"

"She's not a whore," Drayton smiled. "She's the key to this house. Watch this."

He walked over to the door and called outside.

"I'm in the hen house, darling. Come and get me, my little turtledove."

"Are you insane?" Jonson said. "We're not supposed to be here!"

"Relax, I told you. She's the key to the house."

Within seconds, Anne Hathaway Shaxper stood in the doorway, blocking the light.

"There you are," she said coquettishly. She sauntered seductively towards Drayton. "I've been looking all over for you, Michael. My featherbed is so much more comfortable than this old dirt floor, even if it is the second best bed in the house. Willy won't even know we were up there. He spends his days at death's door, but I'm still vibrant, and you know how I have my needs. I've missed you so much. I've been without a man for so long it hurts, and there's only one cure – hey, who is this lug? I thought we were alone."

"Don't be alarmed, Anne. He's a friend of mine."

"How on earth did I miss seeing him? He's a big one, isn't he?"

"Big enough," Jonson said, squaring his shoulders.

"Who are you?"

"I'm sure you've heard of him, my dear. This is Ben Jonson, a playwright from London."

"Sure, I've heard of you. My husband once called you his worst nightmare."

"Yes, that would be me."

"He said you were the bane of his existence."

"See how well he knew me? We're practically brothers."

"Ben, this is Anne Shaxper," Drayton said. "She's the scribe's wife. They've been married forever, if you know what I mean."

"Charmed," Jonson said. He kissed her hand like Fastidious Brisk, the foppish courtier from his play, *Every Man Out of His Humour.* She seemed highly impressed with what she took for his impeccable manners.

"Now I have two strong gentlemen to entertain," she said lasciviously, as she took his arm. "Won't you come inside, where it's warm?"

"Come? Inside?"

"Yes. Come inside the house."

"Oh," Jonson said. "Yes, that would be nice, wouldn't it, Michael?"

"Absolutely."

She offered her other arm to Drayton and the two men escorted her to the house. She removed the key from her bodice and unlocked the back door. Jonson exchanged triumphant glances with his friend as they tiptoed into the kitchen and closed the door behind them.

"Would you care for some breakfast?" the housewife asked, still clinging to Jonson.

"Yes," Drayton replied. He was free to sit down at the table. "Breakfast would be wonderful. Wouldn't it, Ben?"

"Yes, wonderful. Thank you, Mrs. Shaxper," he said, trying to gently extricate himself.

"Call me Anne," she said, feeling his beefy muscles. "My, you're strong. You don't seem at all like those pale and monastic writers Willy always told me about. You must do a lot of physical work."

"When the theaters are closed, I sometimes work as a bricklayer."

"Bricklaying! Well, that explains it. All those lucky bricks."

"Where's your husband, Mrs. Shaxper?"

"Call me Anne. Willy's sleeping on the couch in the front room. That's all he ever does, unless he's raving like a maniac about some injustice from the past."

"Dr. Hall must be out visiting patients."

"That's right. We have the house all to ourselves." Her voice trailed off as she walked towards the pantry. "But first, we'll eat. What a challenge, serving two such ravenous men."

"I hope she's referring to food," Jonson whispered.

"Don't be too sure," Drayton replied. "She has insatiable appetites."

"Then what's she doing, being married to a milquetoast like Shaxper?"

"Not much. She said so herself. You remember; he always said she was lusty."

"Lusty? She's practically in heat! She seems awfully friendly towards you."

"Let's just say I'm an old friend of the family."

"What's that supposed to mean?"

"Someone had to look in on her while William Shaxper was in London all those years."

"What? You!"

"I came back to beg his forgiveness."

"His forgiveness? Look at her! You were probably doing him a favor."

"I don't think the Lord God will see it that way, when my time comes."

"Look here," Jonson said, rising from the table, "maybe you've got time for a tearful confession and an erotic tumble on a featherbed, but I need to find those play manuscripts. Take her upstairs while I talk to the scribe."

"Not so fast, Ben. I got you back into this house, didn't I?"

"So?"

"You said you'd pay my price, whatever it was."

"Oh, all right," Jonson groaned, sitting down again. "You did me a tremendous favor, getting me back in here. So go ahead, name your price. What do you want?"

"*You* take her upstairs while *I* talk to the scribe. Please, Ben, it'll start me on my path to atonement, and I'll find out for you where the manuscripts are —"

"Now wait just a minute! You had this whole thing planned, didn't you?"

"What if I did? You couldn't have gotten back into this house without me."

"Yes, but who's going to help me get back out?"

"Quiet!" Drayton hissed. "She's coming back."

Anne Shaxper returned carrying two large bowls of food. She leaned over and placed them on the table, lightly brushing her ample breasts against Jonson.

"I think I'll go have a few words with Willy, if he's awake," Drayton said, as he left the table. "You two go and satisfy your appetites. Take your time and get acquainted over breakfast."

He turned in the doorway to see a look of dismay on Jonson's face as Anne led him up the back staircase.

CHAPTER THIRTY-THREE

The Scene: New Place, Stratford-On-Avon
April 23, 1616

"Now, unto thy bones, good-night."
— *Much Ado About Nothing*

W hen Ben Jonson staggered into the front room, he was an alarming sight; his hair uncombed, trousers lopsided and shirt unlaced. Drayton laughed, aware of the reason for his disheveled state.

"You look like a flea-bitten mongrel," he said. "What in Lucifer's name did she do to you?"

"I'd rather not say," Jonson replied, as he tucked in his shirt. "What happened upstairs is your fault, Michael. That woman's crazy!"

"Where is she now?"

"Sleeping like a baby in her second-best bed. I put a little something in her wine. It was my only means of escape."

"You can't imagine how many times I wished for such a plan."

"Did Shaxper say anything about the manuscripts?"

"No," Drayton whispered. "He's awake but still a bit groggy from his nap. I was just about to offer him my confession when you came in . . ."

"Were you upstairs rummaging through my things?" Shaxper shouted. "I'll just bet you were! Where's my wife?"

Jonson angrily pointed a finger at him and started to speak. Drayton stepped between them.

"Why don't we all calm down and have a drink?"

"That's a great idea. I'll pour." Jonson stomped over to the table and filled two goblets with sack. He kept one and gave the other to Drayton.

"Perhaps a drink will refresh your memory about the manuscripts, William," Drayton suggested. "I can water it down for you, the way you like it."

"I'm not allowed to drink spirits. It's against doctor's orders."

"Nonsense, it's the perfect cure," Jonson said. "Here's how it works. After I leave, you'll feel better, won't you?"

"Yes."

"But I'm not leaving until you tell me where the manuscripts are. Ergo, if you can't remember where they are when you *don't* drink, you'll probably recall where they are if you *do* drink."

"You're trying to confuse me," Shaxper said warily.

"No, I'm not. There's some science in it."

"Then how come my son-in-law the doctor didn't suggest it?"

"Doctors don't know everything."

"My son-in-law does. He keeps his medical journals in Latin."

"Probably to cover up his mistakes," Jonson muttered.

"What's that? Speak up. I didn't hear you."

"Doctors don't know everything," Drayton repeated, somewhat louder.

"That's right. They don't," Shaxper said thoughtfully. "They like to think they do, but they don't."

"A little watered-down sack can't possibly hurt you," Drayton said.

"It'll get rid of the pain," Jonson added. "It'll make *me* go away."

"In that case, fetch me a drink. What harm could it do? I'm half-blind, I can't taste anything, I have no teeth and I'm partially deaf. I know *you* don't mean me any harm, Michael. Go ahead. Water down my drink. Perhaps it will sharpen my memory."

Drayton walked over to the table and began blending the sack with water. Jonson came up behind him.

"Trade goblets with me," he whispered.

"What?"

"Trade goblets with me. You heard him say he has no sense of taste. Give him my drink and he'll never know it's not diluted. Believe me, I want to get out of here with those plays just as much as he wants to see me go."

"Do you think it'll work?"

"We've got to try it, before that shrew comes downstairs and spoils everything."

Drayton handed the potent drink to Shaxper. He and Jonson watched as the impostor drained his goblet with surprising speed.

"Ah, that's very comforting," he sighed. "Could I have some more?"

"Certainly. It's wonderful to see you so relaxed, William."

"I haven't felt this way in years."

"Now let's discuss the manuscripts."

"Give me some time, Michael. I have to remember where I put them."

"When was the last time you saw them?"

"About three years ago, when I retired to Stratford after The Globe burned down."

"I remember that," Jonson said. "Some imbecile thought it would be a good idea to fire a cannon in the playhouse."

"That imbecile was Burbage," Shaxper sighed. "I never liked the idea."

"As I recall, you gave *Henry VIII* a brand new title. Did you repackage Oxford's old play so you could sell it as a new one?"

"That's not what happened."

"Then tell us what *did* happen."

"You won't believe me if I told you my intentions were honorable."

"That's right, I won't," Jonson said. "So convince me."

"Michael, please, another drink," Shaxper said, color returning to his face. "This is magic. My pain is gone. You can put the empty bottles in the dung heap so my son-in-law won't see 'em. Plant 'em nice and deep. Maybe they'll grow."

"I wouldn't thrust my hands into a dung heap for anyone but you," Drayton chuckled.

"I know. My wife says you've been quite useful around here."

Drayton stared at him, wondering what that meant. He took the empty bottles outside as Jonson poured his nemesis another drink.

"What were we talking about?" Shaxper asked.

"You were telling me how you played false with *All is True*."

"That was my swan song," Shaxper snapped. "I renamed the play because I had prepared a tribute to Lord Oxford revealing him as the author of the Shakespeare plays, but the theater burned to the ground. Fate stole my chance to make an honest confession."

"What confession?"

"That for twenty-eight years, Lord Oxford paid me to pose as Shakespeare."

For a moment, Jonson was speechless.

"Is that how it was!" he exclaimed. "I always wondered why he showered you with so much attention. Just exactly how did your arrangement work?"

"You remember how obstreperous Lord Oxford could be."

"Almost as bad as I am."

"No, much worse," Shaxper said. "He wasn't permitted to become known for writing plays because of his noble rank, but that wasn't going to stop him, especially when the Queen enjoyed his Court performances.

And by the way, they were all gifts to her. He sold his estates to see other men's lands, and found himself conveying their words and customs on the stage."

"Is that where his fortune went? Everyone said he squandered it."

"You, playwright, do you consider the theater a waste of money?"

"No, of course not."

"Neither did Lord Oxford. At first it was considered demeaning for him to offer his plays to the public, but it became downright dangerous when the Queen commanded his history plays to be shown in the playouses. Perhaps it was Fate that brought us together when I sought him out in London as a stage-struck youth longing to become an actor. As it turned out, he needed me just as much as I needed him. First he hired me as his scribe, and then I became his personal secretary and then his business manager and —"

"And then you became Shake-speare."

"Yes, because as the plays grew more popular, audiences kept shouting for the author. What else could we do? By the Queen's edict, appearances by Lord Oxford had been rendered impossible. I was paid to register his plays, negotiate with theater owners and make all of his public appearances. I kept my mouth shut and puffed on my pipe when asked too many questions."

"Is that why the Earl granted you so many favors?"

"I was paid very well," Shaxper boasted. "Lord Oxford had many secrets, but a man with many secrets doesn't inspire longevity."

"Did you just make that up?"

"No, I heard it . . . somewhere.

Drayton returned, poured himself a drink and sat down.

"What did I miss?" he asked.

"Everything," Jonson replied.

"Not quite," Shaxper said. "Here's the worst part of my story: when King James discovered Lord Oxford's most dangerous secret, he killed him."

"That's not true. You've had too much to drink, old friend," Drayton said, gently. "Everyone knows Lord Oxford died of the plague."

"That's a lie. He was murdered in his own bed. I was there. I saw it."

Jonson and Drayton looked at one another in disbelief.

"You think this drink has gone to my head, don't you?" Shaxper cried. "Well, I'm telling you the truth. Midsummer night in 1604, Oxford's house at King's Place was attacked on all sides. They seized his private papers and poured poison down his throat so there'd be no wounds. I stuffed a good number of his plays into my portfolio and escaped that night, always fearing they would come after me. It took a while, but I reconstructed as many of the manuscripts as I could, and sold some of 'em because I had to do it, with Lord Oxford dead and my livelihood gone. A man has to earn a living."

While Shaxper spoke, his wife Anne tottered down the back staircase and went into the kitchen, carrying a bundle of papers. She set them down and ripped off one page at a time, balling them up and stuffing them between the kindling. She picked up a long piece of straw, held it to the torch and lit the fire in the hearth.

"Now I remember!" Shaxper said. "The plays are up in the attic. I put them in the old trunk, the one Countess Elizabeth gave me on her deathbed."

Jonson leapt to his feet.

"How do we get there?"

"Go to the kitchen and take the back stairs. The trunk is at the top, to the left. I'd go, but I feel a bit dizzy. I need to lie down."

"You go," Drayton said. "I'll stay with the scribe."

Jonson raced into the kitchen. He stopped in his tracks when he saw Anne Shaxper ripping pages out of a bound manuscript and tossing them into the fire.

"What's that you're burning?"

"Just some old papers," she sneered. "Why should you care?"

"What kind of papers?"

Before she could respond, Jonson grabbed them from her hands and instantly recognized the handwriting. He dove into the flames, burning himself as he tried to rescue the discarded pages. His screams brought Drayton running.

"Ben, what are you doing?"

"This is the sequel to *Love's Labour's Lost*," Jonson said, his voice cracking. "Do you realize what you've done, you decrepit old harpy? You've burned an original Shakespeare play, written in Lord Oxford's own hand!"

"I didn't know what it was. I didn't think it was important."

"Not important? What's wrong with you? Are you stupid?"

"I burn papers like this all the time."

"She didn't mean any harm, Ben. Stop badgering her," Drayton said.

"Not on your life! She's gone too far this time."

"She couldn't help it, it's not her fault. She doesn't know how to read."

"What?"

"She can't read. No one in Shaxper's family can read. She didn't know what she was burning."

Jonson was furious. He ran into the front room and shook the scribe back into consciousness.

"Why, you merchant of falsehood! You posed as England's greatest playwright and kept your family uneducated and illiterate?"

"I was in London . . . they were in Stratford . . . I had to earn a living . . . there wasn't time to teach them anything."

"Your slovenly wife has just torched an original Shakespeare play because she can't read. It's as if she murdered Lord Oxford all over again!"

Dr. Hall opened the front door and stepped into complete pandemonium.

"What's going on here, Jonson? I told you and Drayton to go away and stay away."

"And I told you I wasn't leaving without the plays."

"Calm down, Doctor," Drayton said, trying to pacify him. "We just found out a moment ago that the plays Jonson has been seeking are up in the attic. I'll help him get the trunk and we'll be on our way."

"Not so fast," Hall said. "I knew it was a mistake to allow you access to my father-in-law, Jonson. Chaos has ruled ever since I let you into this house. Can't you see my father-in-law is a very sick man? Look at him."

"He's fine. He's resting."

Dr. Hall lifted Shaxper's limp hand.

"What on earth have you done to this poor man?"

"We haven't done anything to him. We had a few drinks to celebrate his birthday."

"Yes, that's right," Drayton seconded, "to celebrate his birthday."

"You fed him my best sack?"

"I'll gladly pay you for what we drank, if that's what's bothering you," Jonson said.

"We didn't force it on him. He drank it of his own free will," Drayton added.

"He's not supposed to drink. I swear, I think you both came to Stratford to kill him!"

"That's not true," Drayton protested.

"Give them the trunk, John, and let's be rid of them," Mrs. Shaxper said.

"Oh, all right, go get it," Hall cried out. "Take it out of here, and then leave this house and never come back!"

Jonson and Drayton hurried to the attic before Dr. Hall had a chance to change his mind.

As the doctor solicitously examined him, Shaxper fell from his stupor into a dream.

A smiling Countess Elizabeth summoned him into an old churchyard, where she showed him two stone effigies. He leaned over and read the epitaphs closely, since it had once been his line of work to write them. One effigy was sacred to the memory of Lady Elizabeth Trentham, Countess of Oxford. The other was inscribed to the Honorable Edward de Vere, 17th Earl of Oxford, Viscount Bulbec, Lord of Sandford, of Escales and of Badlesmere, Lord Great Chamberlain of England, also known as the great bard Shake-speare, the appellation he loved best.

The Countess kissed Shaxper on the forehead and told him how well he had served her husband, and suddenly, a ferocious storm blew up. A hundred horsemen galloped in and smashed the effigies to pieces. The Countess wept and a marble obelisk grew from her tears. He marveled that it was decorated with flights of angels after the line in *Hamlet.* But the angels instantly turned into devils and set the obelisk on fire. All of the graves opened up and spread their contagion in the world, and Lord Oxford's bones were scattered in the churchyard, crumbling into dust.

"For Jesus sake, forebear!" Shaxper screamed.

"He's awake," Mrs. Shaxper said.

"Father-in-law, what is it?" Dr. Hall asked. "What's the matter?"

"What will they do to my bones after I die? I don't want them scattered in the churchyard. If they think I'm Shakespeare, they'll dig me up to dance on my grave."

"What's he talking about?"

"I don't know," Mrs. Shaxper cried. "He's not in his right mind."

"Fetch me my quills and paper, John. I'll write my epitaph now."

The scribe took up his pen and began writing. His eyes could barely focus on his work.

"'*Good friend for Jesus' sake forebear*'— that'll scare 'em off. No one will dig me up if I mention Jesus. '*To dig the dust enclosed here.*' — if I describe my remains as dust, they won't see any point in digging me up, will they? — '*Blest be the man that spares these stones,*' - they'll be rewarded for leaving my grave in one piece. *'And curst be he that moves my bones.'"*

Jonson and Drayton set the trunk down in the front room. Shaxper reached out his bony arms towards them.

"Ben! Michael! Please help me!" Shaxper cried. "I don't want my bones thrown around the churchyard! Don't let them desecrate my grave. I heard you talking about how they dug up Lord Oxford. If they think I'm the playwright, they'll do the same to me. Please help me. You've got to tell my story."

He waved the paper frantically in the air and suddenly began gasping for breath. He fell back onto the couch and his breathing became shallow until at last, it stopped.

CHAPTER THIRTY-FOUR

The Scene: Wilton House
May 7, 1616

"My name be buried where my body is,
And live no more to shame nor you nor me."
– Sonnet 72

wo weeks later, Jonson excitedly relayed his discovery to his noble patrons.

"I nearly fainted when I opened your father's trunk, my lady," he said breathlessly, "but if I had, luckily Michael Drayton was there to revive me. We couldn't believe our eyes! Imagine, after all this time, the Shake-speare plays were tucked away in a corner of the scribe's attic."

"Are they foul papers or fair copies?" Lord Montgomery asked.

"Very fair papers indeed, my lord, written in Lord Oxford's Italianate hand. I know it well, believe me. I'd have brought you the entire collection but the trunk is very cumbersome and I wasn't sure you'd have time to peruse its contents."

"Where is it now?"

"At my lodgings. It's quite safe. Drayton's keeping a watchful eye on it."

"I wonder how your father's trunk came into Shaxper's possession."

"Are you implying that he stole it, Philip?" the Countess asked.

"No, my dear. For all I know, it might have been a gift."

"I can understand Lord Oxford making such a personal gift to a servant," Pembroke said. "I've done it myself; so have we all. But I can't believe he'd have given it away with the plays still inside it."

"Perhaps his widowed Countess did, without knowing it."

"Or Shaxper stored the plays there himself for safekeeping so long ago he forgot about them."

"It's impossible to judge his motives," Jonson replied diplomatically. "It seems likely that after the plays were returned by the Stationers' Register, Shaxper did his duty as a secretary and simply filed them away. Once stowed, they probably never left Warwickshire."

"That rings true, especially if Father wrote them at Bilton Manor and Billesley Hall," Susan said. "Both of his old estates are near Stratford, and it would have been easy for him to pass the plays back and forth to his scribe. He always preferred the country because he could work there undisturbed."

"Still, Shaxper held on to the original drafts," Jonson said. "I'll bet he never intended to return them; and knowing our Shake-speare, Lord Oxford neglected to ask for them back. In his mind, they'd already been released to the world."

"That's how Father felt about his plays," Susan sighed.

For a moment, no one spoke. Lord Pembroke interrupted the somber mood.

"Tell us then, Jonson, which plays did you find?"

The playwright became animated again and began talking with his hands.

"First we unwrapped *Othello*, then *As You Like It* and after that *All's Well That Ends Well*. We were like children at Christmas, Drayton and I! We spread the pages on the floor. The paper and ink were in good condition; everything was fresh and crisp, as if he'd penned it yesterday. There were even a few insertions he'd written to be added from time to time, depending on the audience. We all know how he loved to tease them with hidden meanings. Well, the trunk turned out to be a veritable treasure trove. On the bottom lay *Twelfth Night, Julius Caesar, The Winter's Tale, The Two Gentlemen of Verona, Antony and Cleopatra, The Comedy of Errors, Coriolanus* and *The Tempest,* all swaddled in cloth and lovingly protected."

"Impressive! That should make compiling the folio much easier."

"It will, but there are other plays yet to be found, scattered all over England. Lord Oxford's folio won't be complete without the history plays, or *Romeo & Juliet* or *A Midsummer Night's Dream* or *King Lear* —"

"We'll pay while you continue your search," Montgomery said, rising from his chair. "Naturally, one can't expect to publish a folio of this magnitude overnight. I'm sure I speak for my brother when I say we'll be more than happy to pay Drayton to help you, if you find the job too overwhelming."

"Ah, that won't be necessary, my lords. Thank you just the same. I'm quite capable of compiling the folio on my own."

"We don't doubt it," Pembroke said, over his shoulder. "We're all probably safer with fewer tongues to wag about our doings. But we must go and see the King now on a matter concerning the revels. We'll speak with you about the folio in the next few weeks, Jonson. Good day to you, and good work."

The brothers left so quickly, Jonson found himself bowing to the library door. Susan gestured for him to sit.

"What about the scribe?" she asked. "You haven't said much about him."

"What words can I use in front of a lady?"

"Oh, Ben, I'm merely asking if he agreed to contribute any dedicatory verses."

"Not unless the devil has an inkwell."

"What are you saying?"

"William Shaxper is dead, my lady. He died during my visit to Stratford. The doctor said it was a fit of apoplexy brought on by extreme inebriation."

"William Shaxper, drunk? That can't be! Father always mocked him about the way he watered down his drinks."

"Far be it from me to contradict a physician, but it's true. Did you know he had the gall to imply that I killed him?"

"Well, did you?"

"That's hard to say. I suppose God will be the judge of that."

"And where was Michael Drayton all this time?"

"Where was he? By the time we left, he was being treated like a celebrity! Dr. Hall examined a few of his minor complaints, just so he could claim having a famous writer as a patient. It's outrageous, but he considers Drayton a literary luminary. How's that for bad taste?"

"But you're England's poet laureate. What did he think of you?"

"He said he didn't like my attitude towards his father-in-law."

"He must have had great respect for the poor old man."

"Truth be told, my lady, and with my own personal feelings set aside, Dr. Hall is highly educated. He never did praise Shaxper for his literary talent, but might have done so, if the impostor had ever actually written anything on his own."

"Nevertheless, it was kind of you and Michael to stay for the funeral."

"It was only proper, since we were there when he died. Shaxper always liked a captive audience."

"For heaven's sake, Ben, you mustn't say such things about the dead."

"You're right, my lady. One never knows who's listening." Jonson paused to acknowledge God and then continued. "Anyway, Drayton and I served as pallbearers, and we were the only writers in attendance. Aside from Shaxper's family and friends, the rest were local merchants to whom he still owed money. Oh, but he was far from poor, I can attest to that. Everyone whispered about how he'd bequeathed gold rings to each of his theatrical shareholders. He left behind no library or books to pass on, but it wouldn't have mattered anyway, since no one in his family can read. We put his coffin on the hearse for its final ride to Trinity Church and a little while later, the cart bearing your father's trunk drove off in the opposite direction. Death is the only way Shaxper would have parted with those manuscripts."

"Did he have any children?"

"His only son is dead. One of his daughters is married to that Dr. Shed-Blood; the other is the common law bawd of a notorious pickpocket. Shaxper wrote her out of his will and told me it was the best revision he'd ever made on his own. He also said he hoped that his shrew-mouthed wife didn't have one peaceful night's sleep in that lumpy old bed."

"Really, Ben! Such gossip is none of our business."

"But it's the truth, my lady. You can't invent stuff like this."

"How do his neighbors remember him?"

"Now that's an intriguing question. He did pay for some civic improvements towards the end of his life – something to do with moving dunghills away from common areas, I think. But principally, his neighbors remember him for gouging the price of grain during shortages. Someone suggested building him a monument showing him clinging to a sack of grain."

"Who would dare say such a thing about a dead man?"

"Bless me," Jonson laughed. "I think it was his wife."

"I'm sure he wouldn't want to be remembered that way."

"Probably not. But in this life, when we make our own second-best beds, we must sleep in them."

Countess Susan sighed.

"What's wrong, my lady? Oh, blast! I've insulted you, I've said too much—"

"Not at all, Ben. I'm accustomed to your bittersweet indelicacies," Susan said, as she rested her hand on his arm. "For years you've been a faithful friend to me and my father. Still, this talk about death is heartbreaking. I'm not sure if you heard, but Father's grave at Hackney has been desecrated again."

"Yes, Drayton told me. What a despicable crime! Do you know who did it?"

"No, but we've finally found a way to stop it. If I tell you what we've done, you must promise not to breathe a word to anyone."

"I swear, my lady, not a word, on my honor."

Susan hesitated and then looked deeply into his eyes.

"It was Cousin Horatio's idea. A fortnight ago, we quietly moved Father's bones to Westminster Abbey. and buried them beneath the floor in the de Vere family vault. Horatio thinks they will be safe there, as long as his grave is left unmarked."

"Unmarked! You mean the Earl of Oxford is resting in a nameless grave?"

"We had no choice. A quiet reburial was the best we could do. I can't press Cousin Horatio for any more favors. His brother Francis is buried in that tomb."

"I served with Sir Francis in the army. He was a good man."

"And so is Horatio. But you must understand his fear, if Father's story is ever told . . ."

"Perhaps if I talk to him —"

"You mustn't betray my confidence. You've sworn an oath."

"But the Abbey is extremely well guarded. No harm can come to its tombs."

"Still, I must honor Horatio's wish."

"For what, for his silence? He's a war hero. What happened to his courage?"

"It surrendered to age. That tomb will enclose his remains one day."

Jonson struggled with his emotions. He pounded his fist on the library table. "Damn it! Are there no honest men left in the world?"

"I'll know *one*, if you keep your oath," she said, softly.

"Will Lord Oxford have no ceremony, no epitaph to mark his grave?"

"No, just a marker showing that a body lies under the floor."

"Oh, God! What a wretched fate, to have your grave ransacked and your name divested from your finest works! He knew it would happen. He warned us in writing that his name would be buried where his body is."

Jonson covered his face. Susan touched his shoulder.

"Don't be ashamed of your tears, Ben. I've wept oceans of them since Father died. The only monument we can give him now is to publish the folio as a posthumous tribute, the way his Uncle Surrey's sonnets were preserved after his death."

"Do you really think the King will allow it?"

"The prospect looks good. Philip has a solid friendship with King James, and our monarch loves the plays."

"But we still don't know if he loves the playwright. Well, I suppose we'll learn that soon enough," Jonson said.

EPILOGUE

The Scene: Ben Jonson's House,
November 23, 1623
seven years later

This Figure, that thou here seest put,
It was for gentle Shakespeare cut;
Wherein the Graver had a strife
with Nature, to out-doo the life:
O, could he have but drawne his wit
As well in brasse, as he hath hit
His face; the Print would then surpasse
All, that was ever writ in brasse
But since he cannot, Reader, looke
Not on his Picture, but his Booke.

— by Ben Jonson, from
"Mr. William Shakespeares Comedies, Histories & Tragedies,
Published according to the True Originall Copies," First Folio, 1623

J onson wanted to scream the way he had when his children died, but a strange agony silenced him. The unending string of irretrievable losses had grown much worse, now that everything he cherished lay in ashes at his feet.

Fire had ravaged his home, and he was lucky to have escaped with his life. His printed offspring had been less fortunate. Everything had gone up in flames: the decorative volume of his *Complete Works,* his entire library of classics, books his friends had graciously loaned to him, the versification of his journey to Scotland, all of his finished manuscripts and miscellaneous works-in-progress, the tender wards of his imagination that he'd hoped would one day graduate into books.

His earthly creations were gone. And to make matters worse, the entire compendium of Shake-speare plays that had been stored in the trunk smoldered like orange eyes in the corner of the lot where his library once stood. Only the brass nameplate with Lord Oxford's initials survived, and it was so hot Jonson had to use a handkerchief to pick it up.

He didn't know what to say to his patrons. He prayed that they might find a few kind words to say to him, and perhaps provide him with a modest roof over his head and a few meals, at least until he could rebuild. His heart ached and he could scarcely breathe as he surveyed the ruins. He had no possessions anymore, nothing except the clothes on his back and the thick wool cloak that protected him from the winter chill. He wandered through the debris like a pitiful creature, stooping down to sift through the remains with his fingers. Adding insult to injury, people started gathering in the street to gawk at his misfortune. He felt like a churl, an inglorious misanthrope, when he saw that the sky threatened to offer a mixed blessing: rain would disperse the crowd, but it would also blend the ashes of his world into a thick gray mud.

He heard his name as if in a dream.

"Ben? Ben Jonson! Thank God you're still alive!"

He looked up and saw Countess Susan standing over him. Still dazed, he scrambled to his feet. He heard his own voice cracking with grief.

"I'm alive, my lady, although from the looks of these ruins, it might have been best if I had perished with my books."

"Don't talk like that. You needn't worry about a thing. Come and stay with us at Wilton. We'll help you rebuild. We'll see to it that you want for nothing."

"That's very kind, my lady, but you might change your mind when you hear what I have to say."

"What is it?"

"Your father's plays, the true original papers I brought here for safekeeping seven years ago, and all the others I'd gathered from the actors – they're gone, all gone! Everything is in cinders. All that's left is the nameplate from the trunk. Be careful, it's still hot." She stared at it, and for a moment seemed lost for words

"You mustn't blame yourself. The fire was an accident."

"Was it? I'm not so sure. Perhaps the same rogues who plundered your father's grave set fire to my house to keep the folio from going to press."

"Surely you don't believe that."

"I don't know what to believe. All those years of hard work, carrying the plays to the printer one by one, just to keep them safe, and now the originals are as dead as the author."

"Don't chastise yourself. You've suffered your own losses."

"I tried to safeguard his papers, I truly did."

"I know you did. It's not your fault."

"If this fire was deliberately set to stop publication," Jonson said angrily, "the villains made a big mistake. They're one week too late."

"You're not making any sense —"

"I'm making perfect sense, my lady. I had decided to write you this morning and tell you the good news, but as you can see . . ."

"Good news? If you can conjure up any good news out of this, please tell me."

"The published plays are safe. Jaggard told me yesterday that he completed the folio ahead of schedule. He says he'll have it in the book-stalls by Christmas."

"Oh, Ben, I don't know how to thank you. It was an incredible task, just as you said it would be."

"Your kindness and generosity have sustained me, my lady. It's good of you to come and see me in my hour of need."

"Forgive me," she said gently, "but that's not why I came. I didn't know about the fire until I turned the corner and saw the destruction with my own eyes. I came about a different matter, but I have no desire to give you the news of any more catastrophes."

"More catastrophes? What could follow this one? Please, sit down and tell me what's troubling you."

He took her hand and guided her through the rubble.

"I built this brick wall with my own hands when I was fifteen, my lady. I'd like to think that's why it's still standing, but I don't want to tempt fate. Now sit down and tell me your catastrophe. It can't be any worse than this." He gestured at the ashes.

"My brother-in-law Lord Pembroke had planned on coming here today," the Countess said, "but he was forced to send me instead. He's at Court right now, appeasing the King with a variety of promises in order to save my brother's life. You do know that Henry was imprisoned in the Tower nearly two years ago for opposing the marriage of the royal heir to the Spanish princess."

"Yes. He was jailed for speaking his mind."

"And now the Spanish ambassador is demanding his head. Southampton has been carrying messages back and forth to the King, trying to help us win a reprieve. He's very close friends with James, as is my brother-in-law Pembroke. Neither of them can understand why the King is so threatened by Henry de Vere as 18th Earl of Oxford."

"I don't understand it either. Sounds like politics to me."

"Anyway, Southampton seems to have successfully negotiated Henry's release. The King has said my brother will be freed on the condition that our father's name be entirely stricken from the folio."

"That's impossible! The printing is complete. Lord Oxford's name is on it. We can't make any changes now, without turning it into mincemeat."

"But we must save Henry's life. Southampton says the King is terrified. He's gotten it into his head that something dangerous will happen if Father's authorship becomes known to the world. He thinks Father encoded some dark and dangerous secrets into the lines of his poetry. But that's impossible, isn't it?" Susan asked.

"Well, to be honest . . ."

"Isn't it?"

"There are subtle ways to encode messages into poetry."

"Could Father have done such a thing?"

"Certainly. He was a master at it. He knew all about codes. He was a spy, like all the writers in his employ, except that he was sophisticated, cultured and grandly titled, easily welcomed into all the best houses in Europe."

"What secrets did he know?"

"Far be it from me to speculate."

"Something about Henry, perhaps?"

"Who can tell? Like all men, I'll bet he took his darkest secrets to his grave."

Countess Susan probed his eyes as if mining for answers. Jonson shook his head and shrugged.

"Nevertheless," Susan continued, "the King has commanded us to use the Shake-speare pseudonym in our book. We can make no direct reference to Father, his title as 17th Earl of Oxford, or the de Vere family name. Do you understand what that means?"

"Unfortunately, yes. It means that when we print the name Shake-speare, everyone will think that good-for-nothing scribe from Stratford is the author. William Shaxper, the rank impostor who posed in front of the playhouses, puffed on his pipe and couldn't have written a love son-net to a goddess if his life depended on it! My blood boils at the thought. That bogus bard is going to get away with it one more time, all because the King is haunted by ghosts from the past."

"I'm sorry, Ben, but we have no other choice. Father would have surrendered his plays in an instant, if he knew it would save his son's life."

"Any father would do so," Jonson said, thinking of his own lost children."

For a moment neither spoke. Jonson suddenly jumped up and started pacing.

"Jaggard's going to kill me. Can you imagine what our publisher is going to say when I tell him he has less than one month to print the folio all over again?"

"Never mind, I'll speak to him," the Countess said. "Jaggard once dedicated a book to me, and he'd do anything to secure my patronage."

"Still, it's going to be a disaster. He'll have to reprint whole pages. Why, the name change alone is going to leave visible gaps in the type. It's going to be a publishing nightmare!"

"It'll be difficult, but not impossible. At least Henry will be safe, even if Father's name will be buried forever."

Jonson looked pained. He started to speak, but she interrupted him.

"I know how you feel about it, Ben, but there's nothing we can do."

"I can do a great deal," the playwright said. "I'll commission a boy to draw a caricature of a man wearing a mask – that'll serve to hide the identity of Shaxper *and* Shakespeare. I'll write an inscrutable poem that'll make the Oracle at Delphi sound sober. People will think I'm jealous, but have you ever known me to care what people think?"

"Not that I can remember."

"I'll praise the Sweet Swan of Avon and make it sound as if he had a tin ear for Latin and a mildewed ear for Greek. I'll have Shaxper's fellow shareholders Hemminge and Condell write a brash and annoying sales pitch to the reader. The whole thing will look like a hugger-mugger patch-up job, but if the folio looks common, people will think it's the work of a commoner."

"What a shame," Susan said. "It was supposed to have been an enduring tribute."

"Oh, it will be. Your father's plays are immortal. I'll just remind his readers of that fact, and tell them not to pay any attention to the picture or the introductory doggerel."

"Michael won't be pleased at having his poetry called doggerel."

"Drayton? Well, I'll give him a chance to withdraw from the project as a courtesy."

"And the others?"

"Your father's friends? We do need a little sincerity in the book. It can't all be tripe and trumpery."

"Whatever you do, please don't harm my brother."

"On my honor, I won't. King James is too bland to understand riddles and subtleties, but I warrant you he'll be very pleased with the finished product. I'll even devise some convoluted drivel for that ridiculous monument in Stratford."

"Isn't that going too far?"

"Not at all. It'll keep 'em guessing about the authorship for generations."

"I suppose," the Countess sighed. "Still, it's not the memorial I wanted for my father."

"No, nor I," Jonson replied. "But the truth will out. Who would be so foolish as to believe that a merchant from Stratford, with not one word of literary juvenilia or poetic practice to his name, could emerge from the ether to create the greatest plays ever written?"

In a corner of the home's foundation, a gust of wind blew some ashes into a circle.

The long rain had begun.

AUTHOR'S NOTES

Most of the events in this novel happened and were derived from the biographies of Edward De Vere (17th Earl of Oxford), William Shaxper of Stratford, Ben Jonson, William Cecil (Lord Burghley), Queen Elizabeth I, Sir Robert Cecil and others. The story line was constructed from actual events and linked together the same way a forensic scientist builds a compelling case based on evidence.

Some events in the book were dramatized to blend with fact. For example, we know that during a performance of *All is True,* The Globe caught fire and burned to the ground, but we don't know whether Shaxper was prepared to make a speech naming the real author and confessing his own role as front man. Yet we do know that after the fire, Shaxper went home to Stratford and never wrote (or took credit for writing) another play again.

On writing dialogue for historical characters, George Bernard Shaw once said that he preferred not to write what he *thought* the characters had said, but rather, what he thought *they would have said if they had known what they were really doing.* Retrospect and the judgment of history conspire to allow us to speculate on a character's thoughts, emotions and deeds. A writer builds well-constructed scenes that show characters involved in the roles they played as history unfolded. As you read this novel, step into the shoes of Lord Oxford, William Shaxper, Queen Elizabeth I, Ben Jonson and others so that you can imagine how you would have performed if you had been that person.

The title of this book comes from *A Midsummer Night's Dream,* where Titania and Oberon engage in a bitter custody battle over a little changeling boy. In English folklore, a changeling is a sprite that is left in exchange for a human child. The phrase *"A Fault Against The Dead"* comes from Claudius' attempt to convince Hamlet that excessive grief over the death of his father is misguided. Orphaned at age 12, young

Oxford personally suffered such pangs of grief at the sudden death of his father.

Meg and Pinch are fictional characters based on composites from the Shakespeare plays.

The Shakespeare Mysteries by Peter Kline is a major source of the research used in this book. Since J. Thomas Looney's *Shakespeare Identified* and Charlton Ogburn's *The Mysterious William Shakespeare*, a huge amount of material has been discovered about Lord Oxford's life and early literary pursuits. The University of Massachusetts was the first academic institution to award a PhD for research beyond the scope of the traditional Stratfordian viewpoint. This degree was awarded to Roger Stritmatter for connecting underlined passages in Lord Oxford's Geneva Bible with specific lines in the Shakespeare plays. This Bible resides at the Folger Library in Washington, D.C., where Stratfordians make it available only to visiting scholars and for occasional exhibitions, where its timeworn crimson cover is closed, preventing further scrutiny by a curious public.

Lord Oxford's life is well documented. From the time he was four and a half years old, he was educated by Sir Thomas Smith in the full spectrum of subjects studied by the nobility in Renaissance England. At 12, he endured the sudden and traumatic death of his father, followed by the hasty remarriage of his mother. When his older half-sister sued to nullify his inheritance and have him declared a bastard, he wrote a poem (still extant) expressing his fear over the loss of his good name. As an orphan, he became a royal ward in the home of Sir William Cecil, Queen Elizabeth's powerful advisor. Cecil kept a tight hold on Oxford's fortune and eventually married his daughter to him, most likely to secure himself some noble grandchildren and increase the family fortunes when he became Lord Burghley by virtue of his daughter's union.

But Lord Oxford's outrageous behavior and flamboyant antics caused serious problems for Lord Burghley. For example, the robbery

Oxford staged at Gad's Hill is described in *The Famous Victories of Henry V* (with precise details known only by its "anonymous" author) and in Shakespeare's *Henry IV, Part I*. This robbery is the subject of a still-surviving letter written by the victims to Burghley complaining of the unsavory conduct of Oxford's yeomen who had attacked them. Modern Shakespearean commentators never acknowledge the existence of this letter as a key source for the first scene in *Henry IV, Part I* because it represents a personal experience from Oxford's life reflected in a Shakespeare play. There are many other such connections. And as we all know, scandals among the rich and famous are reason enough for a cover-up, especially among disapproving relatives, the Queen of England and the government itself.

Lord Oxford wrote poetry and produced masques in the Elizabethan court. By all accounts he was an excellent musician, dancer, champion of the tilt-yard, scholar and philosopher. Childhood samples of his literary efforts still exist. Many books were dedicated to him, and he was praised as a writer in *The Arte of English Poesy* and *The English Secretary*. Perhaps this public exposure, not desirable for a member of the nobility, is another reason for the use of a pseudonym.

William Shaxper of Stratford left us no known early writings. Except for one well educated son-in-law, his family was illiterate. His sketchy biography has been based on supposition and speculation, much to the chagrin of English teachers and students who have had difficulty associating the grain merchant from Stratford with the authorship of the world's greatest plays. Shaxper's possible kinship to Lord Oxford through Elizabeth Trussel, wife of the 15th Earl, was suggested by Ogburn. It's easy to see that family loyalty would empower Shaxper to protect his noble kinsman Oxford. Surely, the work enabled Shaxper to earn a profitable living and secure some shares in the playhouses.

Even at the time, Ben Jonson and his contemporaries doubted Will Shaxper's authorship of the plays -- and they said so, in writing.

In conclusion, it is important that we connect an author with his or her work, especially in terms of Shakespeare and the world's greatest plays. In doing so, we show students that writers create within the context of their experience and environment. Learning, thinking and writing merge, and the result is a completely unique individual perspective. This can be seen in John Steinbeck's empathy with migrant farm workers, Mark Twain's steamboat life on the Mississippi, Emily Dickinson's reclusive spiritual reflections and Harper Lee's childhood brush with racism. An author's life experience is the framework for a literary masterpiece.

For many years, academics have tried to forbid close scrutiny of the Shakespeare authorship, using vitriolic attacks against those who would know more. But like glaciers melting after thousands of years revealing artifacts buried long ago, the true biographical connections of the 17th Earl of Oxford to the Shakespeare canon are open to discovery.

The best secrets are yet to emerge, whether the traditionalists care to admit it or not.

ABOUT THE AUTHOR

Syril Levin Kline is an educator, journalist, theater director and performer who believes that challenging academic orthodoxy can lead to new insights and discoveries that enhance all fields of learning. She believes that writers create within the context of their experience, and that by helping students connect an author with his or her work, we can enable them to see relationships between their own learning, thinking and writing.

For too long, Shakespeare's true identity has remained an intriguing mystery to students and teachers. In her novel, Syril breathes new life into the literary world of Elizabethan England, enlightening readers with the many connections between the life of the 17th Earl of Oxford and the Shakespeare canon.

Syril has two independent sons, two dependent cats and lives in Silver Spring, Maryland, with her husband Peter, author of *The Shakespeare Mysteries*.

She and Peter can be reached via email at oxfordianklines@gmail.com

She proudly claims Rod Serling, creator of *The Twilight Zone,* as her distant kinsman.

Made in the USA
Middletown, DE
20 December 2019